My cube lit up the space, illuminating rusted desks and broken whiteboards. Everything was in a jumble, tipped over and half buried in the silt and the sand, but even from here I could tell that the metal on the desks wasn't that tarnished. I was just turning back to signal to Gizmo that I'd found something, when a massive lump moved beneath the sand.

ALSO BY LAURA MARTIN

Vanishing Act (sequel to *Float*)

Glitch

Hoax for Hire

Float

Edge of Extinction #1: The Ark Plan

Edge of Extinction #2: Code Name Flood

THE MONSTER MISSIONS

LAURA MARTIN

HARPER

An Imprint of HarperCollinsPublishers

For my four blessings.

You guys are the greatest mission of my life.

The Monster Missions
Copyright © 2021 by Laura Martin
All rights reserved. Printed in the United States of America.
No part of this book may be used or reproduced in any manner
whatsoever without written permission except in the case of brief
quotations embodied in critical articles and reviews. For information
address HarperCollins Children's Books, a division of HarperCollins
Publishers, 195 Broadway, New York, NY 10007.
www.harpercollinschildrens.com

Library of Congress Control Number: 2020951028
ISBN 978-0-06-289439-7

Typography by Ellice M. Lee
22 23 24 25 26   PC/BRR   10 9 8 7 6 5 4 3 2 1
❖
First paperback edition, 2022

The morning before I left the *Atlas* forever started the same as every other. I always woke up early, but thanks to Wallace's snoring, this morning was earlier than most. I winced and peered over the edge of my bunk at him. He lay in the middle of the narrow bunk, his arms splayed wide. For a skinny sixteen-year-old, he had the snore of a man twice his age and size. I debated shoving him off his bunk to teach him a lesson but almost immediately discarded the idea. It was the mean part of my brain that wanted to do that. The nice part of my brain, which would probably wake up any moment now, knew that he was exhausted from working with Dad in the engine room the day before.

It wasn't fair to rob him of sleep, even if he'd robbed me of mine—besides, a quick glance at my watch showed that I was supposed to be up in ten minutes anyway. I lay in bed a second longer, wondering why beds were always the most comfortable right when you had to get out of them, before slipping silently from my bunk and pulling on a threadbare sweatshirt to ward off the ever-present chill of our tiny cabin. I was just easing my way toward the door when my dad sat up.

"Heading out already?" he asked, barely stifling a yawn as he slipped out of bed and past the snoring Wallace to see me off.

"I wasn't planning on it," I whispered, "but somebody sounds like he swallowed part of the ship's engine." I jerked my head toward Wallace, eyebrow raised. Dad glanced over at my sleeping brother and stifled a yawn.

"If you're tired enough, you can sleep through just about anything," he said. "Maybe Gizmo isn't working you guys hard enough." He finished this statement off with a wink, and I grimaced.

"That'll be the day," I said. "He has us starting early today, since we're only going to be able to scavenge for a couple of hours."

Wallace grunted in his sleep and rolled over. Dad held up a finger to his lips.

Sorry, I mouthed silently as I slipped the straps of my backpack over my shoulders.

Dad nodded, wiping the sleep from his eyes with the palms of his hands. He still had a smudge of grease above his right eyebrow, evidence of his hard work in the guts of our ship. It wasn't easy to keep a ship like ours in good working condition, but Dad and Wallace and their crew of fellow mechanics and engineers managed it year after year. They had to—our survival depended on it.

"Be careful down there," he said. "No unnecessary risks."

I nodded, knowing full well that unnecessary risks were some of the only ways you found anything useful these days. All the easy stuff had been picked over fifty years ago when everything first went under. Now we were lucky to find scraps. Today might be different, though, I reminded myself. This particular site hadn't been scavenged yet—at least that's what our boss, Gizmo, had told us.

"No unnecessary risks," I repeated with what I hoped was a reassuring smile. My dad smiled back, and I pretended not to notice the worried crease in his forehead as he gave my shoulders a quick one-armed squeeze. I slipped out the door. I knew my choice of occupation on the *Atlas* was a hard one for him to swallow, especially since we'd lost my mom a few years ago, but we both knew full well that there was no such thing as an easy job these days.

If I'd thought our cabin was cold, the narrow hallway was downright frigid, and I hunched my shoulders inside my sweatshirt as I tried not to think about what the water temp must be today. I'd find out soon enough. Around me the metal of the ship creaked and groaned familiarly as I made my way toward the stairs at the front of the ship. The walls on either side of me showed the jagged marks of years of repairs and reconfigurations, and I ran my finger over one of the many thick welts of metal as I walked. Exactly like scars, I thought. Scars that showed battle after battle that the *Atlas* had fought and won, scars that showed the evidence of its transformations over the years from luxury to lean efficiency. I liked scars. Scars proved you'd survived.

I finally reached the stairs and started making my way up, flight by flight, toward the deck. The chilly damp of the lower level seemed to stay with me, though, and I hurried my pace, hoping that the exercise would warm me up a bit. My legs were burning by the time I finally reached the top deck and walked out into the early morning air of the Mediterranean. I'd asked my dad once why we still labeled sections of the ocean by their original names. It didn't seem to make much sense now that the world was covered by one massive body of water, but he'd told me not to ask such silly questions. That was where he and I disagreed, though:

I didn't think any questions were silly, not when it came to the ocean. I took a deep breath, letting the salty freshness scrub away the musty staleness of the inside of the ship, and headed toward the stern.

The ship was practically deserted this early, but I still kept my head down as I made my way across the worn deck, passing the large chicken coop where the ship's fleet of hens snoozed safely in their nests. They were some of the only domestic animals that had survived the Tide Rising. Animals like cows and sheep required grass to survive, and we didn't have any of that anymore. However, it turned out that chickens could thrive on fish guts and the occasional cockroach, and because of that, we had eggs and the rare piece of chicken in our soup. It was a luxury we didn't take for granted. During the day the hens would peck around, roosting on top of the large storage crates that peppered the deck.

Although, unless you really looked, the crates themselves were almost unrecognizable since every square inch of available surface had a gardening box attached to it. It wasn't much, not like on a grower ship, but the herbs and vegetables we were able to cultivate on deck did help supplement our diet of fish, fish, and more fish. The layout was a far cry from the original deck design, but it worked.

Once upon a time the *Atlas* had been a small cruise ship used for vacations, and if you looked closely, you could still see where there used to be frivolous luxuries like a swimming pool and a running track. The very idea of wasting so much space was laughable now, but I liked to imagine what life was like before, when people sailed on the ocean for fun and not because it was the only way to survive.

We were on the move after having been anchored for two days, and above me on the huge masts the sails were filled with a breeze that moved the massive ship. They seemed disproportionate and out of step with the rest of the ship, for good reason: they had been an afterthought. When the tide had started rising, cruise ships were uniquely suited to take on large groups of people, but they weren't designed to run without fossil fuels—fuels that would be hard if not impossible to come by once the water level rose. So the ship's architects had scrambled to put together a system of sails and rigging that would allow the *Atlas* to maneuver itself using the wind instead of the engines, which would eventually be scrapped and melted down.

A lot of things had needed to be altered or reverted to earlier, less-wasteful forms of technology in order to navigate this new, water-filled world. It had been a bit painful for the human race to take a giant step backward. They'd had to give up so many of the resources, technologies, and conveniences that they'd fought for and rediscover methods of survival carved out by their ancestors, but when your choices are life and death, the decision becomes a lot easier.

I made it to the rail of the ship and glanced around for Garth. He was nowhere to be seen, so I leaned against the rail and watched the horizon, where the faintest line of pink and orange was just beginning to glow. I loved sunrise. I loved sunset, too, but I was usually working or eating when that happened. Sunrise, though, that was mine. She and I had a thing—a standing appointment, you could say—and I mentally forgave Wallace for waking me up early. The few extra minutes of quiet, especially on board a ship that was usually anything but, were a treat. The blaze on the horizon brightened into a warm burnt orange that reminded me of the heart of a fire. I ran my hand over the familiar chips and dents of the railing and sighed. Sometimes it felt like I'd memorized every nook and cranny of this ship. Who knew, by the end of my lifetime I probably would have.

Despite the fact that I had always been fully aware that I would probably live my entire life aboard the ship I'd been born on, the idea still chafed me a bit. It wasn't that I disliked life aboard the *Atlas*—you couldn't exactly dislike the only existence you'd ever known—but that I hadn't chosen it. It had been chosen for me. Just like what I would eat for breakfast was chosen by the ship's cook, how much survival credit I'd receive for the salvage I found was chosen by my boss, Gizmo, and how much electricity our cabin would receive was chosen by the *Atlas*'s captain. That was probably the reason I'd decided to go rogue and become a scavenger: it was literally one of the only ways to get off the ship.

I shook my head and forced myself to focus on the day ahead. A life of choice was a luxury we couldn't afford after the Tide Rising, and that was all there was to it.

"Sorry," Garth said as he skidded to a stop beside the rail twenty minutes later. It wasn't unusual for Garth to be late, but this morning he was an exceptional mess. Half-dressed, with his shirt on backward and only one shoe on, the other held in his hand, he looked like he'd rolled directly out of bed and taken off at a dead sprint. Which he probably had. I raised an eyebrow at him and glanced up and down, not doing a thing to hide my judgment.

"Overslept," he said as he hopped up and down to put on his other shoe.

"Well, if we don't hurry, we're going to have to dive hungry."

"I'm not doing that again," Garth said, already turning to head toward the Atlas's mess hall. "The last time that happened, Gizmo the grump decided to keep us down there for an extra hour on a hunch."

I snorted. "I forgot about that. Didn't you threaten to eat your own wet suit?"

"Let's just say that if Gizmo asks what happened to the chunk by my wrist, I'm blaming it on mice," Garth said dryly, and I rolled my eyes.

Sometimes I wondered if I'd have had the guts to sign up to be a scavenger if Garth hadn't signed up with me. Everyone started to work on the Atlas at age eleven. It used to be nine, right after the Tide Rising, so eleven really did feel like a luxury. As far as jobs went, scavenging wasn't one of the most desirable, that was for sure. You weren't even supposed to work as a scavenger until you were fifteen. It was too dangerous to send someone younger than that into water that seemed to get more and more hostile with each passing year. The pressure of diving that deep could kill you if you weren't careful, and the water temperatures could get so cold you risked hypothermia even with a wet suit.

Despite all that, it was the only job on the Atlas that seemed tolerable to me. Which, considering I was routinely shoved headfirst down small underwater holes, was really saying something. Scavenging was one of the jobs no one really wanted, which is why bending the age requirement was something Gizmo hadn't even blinked at.

I could smell breakfast long before I saw it. You'd think that, having grown up on a diet primarily made up of fish, seaweed, and more fish, I would have become immune to the overpowering smell, but I hadn't. My stomach rumbled regardless as I made my way up to the counter to collect my halibut wrapped in its seaweed wrapper. Garth grabbed a second one when the worker wasn't looking and tucked it into his pocket. That move should have probably grossed me out, but you couldn't be friends with Garth and let that kind of stuff bother you. He'd definitely stored worse things in that pocket. I gulped my breakfast down quickly, barely tasting what everyone on board called a briny burrito as I made my way after Garth down the stairs and toward the back of the ship to the scavengers' dive room. It was time to go to work.

The dive room was already full of the rest of the *Atlas*'s scavenging crew when we came in. Once, the clatter of gear and the overpowering smell of mildew would have overwhelmed me, but not anymore. This tiny room, with its mismatched jumble of wet suits and half-broken dive equipment, was my smelly second home. I mumbled what was supposed to be a hello around my last mouthful of burrito and went straight to my locker.

"You two better hustle if you don't want Gizmo on our case," said Ralph, a scavenger a few years older than me, as he finished zipping up his thick black wet suit. "We'll only have about two hours to scavenge this new town before we have to move on."

"Do we know the name of the town?" I asked, yanking my own wet suit out of my locker.

Garth groaned and rolled his eyes toward the ceiling. "You always ask that, and we never know. Unless it's something big like Chicago or London or something, no one ever cares about the name of the town."

"I care," I said.

"You're weird," Garth said.

"There's that, too," I said, pausing just long enough in my gear check to grin at him. He chose that moment to burp loudly. When I shot him a disgusted look, he threw his hands up defensively.

"What?" he said, his green eyes crinkling up at the corners as he grinned at me. "If I did that in my mask, I'd be smelling it for the next two hours."

"So instead you made us smell it," Ralph muttered as he shouldered past us and toward the back of the dive room, where I could just make out Gizmo with his customary clipboard and scowl.

"What's that?" Garth said, peering at the small metal box I'd just fished out of my bag.

"I'd have shown you this morning if you hadn't decided to sleep in, Sleeping Beauty," I said.

"Beauty sleep," Garth scoffed. "I'd need a beauty coma, and I'd still look like a walrus sat on my face."

I rolled my eyes. Garth was overly self-conscious of his appearance these days. He'd shot up about three inches overnight, and he'd broken his nose a few months ago and it hadn't set right, giving him a crooked and slightly flattened appearance that I barely noticed but he obsessed about. I decided to let the walrus comment slide and held up the tiny rusted box.

"I'm tired of going into a building with nothing but a headlamp," I said, showing him the square with its flashlights embedded in each side. "I used some broken headlamps and patched them together. Now I can just turn this on and toss it in a window or a chimney or whatever, and I'll know if there is anything unpleasant waiting to greet me."

"Makes sense," Garth said. "But I think you're going to get in trouble if Gizmo sees that," he said. "You remember what he said after he caught you with that . . . what was that thing again?"

"A sand sucker," I said, and I felt my face flush the bright, embarrassed red it always got when I was reminded of a failure.

"I believe Gizmo called it a giant waste of time," Garth said.

"That's because it didn't work," I said. "If it had worked, he would have probably liked it."

"Not Gizmo," Garth said. "If it isn't his idea, he'll hate it. Didn't he say if he caught you messing around with junk like that you'd get fired?"

"Something like that," I said as I quickly shrugged my gear on. I tucked my flippers and my face mask under my arm before shutting my locker and turning back to Garth. He wasn't quite finished getting ready, and I tapped a foot to show my impatience.

"Relax," Garth said.

"You know how Gizmo feels about us being late," I said. "It makes him all twitchy."

Garth grinned. "I like making Gizmo twitchy."

"You would," I said as I followed him out of the dive room and down the hall to where I could hear the other scavengers already queuing up. We got in line at the back of the pack just as Gizmo showed up dressed in his flashy blue wet suit. Unlike the tattered and patched black ones we wore, his was pristine, and I couldn't help but be a little jealous of how well it fit his stocky frame. The worse your wet suit fit, the colder you were. I was always cold.

"Good morning," Gizmo said, and everyone grumbled a half-hearted good morning in return. "Today we have some luck on our side. The town we're scavenging was buried under the sand until the recent storm stirred things up enough to uncover it. I don't have to tell you that it means we have some prime scavenging on our hands today. Captain Brown could only grant us two hours, though, as we have a trade meeting scheduled with the *Blue Oyster* and the *Sundial* the day after next and our schedule is tight, which means no screwups." He paused to look each of us in the eye. "Stick to the methods you've been taught," he said with a special glare in my direction. I avoided his eyes, pretending to be preoccupied with cleaning out my face mask.

"Should be a good haul," Garth said in my ear as Gizmo started in on his usual lecture about the price per pound of iron versus copper. I nodded. "Do you ever wonder how many other towns are out there, just waiting underneath the sand for some big storm to stir things up enough for us to find them?" Garth said, looking dreamy-eyed. It was no secret that he loved scavenging more than the rest of us. For me it was a job, one I'd taken to gain access to the ocean that existed beneath the waves.

"But don't you feel like we owe it to the towns somehow to know their names?" I said. "I mean, if we forget their names, isn't it like they were never even there? It seems wrong somehow."

"What seems wrong is only getting two hours," Garth said. "We'll barely be into anything good and it will be time to head back in."

"You'll find something good," I said. "Besides, do you really want just Gizmo in your ear for *more* than two hours?"

"Solid point," he agreed with a smirk. "With all your tinkering, you should figure out a way to turn his mic off somehow."

Gizmo cleared his throat loudly in front of us, and we snapped our mouths shut.

"Better," he said with a scowl that pulled his dark eyebrows so far down they practically connected in the middle. What hair our boss was lacking on the top of his head, his eyebrows more than made up for. "Now, if there aren't any questions, let's do this." He turned and headed out of the room, his own flippers tucked snugly under his arm. We followed obediently down the hall and up the short flight of stairs to the dive deck. Positioned near the bottom of the ship, the deck sat about ten feet above the waves. It had been designed to be levered out from the side when the ship was docked and then ratcheted back in when it was on the move. The result was a flimsy metal platform that barely had enough room for us and the small crane and lift we used to bring up the salvage.

In front of us, one by one, the other scavengers walked to the edge of the deck. Each of them took a few seconds to carefully secure the face mask that fit snugly from chin to forehead before making the jump. The masks not only cycled oxygen through to the diver, but also made a protective bubble around the face that allowed us to communicate with each other via a tiny speaker embedded in the side. They were a far cry from the diving equipment that had been available right after the Tide Rising. My grandfather used to tell stories about clunky oxygen tanks and face masks that didn't even cover your entire face. The human race had quickly realized that diving was essential to its continued survival, though. Only limited resources had been brought onto the boats, and the only way to replenish supplies was to wrestle them from the wreckage beneath the waves.

Desperation often breeds invention, I thought, as I carefully situated my mask so it fit snugly against my chin, forehead, and cheekbones. I wondered if I'd ever invent something so useful. Suddenly the small metal box under my arm felt basic and stupid. It was essentially a glorified flashlight. I let that depressing thought swirl around in my head while I waited for our turn to jump. As the two youngest on the crew, Garth and I were always relegated to the back of the line. A fact that meant we were usually last to the easy-pickings salvage and were stuck dredging up the harder stuff.

Soon enough we were at the end of the deck, and I looked down at the rolling blue waves as the divers in front of me disappeared below the surface. My stomach did a sickening flip, the same one it always did right before I went under. It used to bother me, that surge of fear, but it didn't anymore. Fear was just a part of life, and if I let it eat at me, I'd never get anything done.

"Wanna stick with me today?" Garth asked before sliding his face mask down. I nodded, more than happy to tag along. Garth had a sixth sense about scavenging that I somehow lacked. Sure, I was useful if you had a small dark hole you needed to stuff someone down, but if anyone was going to find something of value on a dive, it was usually my best friend. Garth leaped off the deck, hit the water, and disappeared. I was the last one, and I adjusted my own face mask a final time, stepped forward, and jumped. As I slipped beneath the surface, I placed one hand on my mask so it wouldn't slam upward and break my nose as the water, cold and icy blue, rushed up to meet me.

I kept my feet together and my body tight as I plummeted downward. Below me I saw the rest of the crew already turned and paddling toward the sprawl of wrecked buildings spread out below. Garth was to my left, and I turned and kicked hard to catch up with him.

"Remember," came Gizmo's voice through the speaker in my mask, "iron is at an all-time high. Don't pass up anything." I felt the pressure on my ears as we went deeper, and I took the half second I needed to acclimate. We could dive much deeper than our ancestors thanks to the improvements they'd made on our gear, but some things, like water pressure, had to be dealt with the old-fashioned way. This dive was fairly shallow for us, only about thirty or forty feet below the surface, but it still felt like descending into a whole other world.

The town below us had probably been a small one by pre–Tide Rising standards, but it still seemed huge to me. That was what always struck me about the underwater ghost towns we scavenged: all that space. People used to have entire houses to themselves. Houses with more than one room, and huge areas dedicated to nothing but sleeping or cooking or whatever. It was hard to imagine, but I'd been inside enough of them now that I could almost picture it.

As we got closer, I could see that the houses were only partially revealed, the sand heaped up and mounded around them in the haphazard aftermath of the storm that had unearthed them. The ocean was funny like that, shifting and moving to reveal its hidden treasures. If Gizmo was right, and he usually was, this town had never been scavenged before, which meant we might find some decent stuff.

Garth and I paddled past the rest of the scavengers who'd already laid claim to houses and toward the outer edge of the town, where we had a better shot of finding an unclaimed spot.

"Any of these look good to you?" Garth said.

"I think we should go a bit farther," I said, but my words seemed to bounce back to me. The speaker in my ear buzzed angrily, and I winced.

"Did you hear me?" Garth said.

I nodded and pointed to my mask, making a thumbs-down motion.

"Your mic is busted again?" Garth groaned. "I swear, our equipment is being held together with hope and Gizmo's spit."

"Gizmo's microphone is working just fine, Garth," Gizmo's voice said in our ears, and Garth winced and mumbled an apology that didn't sound at all sincere. Gizmo went on. "If Berkley's mic isn't working, then make sure you two stick together. And if I hear another comment like that, you'll be scrubbing down the dive room for a week."

Garth rolled his eyes inside his mask, but he didn't dare answer back. Gizmo wasn't known for making idle threats, and you never knew when he had the micro-phones set so that every scavenger could hear your response. Our best course of action was to get to work, so I followed Garth toward the outskirts of the town.

"I like the looks of this one," Garth said, pointing to a house on our right, or what was left of it. Since I couldn't exactly argue with his choice, I followed, although I'd rather have taken the house on the left. The speaker by my ear buzzed again, and I winced, wondering if I could just turn it off and claim the whole thing broke if Gizmo ripped into me after this for not listening to his instructions. Garth stopped in front of what was left of the front window and flipped his head-lamp on so he could peer inside. I swam around the back of the house, hunting for an unblocked entry. I ran my hand over the crumbling brick as I swam, and pieces of it fell away, as if the house had been made of clay.

The back of the house wasn't nearly as intact as the front, and I found a convenient Berkley-sized hole in the facade and swam inside. The beam of my headlamp lit up the interior of a surprisingly sand-free space, leading me to believe that either the majority of the windows hadn't broken, a minor miracle, or—and this was more likely—it hadn't been completely buried. Still, if I hadn't known that I was inside a house, it would have been hard to distinguish what I was looking at. The ocean was a pirate that commandeered anything she thought was hers, and she'd turned the inside of the place into a habitat for creatures that liked to make their homes in the dark.

"Find anything good?" Garth said in my ear, and I gritted my teeth in exasperation as he remembered my broken mic and groaned. I got to work, and a half hour later I had a small pile of usable copper piping I'd ripped out of the walls. I flagged Garth down to help me, and together we hauled our find back toward the *Atlas*. Gizmo was positioned directly under the dark shadow of the ship with the salvage net and carefully noted what we dropped off before sending us back out. Around us other scavengers were doing the same, bringing bits of this or that to be carefully noted and added to their total.

Paper money wasn't really a thing after the Tide Rising. With no place to spend it, people used it for a while in place of toilet paper until the human race rigged all the toilets with bidets. My grandparents had been in their forties during the Rising, and after, my grandfather kept a hundred-dollar bill in his pocket just for luck. Sometimes he'd pull it out and show it to me. I loved when he did that, not because I thought the money was particularly neat—in fact, it was so crinkled and worn you could barely see the image of Ben Franklin anymore—but because he'd sometimes talk about Benjamin Franklin and how people like him had shaped the world. He'd ruffle my hair and tell me that no matter what happened in the future, the creativity and invention that had preceded us would always be needed.

It was a lesson the human race had definitely had to learn the hard way. Now, instead of money, we got survival credits. If you wanted to survive, you had to work, and for your work you were paid in credits that could be cashed in for food, clothing, extra heat in the winter, and just about anything else you might need to live your life. My briny burrito that morning had cost my dad a credit, a credit I hoped to more than earn back with our haul today.

Garth paddled toward the outskirts of the town again, and I wished I had a way to tell him that I didn't think we had that much time. Gizmo was already giving the half-hour warning, and as soon as we made it there, we would need to turn around. Garth was a faster swimmer than me, though, and when I finally caught up with him, we were back at the house we'd just left.

"What do you think that is?" he said, pointing to our right, and I followed the direction of his finger to a large mass that was barely distinguishable in the sand.

I gave an overexaggerated shrug and shook my head, trying to send the message that we didn't have time for this, and Garth nodded.

"Super, I knew you'd want to check it out. Great idea." I muttered something uncomplimentary, mainly because I knew he couldn't hear me, and followed him. The closer we got to the mass, the more obvious it was that it was a large building of some sort. Only one story, its roofline almost visible above the sand, spreading back in a T shape.

"I think it's a school," I said, only to have Garth echo me two seconds later. I made a mental note to check my headset before I did another dive mission.

Instead of trying to find a way inside, Garth paddled down to the flat expanse of sand directly behind the building and ran his hand over it. I swam down to where he was pushing at the sand with his gloved hands. Then I spotted it: a slight knob of metal barely visible among the rocks and shells littering the ocean floor. Garth looked up at me, and I saw his wide grin through his mask.

"Jackpot," he said. He put his hand to his ear. "Gizmo?" he said. "You there?"

"Whatcha got?" Gizmo said.

"I think it may be playground equipment," Garth said. "I need the hook."

"Send Berkley back for it," Gizmo said. "And hustle.

The captain wants us out of here." I turned and paddled back up toward the gigantic gray blob of the *Atlas*, my leg muscles burning.

By the time I made it back, a hook and rope in tow, Garth had the top eight inches of the play set exposed. It appeared to be one of those bubble-shaped things with crisscrossing metal bars children could climb around on. It reminded me a little of a fishing net right after it was thrown out over the water, only more symmetrical and, well, metal. It was also bigger than I'd thought it would be, and I said a silent prayer that it hadn't deteriorated too badly. Sometimes when you hooked these things up and the crane started reeling them in, they just fell to pieces. Garth took the hook from me and dove down to wrap it expertly around the middle section of a metal bar.

Deciding that he didn't need my help for this bit, I swam over to poke around the building. The sand had kind of mounded up on one side of it, revealing a long line of windows on the other side. To my surprise, most of them were intact, and I glided down to peer inside to see if they were worth breaking open. Unfortunately, the glass was so covered in scum that it was impossible to see anything. Something about the place felt off, though, and I took a second to look around. I'd been doing this long enough to trust my instincts.

They'd saved me from a run-in with a great white once, and another time from sticking my hand inside a hole where a poisonous sea snake had taken up residence.

Then it clicked, what was bothering me: there weren't any fish. Not a single one was meandering around the building. Turning, I saw that it was the exception to the rule, as rainbow-colored fish of every size and shape poked around the other houses and bits of wreckage. There was something about this building that they didn't like. Had my microphone been working, I'd have mentioned it to Garth, but he was still busy rigging up the piece of playground equipment. I felt something prickle down my spine, and I shivered, imagining a giant spider somehow making its way into my wet suit.

Garth looked up and signaled for me to come help, impatient to start reeling in his find, but I shook my head. It was then that I noticed the hole in the roof. It was big, more than big enough for me to fit through, and I swam up to peer in. The inside was practically pitch-black, with nothing but shapeless lumps and mounds visible in the gloom. I switched on my headlamp, but its one narrow beam didn't do much to illuminate things. It was the perfect time to try out my new light cube.

"What are you doing?" came Gizmo's voice in my

ear, and I knew he was peering at us through his specialized binoculars. No matter how far away you were, you were never really out of Gizmo's sight. "Help Garth with that piece of equipment," he snapped. "We don't have all day!" I turned around and held up a finger to show him that I needed a minute. I heard him huff impatiently in my ear, and I carefully turned my back to Gizmo and the *Atlas* so I could slip the light cube out and turn it on. Light shot out in all directions as I dropped it into the hole.

I watched it sink slowly and hit the sandy bottom about ten feet below. My cube lit up the space, illuminating rusted desks and broken whiteboards. Everything was in a jumble, tipped over and half buried in the silt and the sand, but even from here I could tell that the metal on the desks wasn't that tarnished. I was just turning back to signal to Gizmo that I'd found something, when a massive lump moved beneath the sand.

I froze as the entire bottom of the building seemed to undulate. Something was down there, and that something was big. My mind raced rapidly over all the species I knew of that hid under the sand, but none of them even came close to the size of whatever this was. I watched with horror as first one and then another huge red snakelike coil emerged. I screamed, which was pointless because my microphone was turned off, and threw myself back from the hole and directly into Garth. His hands closed around my shoulders and I twisted frantically, dragging him backward and away from the building.

"What's happening? What is it?" Garth said. "Is there a shark?"

"Did I hear you say *shark*?" Gizmo said sharply, and even though I was terrified, I saw out of my peripheral vision multiple scavengers pop up out of houses, immediately on high alert. We'd lost more than one scavenger to a shark attack, and everyone had a healthy respect for the creatures. I shook my head vigorously, still doing my best to pull Garth back and away from the building. Garth followed, craning his head back to see what had me in such a panic.

"Will you two stop messing around!" bellowed Gizmo in our ears. "I'll slash your credits on that piece of equipment for wasting time, don't think that I won't!" I frantically scanned the ocean for somewhere to hide, but all the houses were too far away to be a viable option. In the distance I saw the rest of the scavenging crew return to the houses they'd just left, following the protocol of scavenging until the last possible minute. I had to warn them, but even if my microphone had worked, my words were frozen inside my throat as panic roared through my veins. I looked back at the wrecked school with its gaping hole in the roof just as two huge luminescent eyes opened up to look right at me.

The eyes blinked, and slowly a head emerged from the darkness of the hole. At first I thought it was a gigantic moray eel—the long snakelike creature that liked to back itself into a hole and wait for dinner to swim inside its gaping mouth. But this creature wasn't the murky lime green of a moray—it was bloodred. It had the same ribbon of body as the moray, but the similarities stopped there. For one thing, this thing was huge—its head alone was probably three feet long—and its mouth, when it opened in a silent hiss, was filled with overlapping rows of needle-sharp teeth. It emerged a bit more, its body uncoiling from the building as it stretched itself to what had to be ten feet and counting.

Gizmo screamed in my ear, the noise so piercing that I cringed from it, causing the creature's eyes to focus back on me. Gizmo's terrified scream came again, and around me I saw the other scavengers pop up from the ghost town, their eyes wide behind their masks as they tried to figure out what had made our leader sound like that. There was a moment where everything seemed to freeze—the divers, the monster, time itself—as we took in this completely unknown but utterly terrifying predator, and then the moment was over and chaos broke loose. Every single diver forgot their training and bolted for the surface as fast as their flippers would take them. Well, everyone except Garth, who stayed at my side, his eyes wide inside his mask. My instincts, all of them, were screaming at me to make a break for the surface, but I knew that would be a mistake. The *Atlas* and safety were too far away.

We'd never outswim the thing. Our best bet was to go literally to ground and hide.

"Don't move," I said, thinking of the moray eel the creature resembled, whose eyesight was incredibly poor. Maybe I'd get lucky and this thing would have the same issue. Even if it wasn't related to the moray, every predator had the instinct to chase down prey once the prey ran. Realizing Garth couldn't hear me, I risked sliding my left hand out to grasp him firmly by the wrist, hoping to convey the same message. His eyes darted toward me and then got wide as he noticed everyone racing for the surface.

"Pressurize!" he bellowed. "Slow down! Do you want the bends? Gizmo! Tell them to pressurize themselves!" Gizmo's voice never came over our speaker, though, and as the monster continued to emerge from the building, the majority of the crew just swam faster. Why hadn't Gizmo told them that? I wondered. He was responsible for the scavenging team, something we'd been reminded of on more than one occasion. To my shock I saw that he was already almost out of the water, abandoning his duties in his desperation to save himself.

I absorbed all this in the matter of a few heartbeats, adrenaline rushing through my system in one heady tidal wave. The monster, which was the only word I could think to call the thing looming over us, turned its head to look at the half-filled net of salvage that was being brought rapidly toward the surface. I saw our opportunity and turned and paddled hard for the ocean's floor, making sure to keep a firm grasp on Garth. My eyes scanned for anything that might save us. Then I saw it: the partially uncovered playground equipment. Garth had made more progress than I'd have thought possible and had uncovered a foot and a half of the equipment, exposing the jungle gym's upper dome.

"Berkley!" Garth yelled, but I didn't turn around. I knew what was behind us. A second later we reached the equipment, and I wiggled, twisting this way and that to squeeze between the bars and down to the sand. I made it inside and turned to help Garth, who was struggling to fit his wide shoulders through the small square of metal. Behind him, rushing toward us, was the monster, mouth open wide. Panicked, I pulled hard. Garth popped through, his flippers sliding inside just as the creature's jaws slammed into the metal equipment. Even through the water, I could hear the screech of the metal as its teeth scraped against it. I lay on my back beside Garth, flat on the sandy bottom of the ocean, the honeycomb web of metal only a foot above us as the creature reared back. It darted its head down again, its massive jaws open. I wanted to shut my eyes, to block out the image of that huge open mouth, but I couldn't. The metal protecting us was already bending and warping under the monster's attack, and I knew it wasn't going to last much longer.

The creature was all the way out of the building now, and I saw the long serpentine body coiling behind it. The thing had to be twenty if not thirty feet long, and it was lashing its body this way and that angrily as it tried to pry us out of our hole. This went on for what felt like forever, but it was probably only a minute or so before the beast decided we were a lost cause and gave up, turning its attention back to the rest of the scavengers and the *Atlas*. I lay there for another second, panting inside my fogged mask, as the monster darted toward the ship.

"Are we dead?" Garth said beside me. "What was that nightmare?" I shook my head. We needed to get to the ship, but my muscles felt wobbly and shaky in a way that made me not trust them overly much. I moved anyway, forcing myself up and out through the bars, using them to steady my trembling arms as I watched the monster. Almost everyone had made it out of the water while the monster was trying to eat us, but the giant bag of metal that we'd been working to scavenge from the ocean still hung limply ten feet below the ship, abandoned in the panic of the situation. The creature didn't notice it, though; it was too busy circling the ship, bumping its nose along the long hull. A moment later it surfaced, its long body propelling it upward so its head exploded out of the water, and I imagined the chaos that must be breaking out on deck. A fresh stab of fear lanced through me as I thought about my family. Were they safe?

A second later, huge crates and odd bits of the ship started hitting the surface and sinking as the monster wreaked havoc on supplies the *Atlas* desperately needed. Someone needed to do something, and fast.

"Berkley," Garth said, "swim for the ship! This is our chance!"

Garth was right, but the second I kicked off, I was brought up short. My left flipper had gotten caught on something, and I turned and spotted the hook and chain I'd handed Garth earlier. It was still attached to the now-mangled playground equipment, its length trailing along the bottom of the ocean floor before bending upward toward the *Atlas*.

I glanced back up as a huge crate hit the water. Yes, someone needed to do something, and that someone might just be me. Reaching down, I grabbed the hook.

"You can't be serious right now. Forget the equipment!" Garth yelled. "Just swim!"

The hook felt reassuringly heavy in my hands as I turned and started swimming toward the monster. I ignored Garth's yell of frustration and exasperation as he saw that I was yet again failing to follow his instructions. The closer I got, the bigger the monster seemed, and I started second-guessing myself with every kick and stroke, but I kept going. If we let this thing keep savaging the ship, there might not be a ship left to escape to, and then we'd all be sunk. Literally.

The monster's long body whipped this way and that so erratically I worried it would hit me and my plan would be ruined. Although a word like *plan* was too fancy for what I was doing. I was winging this on gut instinct and a vague idea that was still forming even as I swam.

I dove underneath the creature, bringing the chain up in a loose U shape underneath it. That was the easy part. This next bit was where it was going to get tricky. For it to work, I was going to have to swim over the top of the creature, and not just once, either. Hesitating wasn't an option, not when any second the monster could plunge back down and see me. So I just did it: I swam hard and fast, the hook clenched tightly in my hand. I made it across and immediately plunged down to swim underneath the creature a second time, praying that it was too busy to feel the slight pressure of the chain lying across its back.

Around me bits of the ship were sinking, hitting

the monster and me as they made their journey down to the bottom of the ocean. If I was lucky, that would be enough to keep the monster from noticing me for another minute. I swam up and over the top of it for my last pass. Reaching down, I clipped the carabiner-style hook over the entire chain rather than to a single link, so that the loops around the creature would tighten like a noose, and then I swam hard for the hanging bag of salvage.

I had almost reached it when I heard Garth yell something in my ear, and I turned to see the monster plunge its head back underwater. My luck had run out. The creature focused on me, sizing up the situation with its yellow orb eyes. Its red skin flashed in the light from above. My heart seized inside my chest, but the rest of me didn't have the luxury of freezing, not if I wanted to survive. I paddled hard for the hanging bag of salvage, and I felt my heart sink when I spotted Garth behind it. He'd taken up refuge behind the bag, probably to make sure I was okay. Now if my plan didn't work, it was Garth's life on the line too, not just mine. The chain that I'd looped around the monster was still hopelessly loose, and any second now it would give one hard shake and the whole thing would slip off and fall to the ocean floor. I couldn't think about that, though. I just had to move.

"What are you doing? Are you crazy?" Garth yelled in my ear so loud it made me wince despite my panic. I wanted to tell him yes, yes I was crazy, thanks, but instead I just grabbed the part of the chain that still looped up toward the ship. Thankfully, the end of it had a safety hook that could be detached so that the ship could free itself in case of an emergency. Well, this definitely counted as one. I detached the top hook, the weight of the chain heavy in my hand as I swam past the bag of salvage and up to where it was hooked to the ship. I clipped my chain to its top loop.

I looked down and frantically gave Garth the signal to drop the bag of salvage. Without that, the plan would never work. "What?" Garth said, staring up at me, his eyes wide behind his mask, and I made the motion with my hand again, yelling "Drop the bag!" even though I knew he couldn't hear me. He nodded, and I heard him repeat my words into his working microphone. Now we just had to pray that someone on board was listening and manning the controls.

The monster chose that moment to attack. It darted toward us like a striking snake, and Garth's scream made my eardrums throb as he ducked behind the bag of salvage. The creature was on us a moment later, its teeth sinking into the salvage net as it shook it this way and that like a dog trying to break the neck of a rat.

"DROP THE SALVAGE BAG! NOW!" Garth yelled again, and this time someone on board followed directions. The bag of salvage metal plummeted toward the bottom of the ocean, exposing us. The monster flicked its tail and opened its mouth in a triumphant hiss. Garth yelped, and we both kicked frantically backward, away from the monster, but there was nowhere to hide. Our only protection was now rocketing toward the bottom of the ocean floor.

The monster was mere inches from us, so close I could have counted the number of teeth in its jaws, when the chain I'd looped around its middle suddenly tightened, and it was yanked downward. The creature writhed angrily as it tried to free itself, but it was no use: the bag of metal it was connected to was too heavy, and the chain was too tight, for it to escape. I felt Garth clutch my arm as we watched the enraged monster twist in on itself. It was time to go. I jerked my head toward the surface, and together we paddled up to the ship.

As we made our way to the ladder, I turned back to look at the monster one last time. It chose that moment to stop gnawing on its chain and look up at me and the ship. I wouldn't have thought that a creature like that could communicate emotion through its gaze, but there was something about the way it stared at me that made me sure that it would kill me if it had the opportunity. I scrambled up the ladder after Garth. As soon as I made it to the scavengers' platform, I felt hands grasp my shoulders, helping me up the rest of the way.

Everything around us was chaos and panic as people rushed here and there, some bending over prone scavengers while others lost their cool completely. Somewhere in there the *Atlas* started moving, slowly at first and then picking up speed as it fled the terrifying monster. The diving platform was reeled in quickly, and I wondered if anyone had bothered to make sure everyone was on board before we departed. Even as I thought it, I knew that it was a stupid question. What mattered was putting distance between ourselves and the monster, and Captain Brown was apparently willing to lose a scavenger or two if needed. I felt a rush of relief that we hadn't loitered in the water a second longer.

"That was incredible," Garth said. He'd ripped his dive mask off, and the red circular ring it left around his face just accentuated his wild expression.

"Incredible?" I repeated. "If by *incredible* you mean *terrifying*, then you hit the nail on the head."

Garth shoved his hands into his dripping hair and pulled, looking back at the shut door as though he'd be able to see the monster again that way. "I'm not sure if

I want to scream or puke. Can you believe we're alive? I can't believe we're alive. I thought for sure we were dead meat down there. I mean, what are the odds of surviving a sea-monster attack? A sea monster! But here we are! Alive!"

"You're also fired," Gizmo said from where he sat, slumped against the wall.

I wanted to check on my family, but Gizmo had other ideas. Despite the fact that he was obviously sick from his fast ascension through the water, he grabbed Garth and me by the back of our wet suits and man-handled us down the hall and into his office.

"You two stay put until the captain gets here," he snarled, slamming the door behind him. A second later there was the dull thud of a lock being turned, and we heard Gizmo's footsteps stomping away.

"No need to thank us!" Garth yelled after him, despite the solid metal door between us. "Well, how do you like that?" he said, throwing himself down into Gizmo's desk chair in disgust.

"Did he say the captain?" I said.

"Maybe he wants to congratulate us for saving the ship," Garth said.

"Or maybe we are in deep trouble," I said, slumping down in the chair opposite Garth.

"We're heroes!" Garth protested.

"We're also the ones who woke up the monster that almost took down the ship," I said. "Well, actually that part was kind of just me."

"Hmm," Garth said. "I hadn't exactly thought of that. How did you wake that thing up anyway? Drop a rock on its head?"

"A light cube," I said. "I showed it to you before we dove, remember?"

"If I were you, I'd keep that bit of the story to yourself," Garth said. "We're already in enough trouble without you admitting you were using one of your whackadoo inventions again."

"They aren't whackadoo," I said defensively. He raised an eyebrow at me as I pulled a face at him. "Well, they aren't all whackadoo," I said. "It worked, didn't it?"

"Yeah," Garth said dryly. "Worked like a charm. That was lots of fun."

I huffed and crossed my arms over my chest. My wet suit was still sopping, and the chill of Gizmo's office was making goose bumps break out all over my skin. Although, I reasoned, that could just be a result of nerves about our impending meeting with Captain Brown. My stomach twisted as I realized that I'd never even had an opportunity to ask whether my family was okay, or if there had been any casualties on board besides the crates. My fear turned to anger as I paced around the tiny office, giving a stack of rusty tin a kick for good measure.

Since Gizmo was head officer in charge of our ship's scavenging department, his office had become a catchall for just about every half-tarnished piece of junk imaginable. Two rusted headlights and a traffic light missing the green and red glass hung on the wall next to a twisted picture frame, two broken rakes, and a shovel that was missing its handle. Old pipes, half-disintegrated kitchen utensils, dog tags, part of a stop sign that just read *OP*, and glass bottles of every shape and size were jammed haphazardly into any available space. He'd even rigged some of the finds to the walls and ceilings with an odd assortment of gnarled wire, misshapen coat hangers, and fishing line.

Even though I was fuming, I couldn't help but notice a few odds and ends that I could use in my current tinkering projects. I felt a pang of sadness over losing the light cube. I'd worked for a month on that thing, and it *had* worked. How was I supposed to know I was dropping it onto a sea monster's head? I spun around to face Garth, who was still brooding in Gizmo's chair, his hands templed in front of his face.

"That was a sea monster," I said.

"No kidding," Garth said dryly.

"No," I said, walking over to stand in front of him, my hands on Gizmo's cluttered desk. "Like a real, honest-to-goodness *monster*. They aren't supposed to exist. I mean, I've read about them in books and stuff, but I've also read about dragons and elves and gnomes and giraffes, and none of those exist either."

"Giraffes?" Garth said, raising an eyebrow. "I thought those did exist before the Tide Rising? Like, they had crazy long necks or eyeballs or something."

I flapped a hand in the air dismissively. "You get what I'm saying," I said. "Sea monsters aren't supposed to be real."

"The one that just about ate us begs to differ," Garth said.

"If that one exists," I said, my thoughts spiraling out in dizzying swirls, "then what *else* exists?"

"I'd guess more sea monsters," Garth said. I turned to look at him. "Well," he said, shrugging, "it had to come from somewhere, so its parents are probably out there too, along with a few sea-monster brothers and sisters, aunts, uncles, and third cousins twice removed."

"Whoa," I said, plopping back down in a rusted chair. I let that sink in for a minute and then turned to Garth. "So why do you think we've never heard about them before? This can't be the first time a ship was attacked."

"That's a great question," Garth said. "Do you think the adults know and they just don't tell us kids so we don't get freaked out? Like, remember when the fresh-water filtration machine broke a few years ago and our parents just pretended we were rationing water because the captain was trying to collect more accurate numbers on water usage?"

I snorted and nodded, remembering how I'd been so annoyed at the tiny cup of water I got with my meals. It wasn't until much later that I realized the *Atlas* had been in a major crisis and my parents had just kept going with smiles on their faces like our survival wasn't at stake.

Before I could think any more about it, the office door clicked, and in walked not only Captain Brown, but Gizmo and four other officers. All of them wore similarly gray, strained expressions as they crowded into the cluttered office. Garth waited a hair too long to spring out of Gizmo's chair, earning him the dirtiest of dirty looks from its owner.

"So, you two are the ones responsible for the attack," Captain Brown said, taking the seat Garth had just vacated. "Tell me what happened." I swallowed hard and glanced over at Garth, but he just shook his head. The story was going to have to be told by me, so I told it, conveniently leaving out the part where I dropped the light box on the monster. Garth was right. We were in enough trouble already. Captain Brown listened to the whole story, his face not betraying any emotion. Finally I finished, explaining about the haphazard hook-and–salvage bag trap I'd made on the fly.

"Why didn't you sound the alarm the moment you saw the monster?" the captain finally asked.

"My microphone was broken, sir," I said. Captain Brown turned to look at Gizmo expectantly.

"Aren't you responsible for checking the quality of the equipment before every diving mission?" he said. Garth scoffed loudly, earning him his second glare from Gizmo in the space of five minutes. Gizmo turned back to Captain Brown, squirming uncomfortably like a fish caught in a net.

"It was an oversight, sir," he said.

"An oversight that cost us precious seconds," Captain Brown said. "We may lose five of your scavenging team to decompression sickness, and the ship had almost no warning of the attack."

"Gizmo didn't warn you when he took off scream-ing instead of alerting the rest of the scavenging team?" Garth said sarcastically.

"That's enough out of you, Watkins," the captain said. The use of Garth's last name made us both squirm. Last names were only used when you were really in for it. "Our ship sustained serious damage, and the cost to fix and replace our lost supplies is going to be astronomical. That's not even taking into account the lost credits of the scavenging crew who will be in pressure tubes for the next week. I get a sense from your tone that you're unaware of who is being held accountable for that?"

"I'm really hoping you're going to say Gizmo," Garth said. Now it was Gizmo's turn to scoff as Cap-tain Brown slowly shook his head from side to side.

"You think this whole mess is our fault?" I said, my insides turning to ice as it dawned on me what he meant. The expense of everything he'd just listed was more than all the credits I'd make in my lifetime—in my family's lifetime, for that matter.

"You can't blame us for this," Garth said, his voice hard. I wished I sounded like that. Instead my own voice had gone up about five octaves and become squeaky with outrage.

"I can, and I will," Captain Brown said. Behind him,

Gizmo was practically beaming at this news, and I shot him a dirty look that he ignored before turning back to Captain Brown.

"We could never earn back that many credits," I said. "Not ever."

"No," Captain Brown agreed. "You can't. However, we have contacted a nearby work ship, and you two will be transferred there in the morning. It won't repay your debt, but it will help."

Garth's face suddenly drained of all color, and I felt the walls of the room closing in on me as I stared at Captain Brown. "A work ship?" I repeated, certain I hadn't heard him correctly. Work ships were the closest thing we had to prisons after the Tide Rising. They were usually reserved for pirates or members of a ship who had committed major crimes. The prisoners of a work ship were forced to do hard labor under pretty terrible conditions until their debt to society was repaid. Something that rarely happened, as conditions aboard a work ship weren't exactly conducive to a long, healthy life.

"Our parents will never allow this," Garth said.

"Your parents have no say in the matter," Captain Brown said, but there was something about the way his eyes flicked guiltily to the side that made me think he wasn't telling the whole truth about that. Did our parents know about his plan? I doubted it. Captain Brown gave a curt nod to the officers flanking him and pushed himself to his feet. "You will remain in Gizmo's office tonight, and we will launch a boat to take you to the work ship at dawn."

"We don't even get to say goodbye to our families?" I said as numb disbelief at what was happening enveloped me. Captain Brown just ignored us and turned for the door.

"I'm going to take that as a no," Garth said. His comment was ignored as Captain Brown and the other officers left. Only Gizmo remained as the door clicked shut behind the rest of the crew.

"Why are we being held here?" I said. "It's not like there is anywhere we can escape to. Why not let us have one last night with our families?"

"Don't you get it yet?" Gizmo said. He shook his head slowly as he studied us. "This isn't so much a punishment as a gag order. Do you think the captain wants you two blabbing about what you saw down there to the rest of the ship?"

"What do you mean?" I said. "Doesn't everyone know we got attacked by a sea monster?"

"You mean the diseased whale that blundered into our ship?" Gizmo said. "Everyone knows about that. They were told about it when the entire ship went into lockdown. Of course, no one saw it besides the scavenging team, but most of our team is currently not in a state to talk, and if they recover, they will be sworn to silence or receive the same fate as the two of you."

"Wait a second," I said. "Why are you covering this up? Shouldn't everyone know about the sea monster? I mean, this could happen again!"

Gizmo rolled his eyes. "Don't be ignorant," he said. "You think this is the first time the *Atlas* has come face-to-face with one of those nasty pieces of work?"

"It's not?" Garth said.

"Kid. You have no clue. And that's the point. We realized a long time ago that keeping the general population of a ship on a need-to-know basis worked in everyone's best interest. The captain and the officers handle sea monsters when they come up, and, thankfully, they only come up every few years."

My mouth dropped open in shock, and I glanced over to see Garth with a similar expression. Gizmo seemed to take pleasure in our surprise, and he grinned at us, revealing his crooked assortment of teeth.

"Why do you think we have such a hard time keeping scavengers on the crew?" he said. "After an incident like this one, I'll lose half the cowards to other jobs, and the other half might not recover from the bends."

"No thanks to you," Garth muttered, earning him another dirty look from Gizmo.

"You know," he said, "I thought I'd feel a little bit sad to see you two carted off to a work ship, but I think I thought wrong."

"You can't really send us to a work ship," Garth protested. "We saved the *Atlas*! If Berkley hadn't gotten the monster all tangled up in the salvage net, you and everyone else would be at the bottom of the ocean right now."

Gizmo's face twisted in a grimace. "I forgot about losing that entire load of salvage. The equipment alone costs more credits than the two of you could make in ten years aboard a work ship, and that's not even counting the salvaged materials the crew had gathered. There was some quality stuff in there. I'll have to remind the captain of that in case he didn't add it to your total."

"Gee, thanks," Garth said.

"You're a real creep, Gizmo. You know that, right?" I said.

"It was either you or me going down for this, kid," he said, turning toward the door, "and it definitely wasn't going to be me." The door clicked shut, and the sound of the deadbolt being locked from the outside felt deafening. My ears rang as I sank down onto the floor, my back against one of the only bare patches of wall in the cluttered office, and I put my head between my knees. A second later I felt Garth sink down beside me, cold wet shoulder pressed to cold wet shoulder. I squeezed my eyes shut, trying to make sense of what had just happened, and failing miserably. It was like trying to add two plus two and somehow make it equal one hundred. It just didn't add up no matter how I looked at it.

"Why?" I finally said, pulling my head up to look at Garth. "Why are they doing this?"

"I have a few theories," he said, glaring at the locked door Gizmo had disappeared through.

"Tell me," I said, desperate to understand.

"Theory one," Garth said, holding up a finger. "Gizmo's the worst boss ever."

I snorted. "That's a fact, not a theory."

"Theory two," Garth said, holding up a second finger. "You heard Gizmo—this is a cover-up. They need to keep us quiet, and the only way to do that is to ship us off. They don't want everyone to panic, and everyone would if they knew there were giant sea monsters out there just waiting to eat our ship for lunch."

"Right," I said. "I guess that makes sense. Besides, the captain wasn't lying about the damages. I bet they are going to cost a fortune, and if he can get rid of us and earn some of it back at the same time, he probably sees it as a win-win."

"But our parents would never allow this in a million years," Garth said.

"Didn't you see the captain's face when I brought that up?" I said. "I'd bet anything they have no idea." Suddenly my insides gave an angry twist as I realized something else, and I turned to look at Garth. "I bet they think we're dead," I said.

"What?" he said. "That's crazy!"

"Is it, though?" I said. "How else could the captain cover this up? I mean, over half the team is in pressure tubes, and we were the last ones out of the water. The only person who even saw us come out was Gizmo, and he had us in this office in less than two minutes. They think we're dead!"

"Whoa," Garth said, and I nodded as I let that sink in. What was my dad doing now? How was he handling the news that his daughter was gone forever just a few years after we lost Mom? "We have to get out of here," Garth said a moment later, already vaulting to his feet to rattle the doorknob.

"We can't," I said, shaking my head as I watched him fruitlessly ram a shoulder into the solid metal door.

"There has to be a way," Garth said, turning to scan the room frantically for any other exit.

I shook my head again. "It's not that we can't find a way out, although that doesn't seem particularly hopeful. It's that we *shouldn't*."

"Did you hit your head down there?" Garth said. "We have to warn our parents."

"And then what? Once they know, they'll just be sent to a work ship too. And what about my brother and your sisters? What happens to them if our parents are sent away?"

Garth stood there a moment, his hands balled into angry fists at his sides, before sagging in defeat and coming over to sink down next to me. "A work ship," he finally said. "Maybe it won't be that bad. Maybe all the horror stories we heard about them were just to scare us into behaving. I mean, my mom herself used to threaten to send me to a work ship pretty much daily when I was three."

"Three?" I said, eyebrow raised.

"I was a rotten three-year-old," Garth said with a shrug. "And if you believe my mom, a horrible four-year-old and the worst five-year-old on the entire ship."

"It took years to become your charming self, huh?" I said, forcing a smile onto my face.

"Masterpieces take time," Garth said with a sigh.

"I'm sorry," I said.

"For what?" he asked, turning to look at me in surprise.

"For dropping a light cube on a sea monster's head,"

I said. "For this entire mess. Maybe if I'd just swum for the ship like you said instead of staying back to tangle the thing up, we wouldn't have gotten blamed for it all."

"Or," Garth said, "we'd all be dead now. I guess we'll never know."

"I guess," I agreed. And with that we both settled in for what would be our last night on the *Atlas*. Garth fell asleep first, his head listing to the side so it rested on my shoulder. I didn't mind, though—even though my wet suit was almost dry, it was cold in the office, and his body heat was welcome. I stayed up for what felt like hours after he'd begun snoring, thinking about that monster. Replaying the day in my head over and over again as I tried to see a way I could have avoided getting my best friend and myself into this mess—and always coming up short. So much for creativity and inventiveness, I thought grumpily as I felt my eyes finally begin to close. Even half-asleep, I couldn't stop myself from thinking about sea monsters.

4

We woke up to the door unlocking. Garth and I both sat bolt upright, our salt-encrusted wet suits squelching weirdly as we clambered to our feet. I was still trying to blink the blur of sleep from my eyes when Captain Brown walked in with two burly ship officers. I noted immediately that each of them was holding a pair of handcuffs as well as a piece of thin black fabric that I feared would be used as a gag. I'd only seen someone sent off to a work ship once before, but the scene was burned into my memory. A man had been caught siphoning food from the kitchens, and the captain had made a show of having him marched through the middle of the ship. He was a warning to the rest of us about what happened when you broke the law.

I doubted that was how we'd be marched out. A glance at the ramshackle clock on Gizmo's wall showed it wasn't even dawn yet. We were being snuck out of here while the rest of the ship slept. I felt like crying, like crumpling into a ball and holding on to the leg of Gizmo's desk so they'd have to pry my fingers off like stubborn barnacles. Instead I stood up straighter and put my shoulders back as I stared at Captain Brown, condemning him for this with my eyes. Beside me I felt Garth's shoulder tremble, but to his credit he stood his ground too. I felt a rush of gratitude that at least I wasn't alone in this.

"Good to see you two have come to terms with your fate," Captain Brown said with an approving nod. "Please stand still."

The officers came and forced our hands behind our backs, quickly cuffing our wrists before slipping the black gags into our mouths. My heart hammered hard in my chest as I forced myself to stay still through this whole process. Struggling wouldn't help, and escaping wouldn't do anything besides bring my family down with me, something I was determined not to do. A moment later we were hustled out the door and into the quiet of the sleeping ship. As we walked, I tried to commit the creaks and groans of the *Atlas* to memory, my eyes scraping over each familiar surface as though somehow that would etch it in my brain forever, because I knew full well that I'd never set foot on the ship again. The thought made my stomach twist uncomfortably, and I remembered how just the day before I'd been chafing at the idea of spending my entire life aboard the *Atlas*. Now I'd have signed up for that life in a heartbeat.

We were on deck faster than I would have liked, and I gasped as I took in the damage the monster had managed to wreak in mere minutes. A huge chunk of the railing and deck had been damaged, and half the supply crates were missing or mangled beyond repair. The captain was really explaining this away with some lame story about a whale? As I stared at the teeth marks, a ripple of fear went down my spine. It wasn't hard to picture what those teeth could have done had they sunk into me. We weren't given time to linger, though: the officers marched us quickly to the far side of the ship, where a few small boats were kept.

One of them was already standing ready and waiting, a small crew on board preparing for launch. I glanced around the deck one last time, simultaneously hoping for a glimpse of my dad and terrified that he'd show up and see what was about to happen. What was worse? I wondered. Thinking your child was dead in some freak diving accident, or knowing they were suffering for years on a work ship to pay off an unpayable debt? Garth was hustled onto the boat first, and I followed, catching my foot on the rail and almost pitching headfirst into the boat before one of the officers managed to catch me. As it was, I barely avoided bashing my face on the opposite rail.

As I leaned over to catch my breath, I saw something move in the dark water below us. I tried to scream, but the gag in my mouth muffled it enough that I was ignored. The water below us churned again, white foam and bubbles erupting from beneath, and terror zipped through me. It was another sea monster—it had to be. I screamed again, jerking from the officer's grasp as I tried to make the new threat known. Finally someone else spotted the churning water and sounded the alarm. There was a flutter of movement as the small boat we were on was hurriedly cranked back in so it was no longer dangling helplessly over the churning water.

A minute later, the thing emerged, blue-black in the predawn light. I thought at first that I was looking at an enormous whale. It was curved and fluid, almost like part of the waves, with a large bulbous front that tapered off to what appeared to be a tail structure at the back. A second later, something moved on top of it, and a light came streaming out the top of a circular hole. A hole that people were climbing out of.

"It's a bloody submarine," said one of the officers.

"That's not like any submarine I've ever seen," said the second officer.

"Pirates?" asked the first as he peered over the rail at the massive vessel bobbing beside us.

"Ahoy, Captain!" came a shout from below. "The *Britannica*, Coalition-issued submarine fifty-four, would like permission to board." Captain Brown hesitated for a minute before giving a curt nod and signaling to the crew to lower a ladder to the waiting sub. Meanwhile, Garth and I stood forgotten, bound and gagged, as two people made their way up the *Atlas*'s ladder and over its rail.

The first one on board was a woman, short and muscular with dark skin and hair cropped so close it stood out in tiny ringlets less than an inch long all over her head. Behind her, in sharp contrast, was one of the palest girls I'd ever seen. She was about my age, with red hair pulled back into a thick French braid that hung over her shoulder like a friendly snake.

"Captain Brown, I presume?" said the woman, striding over to hold out a hand to Captain Brown, who shook it warily. "I'm Captain Reese of the *Britannica*," she said with a wide smile that wasn't returned. "If we could speak in private a moment?"

"Certainly," said Captain Brown. "But if you wouldn't mind moving your submarine, we were about to launch this boat. There is a work ship about three miles south of here, and we have some passengers to drop off."

Captain Reese glanced over to where Garth and I stood and studied us a moment. "They are actually what I came to talk to you about," she said. "So, if you wouldn't mind, this will only take a moment." She stood there expectantly as Captain Brown looked from her to us and back again. Finally he motioned for her to follow him, and they disappeared into the *Atlas*'s bridge. The girl stayed behind and smiled at us. Since we were gagged, smiling back was impossible, but that didn't seem to bother her.

The *Atlas* rocked gently in the water, and I glanced back down at the submarine that Captain Reese had called the *Britannica*. Submarines docked with the *Atlas* at least once a month, if not more. Sometimes they docked to trade with us, and other times they docked so that their crew could stretch their legs and get some fresh air. I usually made a point to avoid submariners, mainly because most of them were downright weird. Although you couldn't really be expected to spend most of your life in a tiny metal tube underwater and not be weird. The *Britannica* was no metal tube, though, and the girl in front of us seemed normal enough, even if her skin was see-through pale.

The minutes stretched on, and the officers around us

shifted uncomfortably, casting nervous glances from the *Britannica* to the deserted deck and back again. The sun was just starting to turn the horizon to a hazy pink when the two captains reemerged. I searched Captain Brown's face for some clue about what exactly was going on, but his stern expression didn't give anything away.

"Change of plans," he told the officers surrounding us. "These two will not be going to the work ship after all. Captain Reese has asked to bring them on as part of her crew."

"But their debt," one of the officers protested.

"Will be repaid by the *Britannica*," Captain Reese said, turning to face us. "That is, if you two agree to join us." Garth garbled a reply around his gag that was far from being understandable, and Captain Brown motioned for the officers to take off our gags.

"What exactly does the *Britannica* do?" Garth said.

"We unfortunately don't have time to discuss that," Captain Brown said sharply. "You either agree to go with Captain Reese and get your explanations later, or we will continue with our plan to turn you over to the work ship. You need to decide now."

His words hung in the cool morning air, and I glanced over at Garth, who appeared just as confused and shell-shocked as I felt. I looked from this strange new captain to the officers on either side of me and back again and realized I was being given a choice. Granted, it wasn't an exceptionally good choice, but for the very first time, I was going to get to have a say in what direction my life took.

I flexed my hands against the hard metal of the cuffs as I felt fear and uncertainty give my heart a painful squeeze. It was the exact same feeling I always got right before I jumped off the *Atlas* into the endless blue of the ocean on a dive. Maybe leaping into the unknown always felt like that, I reasoned as I lifted my chin to look Captain Reese in the eye. Neither of my options allowed me to stay with my family, but even though I had no idea what the *Britannica* did, it had to be better than a work ship.

"I'll go," I said, glancing over at Garth, who nodded.

"Very good," Captain Reese said, motioning for us to head for the ladder. "Let's be off, then. I'd like to disembark before the rest of the ship wakes up, and I know Captain Brown is anxious for us to be on our way as well." I felt the loosening of the cuffs as they were unlocked, and I rubbed at the raw skin around my wrists.

"Are we really doing this?" Garth whispered in my ear.

"Do you really want to go to a work ship?" I whispered back.

"Not even a little bit," he admitted. The red-haired girl headed down the ladder first, and Garth followed. I hesitated a second to look back across the deck of the *Atlas* at the small cluster of officers and Captain Brown, who were all watching us with wary and slightly confused expressions, and took a deep breath in an attempt to calm myself. Ever since that monster had emerged yesterday, my life had felt like it was in free fall, and somehow descending the ladder into the unknown felt like the biggest plunge yet. Captain Reese smiled reassuringly and motioned for me to get on with it, so I did, moving hand over hand down the thick rope ladder.

The girl reached out to grab my elbow to steady me as my feet hit the rock-hard surface of the submarine, and I turned to see Garth already disappearing down the circular hatch in the center of the sub. Captain Reese touched down a moment later, and the ladder was quickly zipped back up into the *Atlas*. A moment later the ship lurched, and I heard the faint call of Captain Brown ordering the men to pull this sail and that rigging to get the ship moving. I felt a gentle hand between my shoulder blades and allowed Captain Reese to guide me over to the hatch. I glanced down, surprised to see a narrow spiral staircase where I'd expected a ladder, and, with one last glance at the *Atlas*, I headed down.

I made it to the bottom of the stairs and watched numbly as two adult crew members worked to secure the circular entrance. For half a second, I debated racing back up the stairs and telling them to let me out, that I'd changed my mind, but I knew that wasn't an option. I caught one last glimpse of the sunrise-pink sky before it was wedged out by the thick metal hatch, and we were ready to dive.

"Take a deep breath," said a voice to my right, and I turned to see the redheaded girl smiling brightly at us. "People panic less when they remember to breathe," she said. I made an effort to wipe away the tears I hadn't even realized were running down my cheeks, but she swatted my hand away and offered us each a small towel to mop our faces with. "Sorry," the girl said, stepping forward to shake my hand and then Garth's so hard and enthusiastically I felt my knuckles pop. "I'm Kate," she said. I nodded, noting for the first time what she was wearing. While Garth and I were still sporting the patched and faded wet suits we'd dived in the day before, Kate was wearing tight-fitting black pants with aqua rubber boots that went up to her knees and matched the *Britannica*'s color perfectly. On top she was wearing a loose-fitting white shirt that accentuated a face that was so pale I could see the veins crisscrossing beneath it like thin blue spiderwebs. The only bright spot of color on her besides her boots were her eyes, which were emerald green and a tad too large for her face.

"I'm Berkley," I said automatically. "This is Garth."

"Good, you've met Kate already," Captain Reese said, coming up to clap a welcoming hand on each of our shoulders. "She's part of your training unit."

"Training unit?" I said. "Training unit for what?"

Captain Reese smiled reassuringly. "All will be explained soon, I promise. I know this is sudden and a lot to take in."

"Don't worry," Kate said. "Everyone is a mess when they come aboard for the first time. Why wouldn't you be? Most people just cry, but there are the special few who puke, too."

"What she's failing to mention is that she's one of the special few who puked," said a voice behind us, and we turned to see a boy come around the corner.

"Thanks," Kate said, making a face at him. "They could have lived without that particular bit of information."

"They could have," the boy agreed, "but why would they want to?" He turned to face us, his movements somewhat jerky and stilted.

"And this," Captain Reese said, "is Max. He's a second-year recruit from the *Iberian*." Max stepped forward and held out a hand for us to shake. He had dark brown hair, which he wore slicked to the side, and light brown skin with a sallow look to it, like he hadn't seen the sun in years. Which, I realized, he might not have. The thought was jarring, and out of the corner of my eye I saw Garth's face twitch.

"You two take charge of the new recruits while we get submerged," Captain Reese ordered. "Captain Brown was very clear that we need to be out of sight as quickly as possible." She turned to us. "Don't worry, you're in good hands." With that she turned and disappeared around the corner. Max looked us up and down, and I noticed that he'd lost the easy smile he'd given us just moments before. His face seemed harder now as his dark eyes studied us. He sniffed. "I bet these two don't last a week."

Kate rolled her eyes at Max. "Ignore him," she advised. "I do. You'll definitely make it at least two. Now follow me. Captain Reese lets new recruits sit front and center on their first submersion, and you're not going to want to miss it." She whirled and headed after Captain Reese.

"Was she joking?" Garth whispered in my ear.

"I hope so," I said, and hurried to follow Kate. We rounded the corner, and I stopped so fast that Garth collided with my back.

"Whoa," he said, peering around me as we caught our first glimpse of the *Britannica*. I'd expected the interior of the submarine to feel claustrophobic, with walls pressing in on all sides and nothing but narrow hallways. I couldn't have been more wrong. The inside of the *Britannica* was huge and almost airy, with a wide-open chamber surrounded by three curved walls of glass that looked directly out into the ocean. The top foot or so of the glass was above sea level, and between the constant roll of the waves I could just make out the retreating outline of the *Atlas*. The sight made my stomach flop sickeningly, and I forced myself to look away. Situated around the rest of the space were different control centers, most of which displayed computer screens full of data I couldn't hope to understand.

"You might want to close your mouths," Max said as he maneuvered himself around where we stood frozen in slack-jawed amazement. "Everyone knows you're the newbies, but you don't have to advertise it by walking around like a whale shark trying to trap plankton."

"Solid point," Garth said, his jaw coming together with an audible click.

"This is the main hub of the *Britannica*," Kate said. "It's where we not only steer the sub but also conduct most of our research."

"What kind of research?" I asked.

"These two don't even know what we do here?" Max said, his eyebrows shooting up in amazement. "Forget a week—these guys will be crying to go back to their ship in a day."

Kate shot him a look and then turned to us. "We research lots of things," she said.

"Sea monsters," Max said. "The *Britannica* hunts and researches sea monsters."

"Smooth," Kate said, rolling her eyes in exasperation.

"I'm not trying to be smooth," Max said. "I'm trying to be honest. They should know what they're getting into while they still have the chance to turn back. If they swim for it, they could make it back to that rust bucket of a ship."

"Sea monsters," I repeated, turning to look at Kate to make sure that Max wasn't just messing with us.

She shrugged almost apologetically. "It's kind of weird that you didn't know the details before you signed on. I mean, when I was recruited, I got the whole spiel from Captain Reese, and then my parents and I made the decision together, but from the, um, circumstances we found you guys in, I'm guessing there wasn't time for that."

"What circumstances?" Max said.

"Don't worry about it," Kate said, arching an eyebrow at him.

"Whatever," Max said, turning away from us. "Get them in their seats. We're about to submerge."

"Is it too late to choose the work ship?" Garth whispered in my ear, and I swallowed hard.

"I think so," I said as I looked at the *Britannica* with fresh eyes. Sea monsters, this thing was designed to hunt sea monsters, and I'd apparently just signed up to be part of its crew. A large school of fish chose that moment to swim so close to the glass that a few of them brushed up against it.

"Glass doesn't seem like, um, a safe choice," I said, momentarily distracted.

"That is no ordinary glass," Kate said with evident pride. "It's built to withstand impacts higher than any metal, and pressure up to a thousand feet. It's safer than most metals too, especially with the way salt wears away at things."

"We know all about the damage salt can do," I said dryly. That wear and tear was what my dad and brother battled day in and day out as they worked to keep the *Atlas* running despite the ocean's attempt to destroy it.

"Gosh, Kate," Max said, rolling his eyes. "You sound like a walking, talking instruction manual, only more chipper and obnoxious."

"Thanks," Kate said, flashing him a grin that showed all her teeth. Max groaned and shouldered past us into the room. He jerked his head hello to a few of the people who were busy at the various workstations, and for the first time my attention focused on the crew members. Most of them were adults, but there were a few teenagers in the group who looked about Wallace's age. We were by far the youngest of the lot, and I noticed that while the crew varied in age and skin color, they all had the same sallow cast to their skin that made it clear that most of their time was spent away from the sun. A few of them turned to inspect us, but for the most part we were ignored as they prepared the submarine to dive.

Thinking of my sixteen-year-old brother made me focus more on the handful of teenagers working alongside the adult crew. Like Wallace, they were all pretty lean and muscular, but on the whole they were about six inches shorter than my gangly sibling, and I had the disconcerting thought that humans might be a lot like plants, and didn't grow very well without the sun.

Kate noticed my glance and flapped a hand dismissively at the crew. "No worries," she said. "You'll meet the gang eventually. There are only about twenty-five crew members on board, including the recruits, and we are kind of like a very odd, mismatched family. You'll learn to love it."

"So," Garth said, glancing around, "there are no actual families on board?"

Kate shook her head. "Nope. Life on a submarine, especially one like ours, isn't exactly a great fit for normal family life. The *Britannica* recruits individuals who show a certain . . . let's say *knack* for what we do, and asks them to join. You two are actually kind of rare. I can't remember if we've ever taken two people from the same ship before. But come on—we need to go snag a seat or someone will give us a lecture."

With that she grabbed us by the arms and guided us over to a long, narrow bench located along the back wall of the hub. Max was already seated, one foot propped up on the bench. He moved it reluctantly, and I sat down next to him with an equal amount of reluctance. If Kate was an overly chipper instruction manual, this kid was the human equivalent of a door slamming in your face. If there really were only twenty-five other crew members, though, I was going to have to figure out how to get along with him. I made a mental note to ask Kate why he already hated us and sat with my back against the cool metal of the sub to watch the *Britannica*'s swirl of activity.

The crew was bustling here and there, flipping switches and calling out commands and bits of information as they went about the business of submerging.

"You'll eventually learn how to orchestrate a submersion," Kate said in my ear. "It's part of your training." I nodded numbly, still not quite sure how I felt about all this. Max was wrong: Garth and I couldn't turn back. I wondered if this whole thing would feel so unsettling if like Kate I'd been able to talk over the decision with my dad. Would my heart still feel like it was stuck somewhere in the back of my throat if I'd had a chance to hug him and Wallace goodbye?

I took a deep breath and pushed the thought away as I reminded myself that I hadn't had the *option* to say goodbye. I'd been stuck between a rock and a hard place, and I'd chosen the unknown hard place instead of the known rock. Now I was going to have to make the best of it. It was what my dad would have told me to do, and I owed it to Garth to put on a brave face. It was kind of my fault he was in this mess, after all.

Despite my mental pep talk, it still felt like I'd left a part of my heart on board the *Atlas*. I kept that thought to myself, my lips pressed tightly together, as I watched. I found my eyes drawn to Captain Reese. She was standing in the middle of things like the calm in the center of a hurricane. She gave an order here, or adjusted something there, and she did it all with an easy smile on her face.

Kate must have noticed my gaze, because she

leaned in again. "Captain Reese is the real deal," she said. "She's one of the only female submarine captains in the world, and she's the best. When Captain Harrison stepped down, the vote was unanimous to elect Captain Reese as his successor. She's a super-skilled diver, too, almost always takes the lead on sea-monster research expeditions, and she single-handedly saved half the crew from a jörmungandr about three months back."

"A jörmungandr?" I said, turning to look at her. "What's that?"

Kate shuddered and shook her head. "You really don't want to know. But you'll find out soon enough once they show you the monster map."

"The monster map?" I realized that all I'd done since boarding the *Britannica* was repeat what Kate said like a half-wit. Kate didn't seem to mind or notice, but just nodded and leaned around me to where Max slouched, his arms crossed over his chest.

"Max," she called. "The monster map is Weaver's first lesson for recruits, right?"

He nodded, not even bothering to look our direction.

"Don't mind him," Kate said, noticing my worried glance. "He's not a fan of new recruits."

Max snorted and pushed to his feet to walk over

to one of the teenagers standing behind a large control panel. We watched him walk away, and I noticed that he had a very distinctive limp, like his right leg didn't quite work right.

"Why doesn't he like recruits?" Garth said.

"He just doesn't," Kate said, a hair too quickly. She wasn't telling us something, and that thought gave me an uneasy feeling in the pit of my stomach.

"Who's Weaver?" Garth asked.

"He's one of the researchers, and the professor for us recruits. You're going to love him," Kate said. "Weaver's weird. But in the best possible way."

"I like weird," Garth said.

"That's good," said Kate. Something suddenly landed in my lap with a heavy thud, and I jumped in surprise, barely stifling a scream. The fat, furry something was doing very uncoordinated circles on top of my legs in an apparent attempt to get comfortable. Its body was small and stocky, with legs that bowed out a bit, and it had a smashed-in, wrinkled face and large ears that stood straight up.

"Is that a pig?" Garth said, leaning over to get a closer look at the thing.

"How should I know?" I said as I held my hands up and leaned as far back as I could in the confined space. The thing was making an odd snuffling sound, and I was worried that it might bite.

"That's just Tank," Kate said.

"What's a tank?" Garth asked.

"Tank is a dog," Kate said with a snort. "A French bulldog, actually, and he's kind of a mascot on board the *Britannica*."

"Seems like a weird choice," Garth said. "Why not a cat?" I pictured the handful of cats that lived aboard the *Atlas*. Despite the fact that land was nothing but a distant memory, rats and mice were still a constant problem aboard boats like ours. Sometimes it seemed like they were more tenacious survivors than we were.

Kate shrugged. "Tank can catch the occasional mouse, but pests aren't really a problem for us. I'd say he's more of a morale booster."

"He's kind of ugly," Garth said.

Kate laughed. "We like him that way." Tank gave a disgruntled snort as though he knew he'd just been insulted and lay down on my lap with what I could only describe as a resigned huff.

"Does he bite?" I said.

"Only toes," Kate said.

"Toes?" Garth said.

Kate nodded. "Yup. He hates them. I think he's convinced we all have worms attacking our feet. Just keep your shoes on when he's around and you'll be fine."

Tentatively I reached out and ran my hand down his back, remembering when I'd tried a similar move with one of the ship's cats and gotten a hiss and a row of four neat red scratches for my trouble. Tank just grunted a little, and I felt something inside me relax a bit.

"You three should shut it," Max commented as he walked back over to plop down beside me again. "You're about to miss the best part."

We turned to watch as Captain Reese gave one final signal and the sub began to sink. A flurry of bubbles erupted from somewhere underneath the *Britannica*, sending up a shower of silver circles that obscured the view for a moment. When the bubbles cleared, I saw the distant underside of the *Atlas*. My breath caught in my chest, and I blinked back tears as the last glimpse of my home disappeared into a swirl of blue-black ocean. There was no going back now.

5

The submarine dove deeper, and I adjusted the pressure in my ears, my training as a scavenger kicking in despite the utter chaos of the last few hours. It was then that I noticed that Max and Kate were looking at me and Garth with odd, expectant expressions on their faces, and I raised an eyebrow.

"What?" I said.

Kate studied me a second and then held out a hand to Max. "I win," she said. "Pay up."

Max hesitated before digging something out of his pocket and slapping it into Kate's hand.

"I'd have bet anything that at least one of them was going to hyperventilate," he grumbled.

"Everyone hyperventilates?" I said.

"Most do," Kate said as she unwrapped the thing Max had handed her and took a bite.

"Really?" I said, surprised. "Like, they didn't realize that being in a sub meant going underwater?"

"It doesn't really hit you until it happens," Kate said with a shrug.

"It's a lot like diving," I said as the sub started moving forward, making its way through swirls of fish.

"How is everyone doing?" Captain Reese said, coming over to stand in front of us. "Now that we're underway, why don't you two step into my office so we can have a quick chat. After that, Kate and Max can show you your bunks and get you settled in before Weaver gives you the official orientation." She motioned for us to follow her and disappeared through a small doorway to our left.

Garth immediately bounded to his feet, but I hesitated, not sure what to do about the sleeping dog. Kate solved my dilemma by reaching down, scooping Tank up, and tucking him under her arm like a giant sausage. Tank blinked up at her blearily. I followed Captain Reese and found myself in a tiny closet-sized office just big enough for the slim desk the captain was sitting behind and the two chairs opposite. Garth was already perched in one, biting nervously at his thumbnail, a habit I hadn't seen in him since we were both eight. I sat down on the edge of the remaining seat as Captain Reese reached over to push the door shut. The room felt close and small, and I shifted uncomfortably as I looked at Captain Reese.

"Did Max or Kate mention what we do here aboard the *Britannica*?" she said, and when we both nodded, she smiled. "I had a feeling they might, and I want to apologize for not being able to paint you a clear picture before bringing you on as recruits. That is not how we normally do things—however, as you can probably agree, we didn't exactly arrive to find you two in normal circumstances."

"That's an understatement," Garth said.

Captain Reese chuckled. "Professor Weaver will go into the nitty-gritty of sea-monster management and research, and you will learn a lot of what we do on the fly and in the course of your duties on board the *Britannica*, so now I'm just going to give you the basics." We nodded, and Captain Reese settled back in her seat and folded her hands in front of her. "The main mission of the *Britannica* is to research sea monsters. And when a monster decides to attack a ship, like the one that almost killed the two of you yesterday, we are commissioned to protect the ship and its crew at all costs."

"Was that only yesterday?" I wondered out loud. It

felt like I'd lived a lifetime since that last scavenging dive.

"It was only yesterday," Captain Reese reassured me. "We received the *Atlas*'s distress call around eight a.m. and came immediately, although obviously we arrived long after the actual attack."

"Wait, you got a distress call?" I said.

Captain Reese nodded. "All ships are equipped with a special distress call for monster encounters. The signal goes directly to the closest on-duty submarine, and if they are capable of helping, they do. Unfortunately, it's a big ocean, and there aren't nearly enough of us to deter every attack."

"How often are ships attacked?" I said.

"Much more often than we'd like," Captain Reese said. "There were close to thirty attacks in our precinct just last year."

"How is that possible?" I said. "Sea monsters aren't supposed to exist."

"And yet they still do," Captain Reese said. "There are at least two hundred different species that we know of, and Professor Weaver estimates there are hundreds more yet to be discovered. In fact, they've become quite the problem," she said, continuing as though she hadn't just said something absurd.

"Wait," Garth said, holding up his hand. "So not

only do you research sea monsters, but you have a precinct? As in there are more subs out there doing the same thing as this one?"

Captain Reese chuckled. "I'm sorry," she said. "I'm getting ahead of myself. I forget sometimes that ship dwellers are kept mostly in the dark about these things."

"That's one way to put it," Garth said with a side-long glance at me. I nodded grimly. The fact that the *Atlas* had kept the existence of sea monsters hidden from us felt like a huge betrayal. It made me wonder what other information the captain and his officers had conveniently forgotten to mention. A shiver of nerves completely unrelated to monsters tingled down my spine as I thought about all the people on the *Atlas* waking up today and grumbling about how a whale could have done that much damage to the ship, and for the first time I stopped feeling bad about not getting to say goodbye and started worrying about what would happen to my family.

"The *Britannica* is one of twenty submarines commissioned by the Coalition to hunt down and research sea monsters," Captain Reese went on, interrupting my thoughts. "About ten years after the Tide Rising, ships started being attacked in such high numbers that something had to be done. The *Britannica* and submarines like it have been assigned to protect certain quadrants

81

of the ocean, to come to the aid of ships under attack and to try to prevent attacks by seeking out monsters."

"To kill them?" I said.

"Only when they pose a threat to the human race," Captain Reese said, "Our main goal is to research and learn about the creatures so we can better protect our ships and the citizens who make their lives on them."

"Did you manage to kill the one that attacked us?" Garth said hopefully.

"Unfortunately, no," Captain Reese said, shaking her head. "The hydra, the monster that attacked your ship, is incredibly fast. So fast, in fact, that the ancient Greeks used to think it had multiple heads. We've proved that theory false, of course, but their speed makes them difficult to capture or kill unless we come upon them actually savaging a ship. We were able to attach a tracking device to the one that had attacked the *Atlas*, a first for us." Noticing our concerned expressions, she smiled reassuringly.

"Don't worry," she said. "It lost the *Atlas*'s trail and is now headed in the opposite direction." I felt myself sag a little from relief. "We will continue to monitor it," she went on. "If it looks like it will cross paths with the *Atlas* again, we will do our best to intercept it. If you two are still with us at that point, you'll be part of that interception."

"Wait," I said. "What do you mean, *if* we're still with you?"

"You're here on probation," Captain Reese said. "If you do well, you will be allowed to become part of our permanent crew. If not, you will be returned to your ship."

"But we can't go back to our ship," I said.

Captain Reese nodded sadly. "I know, which is why I hope this works out."

"But why would you even want us?" Garth said, asking the very question that was on my own lips.

"We have cameras attached to the undersides of most of the ships in our precinct, the *Atlas* included, and we were able to record the majority of your interaction with the hydra. We feel that you both showed an impressive aptitude toward sea-monster hunting."

"An impressive *what*?" Garth said, glancing at me like I might know what in the world the captain was saying. I just shrugged, still trying to wrap my brain around the fact that an entire submarine did nothing but chase down sea monsters. The idea was equal parts baffling and wonderful.

"What did you call the thing that attacked our ship?" I said.

"It was a hydra," Captain Reese said. "A ruby hydra, if we're being specific, which I'm sure Weaver will be during his orientation. Sea-monster specifics are kind of his specialty. He's the closet thing we have to a sea-monster expert."

"A sea-monster expert," Garth said, shaking his head in disbelief. "Too weird."

Captain Reese chuckled, and I found myself smiling back at her. She seemed so much more relaxed than Captain Brown or Gizmo—or any other officer, for that matter—and there was something about her that made me feel less tense. "The majority of people react like your scavenging officer when faced with a sea monster. You two, however, managed to keep your wits about you, and that's rare in anyone, let alone anyone your age. We are training a small group to be the next generation of sea-monster specialists," Captain Reese went on, "and we think you two would be a great addition."

"What about our survival credits, or lack thereof?" I said, thinking of our insurmountable debt. "Our families aren't stuck with our debt now that we aren't going to the work ship, are they?"

"No," Captain Reese said. "Survival credits work a little differently here on the *Britannica*, but due to the dangerous nature of our job, the Coalition has made sure that those who work here are compensated. Captain Brown agreed to accept your credits for the next few years as repayment. And with that, I'll turn you back over to Kate and Max." Captain Reese pushed herself to her feet. "They will give you a quick tour before Professor Weaver takes you to your first lesson." We both stood up in a kind of daze, and she opened the door. Max and Kate were waiting for us, Tank still tucked firmly under Kate's arm. "I know this is a lot to take in," Captain Reese said. "But what we do here on the *Britannica* saves lives, and if you join our team, you'll help save lives too. Who knows, the lives you save might even be your own families'." I was still wrapping my head around that when Kate grabbed my arm and spun me away.

"Come on," she said. "Bunks are this way." Garth and I hurried after her, and Max reluctantly brought up the rear. We wove our way through narrow hallways until we came to a bunk room. Stacked five high, the beds reminded me more of bookshelves than bunks, but I kept my lips shut as Kate showed me the top bunk that was to be mine.

"Go ahead and check it out," she said as Garth clambered into the bunk directly below it. I did, climbing up a bit more cautiously than Garth had and slipping into my bunk. It was narrow, and my face was a mere foot and a half from the ceiling, but it was surprisingly comfortable. There were small cubbies along the back, presumably for our belongings, and I realized with a pang that I didn't have any. The only thing I owned was the ratty wet suit I was wearing.

"Don't worry," Kate said, peering over the edge of the bunk. "The *Britannica* has all the supplies you'll need. I'll grab you a set of my clothes to change into until you get some of your own." She turned to look over her shoulder. "Max, grab some clothes for Garth."

"No," Max said.

"Max," Kate said warningly, and I heard Max huff as he rustled around in his bunk and handed something to Garth. I climbed down, and Kate handed me a stack of clothes, complete with a pair of aqua boots identical to the ones she was wearing, and motioned me into the small attached bathroom. I changed quickly, peeling off the wet suit and giving my chafed skin underneath a good scratch before pulling on the new clothes. Kate was a bit taller than me, so the shirt hung past my hips, but I'd never been so grateful in my life to not be in a wet suit.

I emerged to see that Garth was wearing Max's clothes, and I had to stifle a laugh. Where Max was tall and slim, Garth was shorter and broader, and Max's too-small shirt was stretched over his chest so tightly I was worried it might rip. He shot me a look that begged me to keep my mouth shut, so I did.

"Now what?" he said.

"Now we show you around a bit," Kate said.

"There's no *we* in that sentence," Max said. "You can give them the grand tour if you want, but I have better things to do." With that he turned and maneuvered his way out of the tight bunk room and disappeared around a corner. Kate watched him go, her forehead creased in concern. Finally she turned back to us, rearranging her face quickly into a friendly smile. Tank chose that moment to snort, and we all looked down at the little dog as he turned and trotted out the door at the far side of the bunk room.

"Well," Kate said. "Maybe I'm not on my own for the tour. Please follow Tank."

Tank led us out the door and down yet another narrow hallway. Kate stopped every now and then to point out things like the captain's quarters and two other bunk rooms, one for the adult female crew members and one for the males. Apparently, the coed bunk room was reserved for recruits like ourselves and the teenagers who worked on the crew. Once you were eighteen, you were allowed to move into the adult bunks, which were a shade larger and more luxurious than our accommodations, but not by much. Next up was the submarine's small kitchen, a bathroom, and a few rooms that housed the nuts and bolts that kept the submarine running. I found it hard to remember I was actually in a submarine, though. The *Britannica* felt bigger on the inside than it looked on the outside, and I felt myself relaxing a bit.

"So, how long ago were you recruited?" I asked Kate as I followed her and our roly-poly tour guide down the narrow hall.

"A little over a year ago," Kate said.

"Wow," Garth said, shaking his head. "You've been underwater a whole year?"

"Can't you tell?" Kate said, pointing to her face. "I used to have freckles, you know. A ton of them." I'm not sure what our expressions were, but she flapped a hand dismissively. "Time flies down here. You'll see. They keep us so busy sometimes I lose track of what day it is. Besides, we surface every now and then. After a while this will be your new normal, and you won't even remember your life before."

I felt something inside me twist a little painfully at her words. I didn't want to forget about my dad and Wallace, not ever.

"What was your life like before?" Garth said.

Kate shrugged. "I lived on a small fishing boat. We only had about thirty or so people on board, and most of them were related to me. *Lots* of bickering." She grinned. "Anyway, our boat got attacked by a small ghorch, and the *Britannica* was close enough to pry it off us."

I felt my eyes go wide. "What's a ghorch?" I said.

"Picture a cross between a very large angry crocodile and a whale and you've got a ghorch," Kate said. "In its defense, it was just trying to get an easy meal by ripping into our fishing nets, and then my dad and uncles made it mad by firing a few spears into it. Anyway, it would have been a giant mess if the *Britannica* hadn't shown up when it did."

"And you got recruited?" I said.

Kate nodded. "I actually asked to join. I was bored stiff aboard the *Sailfish*, and I would have given my right arm to go on a few adventures." Noticing our incredulous expressions, she laughed. "Don't look at me like that," she said. "I hated fishing. Enough about me, though. We're on a tour, remember? Down that way is Weaver's classroom, but you'll see that later when he grabs you for his part of the orientation. He'll probably want to show you the large-specimen room, too."

"Large-specimen room?" Garth said. "As in seamonster specimens?"

"What else?" Kate said, and smiled when she saw Garth's expression. "Don't worry," she said. "You'll get used to it eventually. Weaver's classroom is where we do most of our classes, although there are a few on the nitty-gritty of running the sub, and those happen all over the place."

"Classes? But we aren't school-age anymore," Garth said. It was true—we hadn't been to school in over a year.

"On this sub you're always school-age," Kate said. "Captain Reese has this whole speech she gives about how you're never done learning. We have to go to class every day, but when you're an adult, you just have to do this continuing-education thing that seems to involve a lot of research."

"Weird," Garth muttered, and I nodded in agreement.

Tank took a sharp left and disappeared through a wide double doorway, and Kate motioned for us to follow him.

"This is our dive room," Kate said, standing aside so we could file through. I expected to see a similar setup to the scavengers' dive room aboard the *Atlas*. There the dive equipment was stacked somewhat helter-skelter along the walls, and wet suits of various sizes and conditions of shabbiness hung along the wall on rusty hooks. This room had nothing shabby or helter-skelter about it. Along the back wall were open lockers, each one containing a full wet suit with flippers, face mask, and dive equipment. The floor was glossy and clean, with nothing but a few metal drains here and there, and on the far wall was a huge circular metal door.

"Pretty sweet, right?" Kate said with a grin before

launching into an explanation about the advanced technology the submarine used that allowed the *Britannica*'s divers to dive at a higher pressure than the divers aboard ships like the *Atlas* were able to. I was only half listening—there was something about that door that was drawing me to it like a magnet, and I walked over to run my hand over the thick metal that interlocked in the middle like a zipper.

"That's the hatch," Kate said from directly behind me, making me jump. "We use it to exit the sub for underwater explorations. On the other side of that door is a chamber that fills with water and correctly pressurizes us before the outer door opens. I'd ask if you're any good at diving, but the whole ship got to watch you two tangle with that hydra." She let out a low whistle and shook her head. "Max would never admit it, but I think even he was impressed."

"So, about Max," Garth said, crossing his arms to lean against one of the lockers. "Does he hate us for some special reason or does he just have a horrible personality?"

Kate grimaced. "You'll have to forgive him. He's not usually quite that bad."

"I don't *have* to do anything," Garth said, raising an eyebrow. "But explain. Please."

Kate heaved a sigh and plopped down on one of

the benches. Tank immediately vaulted up to sit beside her, and she ran a hand over his head absentmindedly as she studied us, obviously calculating just how much she was willing to reveal.

"Max isn't exactly excited to have you guys joining our team," she finally said. "Mainly because of the reason there are spots available for the two of you."

"Is it because the other recruits got eaten?" Garth asked, and I shot him an annoyed look. "What?" he said defensively. "We're on a sea-monster ship, or sub, or whatever. I feel like that's a completely valid question. So," he said, turning to Kate, "did they?"

Kate shook her head. "No, but close. There was a boy named Luke who was Max's best friend, and he and Max got in a bit of a tight spot with a makara that Weaver was trying to tag, and Luke almost didn't survive it. Max messed up his foot pretty bad, and it still isn't back to normal, which I think puts him in an even worse mood. As for Luke, he and another one of the recruits chose to leave the program. They were sent home two weeks ago."

"How often does that happen?" I said. "Someone getting sent home?"

"Kind of a lot, actually," Kate admitted. "Very few people can hack the kind of life we live, and Luke and Mary-Ann just couldn't."

"So Max hates us for something we didn't do and can't change," Garth said. "Sounds reasonable."

After that Kate led us out of the dive room and down yet another hallway, showing us the seawater-powered generator as well as the small gunnery stations used to defend the sub. She didn't have to tell us what they might need to defend the sub against. Then the tour was over, and we were back at the front of the sub, looking out the glass-enclosed bow at the ocean.

Kate glanced at her watch. "Weaver should be here any minute. Do you mind if I leave you two here? I need to report to my morning shift."

"Shift?" I said.

"Our jobs," Max said, coming up to stand next to us. "You'll get assigned one too. After breakfast you usually have a morning duty, then class or a research diving mission followed by lunch, and then your afternoon duty, dinner, study time, and bed. This sub won't maintain itself."

"Right," I said, "of course not."

"Are these my newest recruits? The ones who single-handedly brought a ruby *Hydramonsterus serpentinius* to the bottom of the sea using nothing but a chain and a bag of junk?" said a voice from behind us, and we turned to see a short round man in a white lab coat walking toward us with open arms as though he was expecting a hug. He had a wide happy face with rosy red cheeks, and a head so bald and shiny it reflected the lights above our heads.

"And you must be Professor Weaver." Garth said, extending a hand.

"It's so, so wonderful to meet the both of you," Weaver said as he pumped Garth's hand enthusiastically.

"It's not that impressive," I heard Max mutter. "All they did was put a bull's-eye on that hunk-of-junk ship they came from." A second later he let out a startled grunt, as though someone had shoved an elbow into his chest. I had one guess who'd done that.

Weaver charged forward and grabbed my hand to shake it.

"I've watched your video twenty times already," he gushed. "I'm dying to know if a ruby hydra makes any kind of detectable noise before it attacks. A chatter or a chirp? Or even a song like a whale? Or maybe just a slight vibration in the water?"

"Professor," Kate said, leaning against the wall, "you should probably do their orientation before you start grilling them. Don't you think?"

Mr. Weaver shook his head and flapped his hands apologetically. "Of course, of course!" he said. "Here I am, getting ahead of myself again. This way, please.

This way." And with that he turned and bustled down a hallway.

I felt a soft shove from behind and turned to see Kate motioning for me to follow him. "Hurry it up," she whispered. "He's probably already forgotten that you don't know your way around here yet. Hustle!"

We hustled, following the faster-than-he-appeared Weaver down hallway after hallway until we came to the red metal door Kate had pointed out to us earlier.

"This is our classroom," he said. I nodded, aware that my mouth was probably hanging open again as I did a slow circle to take in the room. Every single wall—if you could call them walls—was made up of a floor-to-ceiling stack of tanks and aquariums. Bright red and green frogs used suction-cup toes to crawl up the glass of one, while another appeared to have some sort of burnt-orange snake curled up inside. I saw turtles and sea stars, and a particularly toothy fish with one giant eye in the middle of its forehead, and so many other creatures I couldn't have begun to identify.

"This is wild," Garth said as he leaned in to get a better look at a great, bulbous fish that seemed to glow in the dark.

"Why, thank you," Weaver said with a smile. "I take particular pride in this collection. Make sure you don't touch that one, though. The hidden-fanged loogie may look harmless, but it has a specialized jaw with four rows of razor-sharp teeth. It bites first and asks questions later."

"It looks like a blob of snot with eyes," Garth said.

"What do you do with it all?" I said.

"We study them," Mr. Weaver said. "We feed them. We name them." He pointed to a stern-looking turtle that was currently sunning itself on a rock under a orange heat lamp. "This is Phil," he said. "The annoyed-looking seahorse over there is Bob, and his wife, Buela, is probably hiding somewhere in the weeds. She isn't a fan of new students."

I bumped into something and looked down to see a long metal table situated in the middle of the small room. I took a seat, Garth grabbed the seat across from me, and we both turned to Weaver, who was busy fussing with a roll-down projector screen.

"That seems kinda outdated for a place like this," Garth muttered under his breath to me.

"It is very outdated. An antique, really. Or the grandmother of an antique," Weaver said, making Garth jump guiltily. "However, I refused to give up any available real estate for the size of monitor I'd need in here," Weaver explained. "This was my compromise." He gave the screen one final jerk and it stayed in place. With a huff of satisfaction, he pulled out a small tablet and began tapping. A projector lit up over our heads, shooting a beam of light onto the screen, which was now obscuring five huge tanks from view, one of which, I was almost certain, contained some sort of two-headed snake.

"What do you know about sea monsters?" Weaver asked as an antique map was suddenly projected onto the screen.

"Well," Garth said, "up until yesterday we didn't even know they existed. So I'm going to go with not much."

"Same," I said with a nod.

"Okay," Weaver said. "We'll start with the basics. Sea monsters, sea serpents, monsters of the sea, whatever you want to call them, have been around since the dawn of time."

"'The dawn of time'?" Garth repeated, eyebrow raised.

"You're right," Weaver said, "that sounds overly fluffy. I've always liked the ring of 'the dawn of time,' though. Basically, as far back as the human race has recorded its history, there have been records of sea monsters. The problem is that over time these eyewitness accounts became the stuff of myth and legend, and a very dangerous thing happens when things become myth and legend."

"What's that?" I said.

"People stop believing they're true," Weaver said. The map in front of us was old—very old, if I had to guess—with Latin words written across the top in bold lettering. It showed a few land masses, but I noticed one was named Scandia. The land masses weren't the interesting thing about the map, though—*that* was the monsters in the water. The cartographer had liberally filled the blue of the ocean with monsters of every shape and size. Some were whalelike, with flippers and a tail, but the comparison ended there, as their mouths opened to show rows of teeth, and hairlike tufts sprouted out around their heads like lions' manes. Others were more snakelike, and one was in the process of taking down a minuscule ship.

"That's wild," Garth said, his eyes wide. Suddenly he grabbed me and pointed down at the bottom left of the map. "Look, that's our monster!" Sure enough there was the snakelike red monster that had attacked us. I stepped forward, looking at the eerie similarities between an illustration drawn hundreds of years ago and the creature I'd come face-to-face with only yesterday.

"It is," I breathed, stepping closer to the screen.

"This map is the one we keep going back to," Weaver said. "It was created in the 1500s, but we have successfully identified twelve of the monsters on this map, including your hydra."

Our first sea-monster lesson had officially begun. Some of the monsters were as old as time itself, legends that had been seen once and then forgotten as humans convinced themselves that they'd never existed. Others were new discoveries that had come to light after the Tide Rising, and I stared in awe as image after image appeared on the screen. Some depicted huge serpent-like coils unfurling among the waves, while others showed twenty-foot-long tentacles being launched over the bow of an unsuspecting ship. All of which the human race was utterly unprepared for, a fact that had turned from a nuisance to a crisis quickly after the Tide Rising forced everyone out onto the waves.

It was around this time that the Coalition of the Sea, the governing body that formed after the continents were buried beneath the waves, commissioned the building of a fleet of submarines, including the *Britannica*, to work on finding a solution. They were sent out to the areas where the most sea-monster activity had been recorded. Weaver didn't come right out and say it, but it was obvious from the way he talked about the *Britannica* that it was one of the best. From what I could tell, the submarines acted pretty independently, with only a little oversight and direction from the Coalition when needed.

Weaver went on, talking about the recent discoveries they'd made from studying this monster or the other, and I felt a dull throbbing start behind my eyeballs. It was like trying to drink the entire ocean through a straw in a single day, and my brain hurt.

"That's the problem with mythical monsters," Weaver concluded as we took one last look at the ancient map. "They are never content to stay in their legends." With that he announced it was lunchtime, and he ushered us out of his classroom and toward the mess hall.

"Is it really lunchtime already?" Garth said as we followed Weaver down the maze of hallways. I glanced at the tablet Mr. Weaver had given me. On it was a map of the *Britannica*, but it was the encyclopedia of sea monsters that really interested me. According to Weaver, the encyclopedia cataloged the monsters alphabetically, listing things like each monster's approximate weight and size, the amount of young it produced, its estimated life span, and the number of recorded attacks.

Weaver had already taught us a lot about the mysterious creatures, but despite the information overload, I realized that I still wanted—needed—to know more. I felt the itch to investigate that I usually only felt when I was tinkering with a new idea or invention. My grandpa would have said I was having a Ben Franklin moment, and he probably would have been right. There was something about this new flood of monster information that made my imagination buzz.

"What do you think the food's like on this thing?" Garth asked, jarring my attention back to the task at hand.

"I have no idea," I said. The familiar smell of roasting fish hit me a moment later, and my stomach woke up with an angry snarl. I glanced around as we entered the mess hall we'd seen briefly during our tour that morning, taking in the narrow tables, which at the moment were crammed with crew members. I tried to find Weaver, but he'd obviously forgotten about us and headed off to get his own lunch. The far wall of the mess hall was curved and made entirely of glass, similar to the hub, and I jumped as a huge great white shark swam past the window, its teeth so close to the glass I couldn't believe they didn't scratch it.

"Now, that's not something you see every day," Garth said.

"Hey! Newbies! Over here!" someone called to our left, and we both turned to see Kate waving an arm enthusiastically. A moment later she jumped out of her seat and bounded up to us. "Sit with us," she said with a wide smile.

"Sure," Garth said, "but first, where do we get lunch? I'm starving."

"Whoops!" Kate said. "I forgot that you might not know that. Follow me." She quickly ushered us to the other side of the room, where a small square window was cut into the wall. After a quick introduction to a friendly crew member named Brenda, we had our own steaming bowls of food in hand as we sat down with Kate. Max looked up from his own bowl just long enough to jerk his chin in a half-hearted greeting before returning his attention to his meal.

"How was orientation?" Kate asked, blowing on her soup before taking a bite.

"Interesting," Garth said.

"That's an understatement and a half," said Kate. "I remember just how weird that orientation with Weaver was. 'Hi, welcome aboard, there are sea monsters everywhere and you're going to help hunt them down.'" She shook her head. "Subtlety is not a strong point around here, and between you and me," she said, leaning forward conspiratorially, "it just gets weirder."

"Lovely," Garth said, digging in and taking a big spoonful of his soup. I followed suit and was pleasantly surprised. The food on board the *Atlas* was just okay: it had all the things you needed to stay alive and well nourished, but that was about all that could be said for it. This soup was actually good—great, even.

"And how often do you, um, stumble upon sea monsters?" I asked.

"More than you'd think," Kate said. "When it comes to sea monsters, it turns out that you just have to know where to look. But since we are the youngest recruits, we don't see as much action as the teenagers or the crew. Weaver lets us go out on field trips after the fun is over sometimes, but for the most part you'll spend the next few months watching and learning as much as you can."

"Kate's lying," Max said. "She's trying not to freak you out any more on your first day, but we were on the team for the last three research dives as well as a recovery expedition after a ship got taken down by a terrible dogfish."

"Wait," I said. "Isn't that the sea monster in *Pinocchio*?"

"Whoa," Max said, raising an eyebrow. "The new girl may actually know her stuff."

"The new girl has a name," I said. "It's Berkley, and I wouldn't go that far. Garth and I have a lot to learn."

Max sniffed, but his expression softened a little. "Right," he said. "Well that monster isn't just in fairy tales. It's also infesting the North Atlantic."

"Don't worry, it's not five stories tall like the book says," Kate said. "It also doesn't have three rows of teeth."

"It has four," Max said.

"Really?" Kate said. "I thought it was five." She shrugged. "Anyway, it's only about two stories tall."

"Oh good. Only two stories," Garth said, glancing over at me with a *what did we get ourselves into?* look.

"So, when do you think we'll see our first monster?" I asked.

"That's easy," Kate said with a grin. "Tomorrow morning."

6

I woke up and stared at the ceiling over my shallow bunk. Below me I could hear Garth's thunderous snores weaving in and out of the chorus of breathing and grunting from the other sleepers, who slept stacked on top of one another like so many dishes in a cupboard. The night before, I'd briefly met the five teens who shared our bunk room, and I'd been happy to see that, unlike Max, they didn't seem to have a problem sharing their space with new recruits. There were three girls and two boys, and from the way they joked around and teased one another while getting ready for bed, it was clear that they were friends.

I'd glanced over at Max and noticed that he was watching the group with a kind of sad longing. He caught me looking and immediately adopted his now-familiar scowl, and I remembered what Kate had told us about how he'd lost his best friend. The odds were that he'd never see him again, not with the way the *Britannica* constantly zigzagged across the ocean. I wondered if he blamed himself for Luke's decision to leave the program, and I had to keep myself from glancing at his injured foot. I could more than relate to that kind of guilt, and I decided that I was going to give Max and all his grumpiness a little more grace than he seemed to deserve. My dad had told me right after Mom died that sometimes when people were the most unlikable, they needed your kindness the most. Wallace had become a real jerk for a while after we lost Mom, but he'd eventually turned it around. Maybe Max was the same way.

My thoughts shifted from the night before and back to the here and now of my first morning aboard the *Britannica*. My eyelids felt fuzzy, which wasn't much of a surprise since it had taken me what felt like hours to fall asleep. Around me the submarine creaked as its metal and glass muscles flexed, keeping the ocean waters at bay as it sliced through its briny depths like a hot knife through butter. It wasn't time to get up yet, but a lifetime of waking up early was hard to break, so I rolled over in my bunk, careful not to whack my arm on the ceiling, and pulled out the tablet Weaver had assigned me. I carefully pushed the button to wake it up, and smiled when a dim yellow light illuminated the inside of my bunk.

It took me a second to find the sea-monster ency-clopedia, but I finally did and clicked it open. The first entry was an account from a crew member of the *Britannica* from almost twenty-five years ago. As my new cabinmates snored, I tapped to the *H* section and pulled up the profile of the monster that had attacked us. The first image was a close-up of the illustration from the monster map Weaver had shown us the day before, followed by a few blurry images of the monster itself and a recording of the ships it had attacked and damaged. I noted that the newest entry was about the *Atlas* and blinked in surprise when I saw my name as well as Garth's listed in the account.

The profile went on to discuss how many eggs a female hydra could lay in its lifetime, as well as the fact that it was lethally poisonous, its bite capable of stop-ping a whale's heart in seconds. I swallowed hard as I remembered just how close I'd come to those poison-ous teeth. I was about to flip to the next monster on the list when the end of the article caught my eye:

The ruby Hydramonsterus serpentinius is one of the few monsters that appears to hold a grudge. If it is attacked by another sea monster or even by a ship,

for that matter, it will hunt that monster or ship down
relentlessly until it can be found and destroyed. For this
reason, it is imperative to kill a ruby Hydramonsterus
serpentinius after any kind of altercation.

I looked up from the tablet and clapped my hand over my mouth to stifle a gasp. The monster that I'd accidently unearthed, the monster that had viciously attacked our ship until I'd managed to detain it long enough for us to escape, was going to hold a grudge against the *Atlas*. A grudge that would cause it to hunt down the ship until it found it. My mind flashed to my family, and I felt myself go cold as I remembered Captain Reese's final words after our meeting in her office: that the very lives we saved might be those of our families. She'd known. Any uncertainty I'd been feeling about being on the *Britannica* disappeared in that moment. I no longer needed to make the cut here to avoid a future on a work ship; I needed to make it here so I could save my family.

The bell clanged a half hour later, and I powered down the tablet before launching myself out of my bunk. Unfortunately, I was distracted by my recent discovery, and I almost landed on Max, who shot me a dirty look out of sleep-bleary eyes.

"Do that again and I'll use that fluffy hair of yours

to scrub the deck," he growled.

"Do submarines even have a deck?" I said as I quickly scooped what he'd so nicely called my fluffy hair into a thick braid that trailed down my back. It wasn't my fault that I'd inherited wild curls that stuck out in all directions unless something was done with them.

"Chill out, Max," Kate said from her own bunk as she stretched her arms up toward the ceiling.

"Berkley's head would make a terrible mop," Garth added as he climbed down. "Far too cumbersome, and noisy."

"Gee, thanks," I said, wondering when I was going to be able to find a time to tell him what I'd learned. Maybe we could go to Captain Reese and ask her to do something. I wasn't sure what that something might be, but not doing anything didn't feel like an option either.

"This is way too much talking for this time of the morning," Kate said, grabbing my hand and dragging me past the boys and out the back door of our cabin. "Go brush your teeth," she shouted over her shoulder at Max. "Your breath smells like seal puke."

"What does seal puke smell like?" I asked as she took a left, never letting go of my arm.

"Fishy," she said, pushing open the door to the girls' bathroom. I'd learned yesterday that it was attached to the dive room, and I had to stifle the urge to take another peek at the equipment.

"What's the rush?" I asked as she hurriedly turned on two of the showers and rushed to grab us each a towel.

"Do you like hot water?" she said.

"Um, yeah?" I said, confused, as she ducked into her shower stall and pulled the curtain shut.

"Well, you're out of luck," she said. "But if you want lukewarm water, then you better hurry. This sub is state-of-the-art, but if you aren't one of the first five showers, you are going to freeze." I quickly took her advice as the door to the bathroom opened and five other crew members hurried inside.

A few minutes later I was done and slipping on my own pair of *Britannica*-issued aqua boots for the first time.

"What do you think?" Kate asked, smiling as she watched me admire my new outfit in the mirror.

"I'm not sure," I said honestly. "How long does it take before all this starts to feel, I don't know, normal?"

Kate snorted. "I hate to break it to you," she said, "but we don't really do normal here." I must have looked unsure, because she put an arm around my shoulder and gave it a quick squeeze before whipping her hair up into a wet bun on top of her head. "Don't worry," she said. "You'll get used to it, I promise. I'm just happy to have another girl recruit. Max hasn't exactly been a ray of sunshine recently."

"Thanks," I said, glancing around at the other crew members getting ready around me. I'd grown up on an overcrowded ship where personal space was rare, but life on the *Britannica* was even more close.

"You okay finding your way to the hub?" Kate said. "You're supposed to report there for your morning work assignment."

"Sure," I said, feeling fairly confident that I could find my way back. "Where are you going?"

"Early-morning cleaning of the large specimen tanks," she said, and rushed off before I could say anything else. I wondered if I was going to get to see the large-specimen area anytime soon, but I pushed the thought aside as I made my way into the maze of passages.

"Good morning, Berkley," said a voice behind me, and I whirled in the tight hallway as Captain Reese emerged from her quarters. Unlike the recruits that I bunked with, she had her own small cabin, probably a quarter of the size of the one I'd shared with my parents and brothers back on the *Atlas*, but still a luxury here where every square inch mattered. I noticed with envy the way her curls stayed in place, bouncing a little as she shut the door behind her. Maybe that was what I needed to do, I thought: just chop off the whole mess and only leave a couple of inches behind to do what they would. I discarded the idea almost immediately. While her curls were perfect little springs, mine would just fuzz out and make my head look like the mop Max had so kindly compared it to that morning.

Captain Reese smiled at me, and I found myself smiling back. Her gingerbread-colored skin made a sharp contrast to a lot of the other crew members, whose skin had taken on translucent paleness from a lack of sunlight. I'd never really thought about what a life spent below the waves without sunlight would do to a person, and I glanced down at my own golden, freckled skin and wondered how long it would take before all evidence of my life aboard the *Atlas* faded away. Kate had mentioned something about vitamin D supplements and special light bulbs aboard the sub, but it hadn't made me feel much better.

"Heading to the front?" she asked. I nodded. "Lovely," she said. "I'll come with you. We'll see what kind of progress Officer Wilson has made while we slept." I quickly flattened myself against the narrow passageway so she could slip by. She probably wouldn't have minded following me, but I knew myself well enough to realize that I'd be a jumpy bundle of nerves, tripping over things that weren't there, if I was leading the captain through her own submarine. No thanks.

The sound of toenails clicking on metal resounded to our right, and we turned as Tank came trotting around the corner, a large biscuit of some sort held proudly in his mouth. Tank reminded me a lot of Garth: stocky, smashed-up nose, and a bit bowlegged. Not that I'd ever tell him that. Tank trotted by us, head held high. He might as well have shouted, *Make way, people—I'm busy!*

"Sometimes I think he believes that *he's* the captain," Captain Reese said, shaking her head.

As the little dog headed off down the hallway, I glanced over at the *Britannica*'s captain. I needed to ask her the question that had been needling me for over an hour now, and I had no idea if I'd get a chance to talk to her one-on-one again anytime soon.

"I have a question," I said, the words tumbling out in a rush before I could lose my nerve.

"I have an answer," she replied with a quick smile.

"I was looking at the monster encyclopedia this morning," I said, gesturing to the tablet in my hand, "and it said that hydras hold grudges? Is the one that attacked the *Atlas* going to attack it again?"

Captain Reese sighed and put a hand on my shoulder. "I was hoping you'd have a chance to get adjusted a bit to life here before you ran across that bit of information. It's why I didn't mention it earlier. Unfortunately, I don't have a good answer for you. The truth is that we don't know. Sea monsters in general, and the hydra in particular, are still very much a mystery. It's why we devote so much time and effort to research. The more we know, the better we can protect ships and the people who live on them. All I can tell you for sure is this—we attached a tracker to the hydra, and we should be able to give the *Atlas* fair warning of any future attacks."

"Just a warning?" I said, feeling my heart sink.

Captain Reese nodded. "We can't follow one ship around just in case it gets attacked. Our job is to protect as many ships as possible." My hands clenched into tight fists as I tried to process this, and Captain Reese noticed. "What I told you yesterday still holds true. Learn everything you can from Professor Weaver, work hard, and you might contribute to the breakthrough that helps protect your ship. It's all any of us can hope for these days." I nodded and followed her silently down the hall, my brain churning. Being able to warn the *Atlas* was good, but it wasn't enough. There had to be more I could do, and I felt the familiar itch in my fingertips to fix the problem at hand, only this time I knew it was going to involve more than making a nifty flashlight.

A minute later we made it to the front and entered the glass-enclosed hub. My eyes were immediately drawn to the ocean as we sliced through water so deep the sun's rays hadn't found it yet. There was nothing to give away that it was actually morning except for the faintest hint of lighter blue water directly above us. The sub's powerful headlights were turned on, casting two thick beams of light that occasionally illuminated a school of fish or the body of an octopus or squid as it hurried to get out of our way.

"Anything interesting to report?" Captain Reese asked, jarring me from my admiration of the sub and back to the task at hand. Officer Wilson turned from where he was inspecting a computer monitor over a sailor's shoulder and smiled at Captain Reese. Like most of the crew on board the *Britannica*, he was short, with a wiry, muscular frame that made it easy for him to maneuver inside the sub. He was older than the captain by a good ten years, or at least the gray-and-white hair at his temples made him appear that way. I was terrible at guessing the ages of adults. They all just looked like different variations of old, and it was rude to ask, so I never did.

"Unfortunately, no," said Wilson with an apologetic shrug. "The cetus is proving trickier to track than we expected."

"Legends usually are," said Captain Reese. "What is our exact location?"

Wilson turned to the monitor he'd just been consulting and shrugged. "We're weaving our way between and around submerged islands at the moment, Captain. We've been angling ourselves toward the ruins of Athens, since the last rumblings of the monster came from that direction. If nothing turns up in the next day or so, we'll make our way over the top of the old coastline for a bit to see what we can see."

"Very good," said Captain Reese. I thought I'd been forgotten, and I was puzzling over what in the world a cetus was when Wilson turned to me. "What can the new recruit tell us about the cetus?" he said.

"Um," I said, shifting nervously from foot to foot. "I'm not sure yet, sir," I said. "This is my first day."

Wilson shook his head, and I felt myself shrink a bit.

"Perfectly fine," Captain Reese said. "No one expects you to know all your monsters on the first day." She raised an eyebrow at Wilson, who'd already turned his back on us to look back at the monitor.

"Who's asking about the cetus?" Max said, coming up behind us, his hair still wet from the shower.

Wilson turned to Max and jerked his chin up. "Why don't you show the new kid how it's done. Tell us what you know about a cetus."

"Weaver just did a lesson on it a few days ago," Max said. "There isn't much to know. It hasn't been heavily researched."

Wilson snorted. "You could say that about any of the sea monsters we track."

Max seemed unfazed by Wilson's bluster and shook his hair back out of his eyes. "Cetus was a monster from Greek mythology," he said. "Which is why we're hunting near what used to be Greece. Odds are his descendants are still mucking about somewhere nearby. Legends always have some basis in truth, and if you start your hunt near their origins, you usually have the best luck."

"Not usually," Wilson interrupted. "Always." It was weird to hear Max talk about Greece. I mean, I knew what continents were and countries and all that from school, but people didn't use them to navigate anymore. On the *Atlas* we moved about based on weather patterns and fishing opportunities.

Captain Reese motioned for Max to continue.

"The legend says that Cetus was a monster sent by Poseidon to devour Andromeda," Max said, and then paused and glanced over at Captain Reese. "Do I need to go into the whole bit about how Poseidon was the god of the sea and Andromeda was the daughter of King Cepheus?"

"Not this time," Captain Reese said.

"So anyhow, Poseidon was mad that Andromeda's mom had said she was more beautiful than all the nereids in the ocean. Luckily for Andromeda, though, Perseus saved her."

"Nereids," Wilson said, and shuddered. "If I ever see one of those again, it will be too soon."

"You can say that again," Captain Reese said with a smile and a nod of approval at Max. "What are the practical applications for actually capturing a cetus?"

"Well, the odds are that they live deep, probably in a cave under one of the islands. In the legend, Cetus is stopped by Medusa's head and turned to stone, but he was likely just blinded with the use of a bright light. So we'll probably use that when we are hunting the rest of them," Max said, and I wondered if I'd ever be able to rattle off sea-monster information like that, all cool nonchalance and confidence.

"Good to see that Weaver is doing a good job with the recruits," Wilson said, nodding his head in approval.

"What the legend doesn't mention is what Cetus looked like," Captain Reese said, "but I have a feeling we'll find that out soon enough." She pointed out the front of the glass, and Officer Wilson pulled back the throttle, slowing down the *Britannica* so the headlights could shine on the large outcropping of rock on our right. There, carved in the side of the rock, were claw marks. For a moment we hovered there, the only noise the low thrum of the *Britannica*'s engine.

"What's the measurement on those?" Captain Reese asked, breaking the silence.

Officer Wilson quickly tapped a few things into his computer, and an image of the claw marks appeared on his screen.

"They appear to be about five feet long and a foot and a half wide," he said.

"And what are the calculations for an animal capable of making claw marks of that size?" she asked.

Wilson typed a bit more and then sat back and whistled. "It looks like we have at least a twenty-five-footer, Captain."

Captain Reese nodded and turned to me and Max. "Don't worry about a work assignment this morning, just go grab your breakfast while you can," she said. "I have a feeling it's going to be an interesting morning."

I nodded and turned to follow Max back into the depths of the submarine, not quite sure yet how I felt about interesting mornings.

The salty smell of boiled kelp wafted down the tunnel, and my stomach gave an angry snarl. Garth and Kate were already seated at the table, their plates piled high.

"What's with you two?" Kate asked, raising an eyebrow as I sat down with my own plate, elbowing Garth to make myself a bit more room.

"We were up in the hub when Captain Reese spotted claw marks," Max said around a mouthful.

Garth choked on his bite of kelp and spit it back onto the plate. "Claw marks?" he said.

Kate let out an appreciative whistle. "Nice. How big?"

"Big enough," I said.

"Think we'll get to take a look at them?" Kate asked Max.

Max shrugged.

"They have to belong to the cetus," Kate said. She gave her plate a shove to make some room and yanked her tablet out of her backpack. Next came a pair of thick black glasses, which she crammed onto her face so she could peer down at the screen. She noticed my glance at the glasses and shrugged. "Staring at a screen gives me a headache without these. Now, where is that textbook Weaver showed us on Greek mythology?"

"Do you know what they're talking about?" Garth whispered as Max leaned in to look at Kate's tablet, his head cranked to the side as he tried to read whatever she'd pulled up.

"Sort of," I said. "Apparently, the kind of sea monster we're after is a descendent of some mythological one called Cetus, and from the way everyone reacted to those claws, it must have a pretty impressive set."

"Does anything else in the ocean have claws?" Garth asked.

Max shrugged. "Don't look at me. Kate is the brains around here. I'm just the good-looking one."

Kate snorted and reached over to give Max's head a stiff-armed shove. Max almost face-planted into his

121

steaming plate of seaweed but caught himself at the last second and glared at her.

"Last time I'll give you a compliment," he muttered. I smiled. Max was prickly, all right, but there was something about the way the two bickered and shoved at each other that reminded me of the way Wallace and I used to annoy each other back on board the *Atlas*. I pushed that thought to the back of my brain. If I thought about missing him, I'd think about how much I missed my dad, and then that would spiral into thinking about the danger they were both in.

"Doesn't matter anyway," Kate said, sitting back from her tablet. "By the time we get done with our morning duties and then class, the dive team will be back, and Captain Reese will have the sub underway." Despite her words, she kept tabbing through the textbook, and picture after picture of creatures that might or might not be Cetus flashed onto her screen. The images had been pulled from texts, paintings, and tapestries so old—from the time of the Roman Empire and before—that the dates and names of the creators had long ago been lost. I knew from my own brief studies that morning and from Weaver's crash course the day before that these relics used to be housed in fancy places like the Vatican or stored behind protective glass in famous museums. All of them were gone now.

When the waters had started rising, there had been a panic to save books as well as other precious works of art and history, and plans had been devised to build subs and ships to house them. It didn't work, though. The water rose too fast, and eventually everyone agreed that any available space aboard a boat or sub needed to go to living, breathing people and their small allotment of belongings, and not to useless stuff that would undoubtedly mold and disintegrate. It had been a huge loss to the human race, with the only consolation being the images that were hastily taken and uploaded so that the artwork might be remembered long after it became fish food.

I peered over Kate's shoulder at her most recent find, which showed Cetus with a head very similar to a lion and huge front fins that were indeed capped with claws. The back half appeared to be some weird combination of a whale or a shark. It was no wonder that for hundreds of years people had written off images just like this one as pure make-believe. The creature staring back at us from Kate's screen seemed like something from a fairy tale. I knew different, though. Fairy tales didn't leave deep gouges in coral reefs.

"So, is the *Britannica* trying to kill the cetus?" Garth asked Max, and I looked up from the tablet.

Max shook his head. "This is a research-only

mission. The cetus is one of those monsters that seem to have been around for forever, and Weaver thinks that studying the more ancient species will help us with some of the new weirdos that have cropped up."

"Weirdos?" I repeated.

Max chuckled. "Just wait. You'll see some real doozies if you hang around long enough."

"Are you still betting on how long we'll make it?" I said, eyebrow arched.

Max shrugged. "Don't take it personally," he said. "I bet on everyone. It keeps things interesting."

The bell clanged, and I quickly shoved the last bite of my breakfast into my mouth. Kate snapped her tablet shut and shoved it in her bag as we clambered out of our seats. Max eyed her half-eaten breakfast and reached over to snag a bite. Kate saw him coming and smacked his hand away before picking up the whole dripping mess of seaweed and shoving it into her mouth.

"That's disgusting," Max said.

"That's smart," she said around her massive mouthful as she shouldered past us, heading for the tunnel on the far right.

"See you in class!" she said before disappearing around a bend. Garth and I turned to look at each other as everyone hurried out of the mess hall.

"Do you know where we go?" he asked as the last person rushed past us and down one of the five hallways that connected the mess hall to the rest of the sub.

"How in the world would I know that?" I said.

"Didn't Weaver say there was a schedule somewhere?" Garth said.

"On our tablets, I think," I said, turning to dig out my own tablet. I should have asked Kate about the schedule for the day, or at least where to find it, instead of gawking at sea-monster pictures like an idiot.

"Which one of you is Berkley?" said a voice behind us, and we both jumped and turned to see a weathered old man standing in the center tunnel. His hair was white and cut close to his head in the buzz cut that so many of the sailors seemed to favor, and his eyes were a piercing blue. He was small-boned and slightly hunched, but there was something about the way he held himself that made it clear he didn't mess around.

"Her," said Garth, pointing at me.

"Right," said the man. "You're assigned to work with me this morning." He jerked his head at Garth. "Someone will be along for you shortly, recruit. Just sit down and cool your heels."

Garth promptly plopped down in his seat, his butt making a loud *thwump* in the empty room.

The man looked at me, eyebrow raised. "Do you listen as well as that one?" he said. "Otherwise I may swap."

"I'm a very good listener, sir," I said, standing up straight.

"Right, then," the man said, turning to walk back down the tunnel. I hesitated for a moment until I felt Garth's foot on my back as he gave me a solid shove.

"Thanks," I hissed over my shoulder as I hurried to follow the gnarled figure, who moved with surprising ease through the network of hallways.

"The *Britannica*'s primary job is to hunt down sea monsters," the man said, never slowing his pace. "But we don't have the room on board for more than one crew. Around these parts you're expected to do just about everything, so you'd better get used to it. I'm sure you were expected to work aboard whatever wretched hunk of floating junk you came from, and it's the same here. Today I'm going to teach you how to work on the bomb."

"The bomb?" I repeated, the little hairs along my arms standing on end at the word.

The man flapped a hand dismissively over his shoulder and took a sharp left that had me scrambling to keep up. "It's not a real bomb," he said. "I always forget you new recruits don't know a jellyfish from a

126

jelly sandwich. It's what we call the sub's oxygen generator." He suddenly whirled to face me, and I came
within inches of running right into him.

"Hector," he said, holding out a hand. I shook it,
wincing a little at his grip. With that he opened up a
door that I hadn't noticed before and led me inside.
The room was small and close, and I could hear the
low hum of machinery. It reminded me a little of the
systems room aboard the *Atlas*, with its smells of oil
and grease and metal.

The bomb was hard to miss. Made completely of a
tarnished brass that had turned a lurid green, the oxygen generator was a mess of dials, switch panels, and
large tubes.

"We pump in seawater and, wham-bam-kapow, it
turns it into oxygen," Hector said. "The fancy-pants
name for it is electrolysis, but what you need to know
is that without this thing, everyone dies."

"Right," I said. "What can I do?"

"Desalination filters need scrubbed," he said with a
jerk of his head toward the left side of the generator.
I nodded and followed him as he began deftly flipping switches and turning knobs in preparation for the
morning's work.

"Here," he said a moment later, handing me a long,
slim cylinder that he'd pulled out of the generator. "Get

going on this one." He jerked his head over to where he already had a deep pan of water and brushes waiting, and I nodded and got quickly to work. Hector joined me with his own cylinder a minute later, and we worked together in companionable silence for a few minutes.

"We spotted claw marks this morning," I finally said, because if I didn't talk about it, I was worried I might bust.

"Did ya now?" Hector said, never looking up from his task.

"Big ones," I said.

"They usually are," he said, holding his cylinder up to the light before plunging it back into the water. "The monsters with claws are the meanest," he said, "but they are also usually the slowest. Claws are utter rubbish when it comes to swimming."

"Really?" I said.

He nodded. "The ones with the claws don't need to be fast, though," he said. "They can shred you into ribbons with one swipe."

I wasn't quite sure how to respond, so I just got back to work. I glanced over at him out of the corner of my eye a few minutes later. His sleeves were rolled up past his elbow, and faded black tattoos of monsters were visible, swirling up his arms. He noticed my glance and smiled a smile that revealed more than a few gaps in his teeth.

"It used to be a tradition for crew members to get a tattoo of each monster they helped capture or kill."

"Used to be?" I asked, staring at a tattoo of a monster that appeared to have more than one head.

"Eventually us old-timers ran out of room," he said with a smirk. "I have more sea-monster know-how and whatnot in my left nostril than you will probably have in your entire life, and you'd best not forget it."

"Yes, sir," I said, wondering who Garth had ended up with and if he'd be willing to trade.

A bell clanged a few minutes later, and Hector calmly took the cylinder I'd been working on out of my hand and jerked his head toward the door. "Better get to class."

"Thanks," I said, but as I hurried down the hallway, I couldn't help but think about the pain in Hector's eyes right before he'd turned back to his work. Someone he knew had been shredded by a monster with claws—I'd put money on it. The thought made my stomach churn uncomfortably, so I pushed it away. It was time for my first class.

8

The *Britannica*'s classroom was tucked into the side of the submarine, and to my surprise I was able to find it with only two wrong turns. It helped that I ran into Garth halfway there. He was dripping wet, covered in an oily blue-black substance, and grumpy. When I asked what had happened, he just grumbled something incoherent and wiped at his face with a dripping sleeve. I decided that my job with Hector hadn't been that bad.

We were almost to Weaver's classroom when Kate popped out of a trapdoor on the floor like an over-grown sand crab. The gear room was just visible as she scrambled up the ladder to follow us. Smudges of oil and grease liberally coated her aqua jumpsuit, and I wrinkled my nose at the smell as I hurried after her.

"Five seconds until you are late!" cried Mr. Weaver's voice from the end of the passage. We picked up the pace, practically flying down the hall and into the tiny aquarium-filled classroom.

Kate flopped down at the table and pulled out the chair next to her for me. "You don't want to be late," she said. "Like, ever. Late recruits get clean-up duty, and trust me, you don't want clean-up duty."

"Everyone, please sit down," Weaver said. "We have a special opportunity today, but we have to get through our regular lesson first." At that moment Max came bursting through the open door, sweat dripping down his face.

"Have fun cleaning up," Kate said, grinning wickedly. "I hope it's something messy."

"Crumb and fish guts," Max said, slumping into the empty seat beside Garth. He scowled at the table for a moment and then glanced over at Garth with a raised eyebrow.

"Is that terrible smell coming from you?" he said.

"Let's just say that cleaning the large-specimen tanks has a steep learning curve," Garth said dryly.

Max snorted. "Elmer dunked and inked you, didn't he? That old octopus is about as mean as they come."

"Enough chitchat," Mr. Weaver said. "It's time to get started." A moment later something wet, squishy, and very much alive landed in the middle of the table. Everyone sat back as the thing made an awful squelching noise, its tentacles thrashing around so wildly that one whacked Garth across the face.

"Blech," he said, scrubbing at his red cheek with his sleeve.

"What is it?" I asked.

"Looks like a squid," said Kate, who had the luck of being closer to the thing's head, where there was a lot less action.

"I love a good calamari," Max said, leaning forward to pin down one of the long, thrashing arms with a finger. "Can we fry this guy up after we inspect him?"

"That's exactly where he's headed when we're done," Mr. Weaver said. "But first, he's today's lesson, so if you could hold off eating him until we're through, Max, I'd appreciate it."

I leaned back, well away from the tentacles of the squid, and tried to squelch my disappointment. I'd really been hoping for a cetus lesson. I mean, squids were fine and all, but they weren't the legendary sea monster we were supposedly hunting.

"Who can tell me about the kraken?" Weaver said. The room fell silent except for the wet slapping of the squid's long arms on the table. With a quick movement

Weaver scooped it up and plunked it into the five-foot-long tank behind him. I blinked at the wet table a second, gathering my thoughts. Unlike the cetus from that morning, I actually had heard of the kraken before.

"The kraken is a monster first found in Scandinavian folklore," Max said. Weaver gave him a nod of approval as he forged on. "It's reported to be some kind of cephalopod, like a squid or an octopus, and big enough to take down entire ships."

"There's one in *Twenty Thousand Leagues Under the Sea*!" Garth said. "It snatches a sailor clean out of the *Nautilus*! Blam! One second he's there; the next second he's a goner." He sat back with a sigh. "Gosh, I love that book. Captain Nemo is just great. The entire time you can't figure out if he's a good guy or a bad guy or crazy or what."

"My favorite Nemo is a little orange clown fish," Max said.

"Not that debating the merits of Nemos isn't fascinating," Mr. Weaver said, "but I'd have thought that you'd want to get through this lesson so you could hear about the unique opportunity Captain Reese has granted us."

"What opportunity?" I said, all thoughts of the squid and its giant legendary counterpart momentarily forgotten.

"Well," Weaver said, followed by an overly dramatic

pause as he savored our anticipation, "I did receive special permission from Captain Reese to take you all out on a dive inspection of the claw marks that were spotted this morning." Kate cheered, and Max pumped his fist in the air, whooping loudly. Weaver flapped his hands to quiet them down and smiled. "It's not often that we are shallow enough for a recreational dive, and it was an opportunity too good to miss. Now, let's finish our lesson on the kraken, shall we? Everyone grab your tablets and open up the lesson I just sent you. If this hunt for the cetus is a bust, we may head north and see about the kraken that was spotted there."

There was a flurry of activity as we all got our tablets out and ready. The next hour flew by, and by the time I slid my tablet back in my bag, I had over two pages of notes, and I realized that I'd missed being in school. There was something exciting about learning something new, especially when that something new was a Norwegian folktale the size of ten ships. I also had a very strong desire to read *Twenty Thousand Leagues Under the Sea*, despite Garth and his big mouth having spoiled the bit with the kraken.

I was too excited to worry much about it, though—it was time to dive. The dive room smelled comfortingly familiar, and I inhaled the smell of musty rubber and brine with a smile on my face. Within moments my bare feet were covered in a fine grit of dried sea salt, and I could almost convince myself that this dive was going to be just like the countless others I'd done on the *Atlas*. I quickly collected the wet suit with my name on it, zipped it on, and bounced on the balls of my feet as I waited for Kate, Max, and Garth to suit up with what felt like a painful slowness.

"You pumped?" Garth said as he came to stand next to me. "You look pumped."

"Sort of," I said. "I mean, you and I know squat about sea monsters, but this? This we know. It will be nice not to feel like a fish out of water, even if it is only for a few minutes."

"I don't know," Garth said. "Diving feels sort of, I don't know, pointless if we aren't scavenging. I'm going to miss the thrill of the hunt."

"Sea monsters aren't thrilling?" I said.

"Sea monsters are terrifying," Garth said. "There is a big difference."

Weaver entered the dive room and did a quick head count before walking over to check out the gear we'd be using for the dive.

"It's going to be cold," Max grumped as he hobbled over to us. He was already wearing one of his black flippers, but the other one was clutched in his hand, and I glanced down at his bare foot and grimaced.

The entire thing was a mottled blackish green, and two of his toes were a pretty solid black color. There was also a fairly impressive and only partially healed gash snaking up his foot to disappear inside the cuff of his wet suit.

Max noticed my glance, and his lip rose in a sneer. "Before you ask, I can swim just fine, probably better than you."

"I wasn't going to ask," I said.

"Easy," Kate said, coming up behind Max and placing a calming hand on his shoulder.

"You take it easy," Max said, shrugging her off to go stand by the hatch door, as far from us as humanly possible.

"I'm sorry?" I said, not sure exactly what I'd done wrong.

"Nothing to apologize for," Kate said. She leaned in, dropping her voice so it wouldn't carry. "The accident with Luke was pretty bad. Max is lucky he survived it, and he's doubly lucky that Captain Reese didn't decide the whole thing was his fault."

"Was it his fault?" Garth asked.

Kate shrugged. "Hard to say. But either way, I think Max just feels he has a lot to prove."

"He doesn't have anything to prove to us," I said. We hadn't proved ourselves at all yet, and honestly, the only thing we'd done to earn our way onto the *Britannica* was avoid getting eaten. Well, that and make a sea monster mad enough to hunt down the *Atlas*, I thought with a wince.

"Zip me up, will you?" Garth said, turning so I could see the wide gap between the teeth of the zipper.

"Um," I said, glancing over at Kate for some assistance. She took one look at Garth and burst out laughing.

"Oh boy," she practically choked. "They didn't assign you the right size wet suit." She glanced around, but there weren't any spares hanging anywhere. "We will just have to make this one work for now," she said with an apologetic grin. "Can you suck it in?" she asked, grabbing the two sides of the wet suit and forcing them together so I could zip.

"I am!" Garth said.

"Suck it in more," Kate said. "Geez, you have broad shoulders—do you have to walk through the halls sideways?"

"Almost," Garth grunted as I zipped up the final few inches.

"Okay," I said, stepping back. "You can exhale now."

"Can I?" Garth said, running a finger around the neck of the wet suit. "I feel like ten pounds of tuna in a five-pound can."

"Funny," Kate said. "I was just going to give you that exact compliment."

"All right!" Weaver called, and we went instantly quiet. I could feel the thrum of excitement in the room as though we were all rubber bands on the brink of snapping. "It looks like everyone is geared up, so I'll go over a few last reminders before we enter the hatch." He turned to Garth and me, eyebrow raised. "I'm told you two are experienced divers. Is that correct?" We both nodded, and he seemed satisfied. "Like I was saying, we are fairly shallow, all things considered, but you will still be exiting the *Britannica* at around seventy feet below the surface. Remember that once the hatch fills with water, we will remain in the hatch until we have been correctly pressurized. Then and only then will the outer hatch open, allowing us to leave the sub to investigate the claw marks."

I felt my hand shoot into the air almost as though it was acting on its own. "What about the cetus?" I said. "We aren't going to run into it out there, are we?"

Garth shifted nervously next to me, but Weaver flapped his hand dismissively. "Do you really think we'd send you out into sea-monster-infested waters?"

"Yes," I said, the word slipping out of my mouth with a point-blank starkness that startled even me. Everyone turned to look at me, and I felt my face turning red. "I mean, isn't that why we're here?" I said. "Isn't getting sent out into sea-monster-infested water the end goal?"

"That is a very good point, Berkley," Weaver said. "However, this entire area was explored this morning by the Britannica's diving crew to ascertain whether or not a cetus was still in the area. They deemed the area clear. As an added precaution we always have four scout divers—located to the north, south, east, and west of the Britannica—who will give us ample time to get to safety if they spot anything awry. We try very hard not to send any of our recruits out unprepared and unarmed."

"Right," I said. "Sorry."

Weaver went on, lecturing us about staying close to the group, the amount of time we would be out in the open, and procedures to follow in case any of our equipment started malfunctioning.

"I hope the new kids don't panic," Max whispered behind me, just loud enough that I could hear.

I debated letting that comment go. I had promised myself that morning to give Max and his crummy attitude some grace, but I found myself turning to face him, my own glare firmly in place. "If you need to worry about the new kids, worry that we are going to show you up and make you look bad," I said, turning back to face Weaver, who was thankfully distracted with something on the panel that worked the hatch.

"That was a bit cocky," Garth whispered, "even for you."

"I mean it," I said, setting my jaw. "We can do this, and we are going to do this well. Our families are depending on it."

"What does that mean?" Garth said. "Our families have no clue what we're doing, thank goodness." He gave an exaggerated shudder as he looked at the hatch door looming in front of us.

"I'll tell you later," I said dismissively, realizing that I had almost said too much. I wasn't sure yet how much I should tell Garth about the hydra that was potentially stalking the *Atlas*, and now wasn't the time to drop that kind of information on him. My determination to succeed here, at this new, weird challenge that had been put in front of me, solidified inside my chest. I wanted to save my family, and from the sounds of it, that meant two things. The first was that I was going to have to make it as a crew member aboard the *Britannica*. I wouldn't do my family any good if I got kicked out of the program and ended up helpless on some random ship, or, worse, on a work ship. The second was that if there was a way to protect ships like the *Atlas* from monsters, it was going to be something the *Britannica* and its crew discovered by actually studying the things. I'd always been good at figuring out problems. I knew how to tinker with bits of this and that until I found something useful. This was the same thing, I told myself, only instead of bits of metal and wire and broken junk, I was going to be figuring out sea monsters.

"If no one has any questions, please put your masks on and make sure your air converters are working *before* you enter the hatch." He said this last line with a meaningful look at Kate, whose face immediately turned bright red.

I felt all the blood run out of my face and collect somewhere at my feet as I thought about what he'd said. I checked the tiny air converter on my mask once, and then three more times, just to be safe. Standing in that hatch while it filled up with water and realizing that the machine that would convert ocean water into air wasn't working was not something I wanted to experience for myself.

"Don't be so twitchy," Garth whispered next to me, his face muffled inside his mask. "It will be fine. If you could dive with the junk we used on the *Atlas*, you can dive with this." I nodded, but it made me feel better that two adult crew members walked in just then to check and then double-check each of us before we made our way over to the door on the far side of the dive room.

"Remember to stick together," Weaver said as we

all filed into the hatch. The five of us stood shoulder to shoulder as Weaver hit the button to close the door.

"Masks on," he called, and everyone jostled one another to comply. "Give me the thumbs-up when you're ready," he said, and four thumbs went into the air. He placed a hand to his ear and looked at the floor. A second later there was a slight crackling sound in my own ear as Weaver's voice came through my earpiece.

"If you can hear me, hold up two fingers," he said. Everyone put two fingers in the air. Garth and I shot each other a knowing look. This was already very different from a dive aboard the *Atlas*. Weaver went through a few more checks to ensure that he could hear us as well. Finally he nodded and hit another button. The room hissed as water started pouring in from the ports along the floor. Within seconds it was up to our knees and then our waists. I bit my lip so hard I drew blood. I'd never stood in a room as it filled rapidly with water, and I could already tell it wasn't a sensation I'd ever grow to enjoy. The water reached our necks and then crept up over our faces and heads until we stood completely submerged. The entire room hummed, and I felt the subtle pressure change begin. I cleared my ears once, twice, three times, and then it was over. A heartbeat later the door on the opposite side of the room slid open, and we looked out at the endless expanse of the ocean.

"Move out," Weaver said, motioning with his hand before turning and paddling out of the hatch. Max and Kate followed immediately, with Garth and me bringing up the rear.

Everything that had tightened inside me in the hatch seemed to loosen the moment I entered the vast blue ocean. I glanced up to where the sun was turning the water into dazzling shades of aquamarine and imagined swimming straight up to feel the warmth on my face. A movement to my right brought my head snapping back down, and a swirl of silver fish went swimming past. Below, the water was teeming with life as bright, rainbow-colored fish darted in and out of the nooks and crannies of the ocean floor.

"No stragglers, Berkley," said Weaver's voice directly in my ear. "Please keep up with the rest of the recruits." I looked up to see the entire group twenty feet away, staring right at me. My face heated, and I kicked hard to rejoin them. I'd always prided myself on being a fast swimmer despite the fact that I was short, and my legs churned through the bubbles erupting from the back of my face mask.

"Like I was saying," Weaver said when I'd caught up, "while these claw marks are impressive, based off legend and lore, I don't believe they are quite large enough to be from a full-grown cetus." He ran a hand over the gouges as we all huddled closer to get a better look. The marks were even bigger up close, and I felt my heart thump at the thought of the monster that had made them. Weaver started discussing the calculations and equations used to determine the actual size of the creature, and my eyes wandered back out across the ocean. After years of working as a scavenger, it was odd to focus on just one thing. I'd been trained to notice the unnoticeable and find the unfindable, and it seemed old habits died hard.

I wondered a bit at myself as I gently moved my arms around to stay floating beside the rest of the group. I'd expected to be scared on this first dive with the *Britannica*—after all, the last time I'd been in the water I'd almost been eaten, and since then I'd learned of an entire encyclopedia of monsters capable of turning me into lunch—but somehow I wasn't. This felt a lot like any other dive Garth and I had made, albeit with much better equipment, and I decided to attribute my composure to the rock-solid determination I'd felt right before we'd entered the hatch.

Maybe I should even thank Max for being such a jerk, I thought with a slight smile. Of course, he couldn't have known that the best way to motivate me was to tell me I couldn't do something. My mind flashed back to Garth double-daring me to zip-line down one of the ropes on the *Atlas*'s rigging when we were ten. I'd done it and gotten caught and punished. When my dad had asked me what in the world had possessed me to do something so dumb and reckless, I'd had a hard time answering. Garth would have still been my friend if I hadn't done it, so it wasn't that. It was that I'd had to prove to myself that he wasn't right, that I wasn't a chicken. This felt similar.

In the distance I could see what used to be the shoreline of Greece, but its former life was nothing but a distant memory, and it was now just another part of the ocean. A few stone buildings remained, their windows and doors long gone. Rainbow-colored sea urchins, plant life, and sea stars had utilized the crumbling facades, and the underwater city had a beauty it never could have achieved on land. The scavenger part of my brain wondered if there was anything of value left in those colorful wrecks. In a few more years even less of it would remain. The ocean was ruthless like that. Her salt ate metal, her tides wore down rocks, and her sand scrubbed away all remaining traces. It was beautiful, though, if you could look past the sadness of losing an entire way of life.

"Berkley," came Weaver's voice in my ear. "Focus, please." I snapped my head back to look at him. "We hypothesize that the cetus is much like the other clawed monsters we've captured, and therefore most likely feeds primarily on sharks, whales, and other large fish, including some of the giant squid we talked about this morning." Weaver ran a gloved hand down the claw mark almost reverently.

I sensed a movement to my left, and even though I knew I should keep my focus on Weaver after getting reprimanded twice, I still turned to see the *Britannica*'s southern scout swimming in from wherever he'd been investigating. My head automatically turned to the right to see if I could spot the northern scout, and I felt my heart spasm in terror. The scout was there, swimming leisurely back toward the sub, completely unaware that she was being followed by a creature so large she was in danger of being swallowed whole.

I screamed. Everyone around me jumped as my scream burst through their earpieces. Terror stuck the words in my mouth, and all I could manage was to flail frantically at the oncoming monster, which was definitely not a cetus. No, this was a creature I recognized, although it was so big that I was fairly certain it could eat a cetus for breakfast. Everyone froze for one agonizing heartbeat as they took in the behemoth shark bearing down on us. Weaver's eyes went wide inside his face mask.

"Swim for the *Britannica*! Now! It's a megalodon!"

9

"**S**wim for the *Britannica!*" Weaver bellowed again, so loudly his words seemed to bounce around inside my head. Adrenaline ripped through my system like a tidal wave, every nerve standing on end. Everyone listened, making a beeline for the sub, but I could already tell that we'd never make it. A shark that big had to be capable of swimming at breathtaking speeds, and I glanced back to see the northern scout barely avoid being eaten thanks to some fancy maneuvering and a whole lot of luck. Suddenly the water around me reverberated as the *Britannica* shot something into the water. For a split second I thought they were firing on the megalodon, but whatever they shot went wide.

"How in the world did they miss that thing?" Garth's voice came in loud and frantic in my ear. "It's gigantic!"

"Swim!" Weaver repeated. "They are creating a distraction for us. We don't have the equipment to bring down a monster that size. They're buying us time."

Then the distraction detonated. A hundred feet to the right of us something erupted, sending a shock wave through the water that I could feel in my teeth, and suddenly the ocean was red.

"What was that?" Garth said as the red bloomed through the water, spreading in inky scarlet swirls.

"Blood bomb," Kate rasped. Before I could wrap my brain around what a blood bomb might be, a miracle happened and the megalodon changed course, the blood a siren song it couldn't ignore. The smooth silver-gray body passed over our heads, throwing us into its immense shadow for a moment, and despite the panic of the situation, everyone craned their necks to watch it pass.

"The blood bomb won't work for long," Weaver said into our earpieces as he herded us back toward the *Britannica*. "Get in the hatch. I don't want to close it until we have everyone." He didn't have to say why he didn't want to close it. He'd explained before we entered the first time that it took minutes to pressurize the water and then drain it. Minutes that would leave any stragglers locked outside the *Britannica* with the monster.

And what a monster this was. We were dwarfed by the megalodon—like a mouse by a cat—which took my breath away in a way the encounter with the hydra hadn't. The megalodon was bigger than the hydra by at least ten feet or so, and there was something about the familiar shape of a shark that hit me harder than the strange snakelike hydra had. It was a predator I knew, one I'd grown up knowing, and now it was feet away from me and bigger than I ever could have imagined.

The water in front of me churned as everyone paddled for all they were worth. Pinning my arms to my sides to make myself more aerodynamic, I kicked hard, my leg muscles burning. The hatch was open, a gaping square of light that promised safety, but I couldn't help myself, and I looked back. The megalodon had turned, no small feat for an animal of that size, and was swimming toward us through the red-tinted water with single-minded focus. It knew it had been tricked, and it wasn't happy about it. Turning again, I saw that Kate had made it into the hatch, and Weaver hovered just inside the entrance, waiting to pull each of us in as soon as we were close enough.

The water around me seemed to reverberate as four thin black torpedoes shot out from the *Britannica* and hurtled toward the approaching shark. Suddenly they exploded, and four black cabled nets flew out in every direction. The black netting wrapped around the mega-lodon's face and jaws, snagging on its rows upon rows of teeth before streaming back and around its fins.

"That's never going to hold it," I said, amazed by the stupidity of firing a net at something that massive.

"It's electric," Kate said in my ear, her breathing harsh and jagged. A second later I saw what she meant: the monster jerked sharply to the left as the nets were activated, sending volts of paralyzing electricity through their webbing. The shark thrashed, throwing its head one way and another, and shredded the net like it was nothing but a spiderweb. I felt someone grab my arm, and I turned to see Weaver yank me the last few feet into the hatch with everyone else. A quick glance showed that all four of us recruits were in, but to my surprise Weaver still stood at the entrance, his hand poised over the button that would close the hatch, his face tight behind the mask.

Then I saw it—the scouts. Three of them were almost to the hatch, but the fourth, the northernmost scout, was nowhere to be seen. The small square of the hatch entrance showed nothing but clear ocean as the three scouts ducked inside. Still Weaver waited at the entrance, his hand hovering over the button that would seal us safely inside the *Britannica*.

He waited too long. One second the square of visible ocean outside was clear, and the next the megalodon was ramming itself snout-first into the hatch. It barely missed Weaver, who threw himself away from the entrance just before impact. As it was, one of the shark's teeth caught his side, shredding his wet suit and sending a plume of blood into the water. Weaver put a hand to his ribs and pressed himself against the side of the hatch, and Max yanked him further back before any more damage could be done. The megalodon's head was too big to fit all the way inside, but even so, its rows upon rows of teeth were so close that I could have reached out and touched them if I hadn't valued keeping my hand attached to my body.

The lights flickered, and the sides of the hatch seemed to bend outward as the shark gained another few inches. My mind fogged with panic, and the electric zing of adrenaline hummed uselessly through my veins. I wouldn't have thought it was possible for things to get any worse, but then the lights went out. I wasn't sure if we'd lost power or if the crew on board had decided to turn the lights off to hide us and confuse the shark, but either way the inside of the hatch was suddenly pitch-black.

The metal under my feet vibrated as the *Britannica* shot something else into the water. A second later the megalodon jerked to the right and pulled its face out of the hatch. The shark thrashed angrily in the water, and I saw a small black object embedded in its side. Seconds later, the thing exploded. The water turned an impenetrable red, and I had no idea if I was seeing another blood bomb or if the shark had been injured, but I didn't care.

"Somebody shut the hatch," said Weaver's voice in my ear. "Somebody," he repeated, his voice not much more than a gasping sort of croak, "hit the button." No one moved. It was as though we'd been frozen in place as we watched the red water churn in front of the hatch opening. Now that we couldn't see the shark, it was almost worse than when it had been inches away from us, and we all stared at the water, waiting. I looked to my left and right, trying to see Max, Garth, or Kate through the dark water, but it was impossible.

I thought about those teeth inches from my face. It was just a matter of time before the shark remembered the hole we were all hiding in. The last thing in the entire world that I wanted to do at the moment was move from my spot on the wall, but despite the terror coursing through me, I recognized this moment for what it was: an opportunity. Just like the fear for my family had forced me into action when the hydra was attacking the *Atlas*, my determination to prove myself pushed its way past my terror now. Captain Reese needed to see that we had what it took, and I was going to have to prove that I did if I wanted to protect my family. It was time to move.

It took everything in me, but I inched my way to the right, sliding toward the far wall of the hatch and that little red button. I felt someone try to grab my arm, and I shook them off without looking back. Odds were it was Garth trying to stop me, but there wasn't time for that. Either we shut the hatch or we waited for the megalodon to come back and pry us out of the *Britannica* like a clam from its shell.

My hand slipped over the edge of the hatch and out into open water, and I jerked backward. I'd gone too far. Turning back, I ran my hands over the wall, cursing the blood bomb and the loss of lights that had made the water impenetrable.

Suddenly I felt something beside me, and I whirled in the dark, my hands coming up defensively before I realized it was just another diver.

"It's me," Kate's voice said in my ear. "Hit the button!"

"I can't find it!" I said, my hands pawing over the seemingly empty wall. Kate joined me, and a second later so did one of the scouts, and together we searched. For a moment there was nothing but a bunch of fumbling hands, and then my hand found the button at the same time as Kate's, and we pushed. Nothing happened. I hit it again. Still nothing.

"Maybe the shark busted something when it attacked," I said. "Is there another way into the *Britannica*?"

"No," Kate said, her voice half wail, half sob. "Not while we're underwater. If any of the other entrances are opened, we'll be flooded and sink."

"Hit it again," instructed the scout. I did just as I sensed movement to my right and whirled, expecting to see the open mouth of the shark bearing down on me. Instead I spotted the northern scout paddling into the hatch.

"It's about time!" said the scout who'd been helping us find the button as he grabbed the northern scout by the arm and pushed her toward the back of the hatch.

I glanced back and saw Mr. Weaver grab the late scout in a tight hug despite the fact that one of the other scouts was attempting to stop his side from bleeding, and I realized the water was clearing. Turning, I looked back out the hatch entrance, searching for the shark. A moment later I spotted it: it was circling around and heading back toward the sub, because of course if we could see it, it could see us. The lights in the hatch suddenly sprang to life, and black spots erupted in my vision from the brightness.

"Hit the button!" Weaver rasped in my ear, and I turned to discover that the button was now glowing a hopeful shade of green. I hit it and the hatch door shuddered and began to move. Through it I could still see the speeding form of the massive shark, and the scout who'd helped us find the button grabbed our wet suits and jerked us toward the back of the hatch. Garth and Max reached out their hands to pull us in the last few feet, and I turned in time to see the hatch door slide shut.

I grinned triumphantly at Garth, but a second later the entire sub lurched as the megalodon hit the side of the *Britannica* with such force that the door bent inward. I screamed, but the sound of everyone else's terrified shouts in my ears drowned me out. The hatch's lights flashed, showing us that the depressurization process had already begun, and I quickly cleared my ears. The water had just started to drain out of the hatch when the second impact came, throwing half of us off our feet so our heads slipped back under the quickly retreating water.

"Keep your masks on," Weaver said, and I looked over to see him being supported by two of the scouts, his face a sickly gray behind his own mask. The third impact came when the water was at our waists, and everyone held on to one another or the wall to steady themselves. The metal of the hatch door bowed in a bit more, and I wondered how much more it could take. If it burst open, we'd be worse off than when we started, not only because there would be no way to escape the shark, but because the sudden pressure change could kill us.

The water was down to our knees when the entrance to the sub behind us opened, allowing the foot of remaining seawater to rush into the *Britannica*, soaking the dive room and the feet of the waiting medics and crew, who immediately began shouting at us to get inside. We stumbled over our flippers and one another in our rush to make it into the safety of the submarine. The last one to make it inside was Weaver, who was apparently unconscious, as he was being dragged by the scouts. Before they'd even cleared the door, one of the crew hit the close button.

The door to the hatch was beginning to shut just as yet another impact rocked the sub, knocking those who weren't already sprawled on the floor to their knees. The inner door was almost closed when the outer door ruptured, and water came flooding into the dive room. Two crew members threw themselves against either side of the door, and by some miracle they managed to force it shut, but not before gallons of seawater had made it into the now completely drenched dive room.

Another crew member hit the intercom button on the wall and yelled, "Hatch is secure. Go!"

The *Britannica* rumbled beneath my feet as its engines came to life, shooting us into the ocean and away from the megalodon.

"Did that really just happen?" Garth said, yanking his mask off and dropping it unceremoniously into the six inches of water surrounding our feet. I expected everyone around us to be in various states of hysterics or shock similar to the fallout after the *Atlas* was attacked, but to my surprise the scouts were actually laughing, clapping one another on the back as they took off their gear.

"Get used to it, rookie," Max said as he spit into the water at our feet and wiped his face off on his sleeve.

"That's one impressive rookie," said a voice behind us, and I turned to see the scout who'd helped Kate and me find the hatch button. He pulled off his mask, and I saw it was one of the teenagers from our bunk room. He was maybe sixteen or so, with shaggy black hair and a wide grin that showed off dimples. He tucked his own mask under his arm and held out a hand to me.

"I haven't had a chance to introduce myself yet; you were already in your bunk by the time the gang and I turned in last night. I'm Ryan."

"Berkley," I said, shaking his hand.

"It's not every day we get attacked by a meg. I'm impressed you had the guts to go for the hatch button."

"Some of us had the guts, but we were too busy trying not to get swallowed whole," said a teenage girl as she dropped her own mask onto a nearby bench and shoved her wet hair off her face.

"Were you the northern scout?" I said.

She grimaced. "Unfortunately," she said. "I'm Megan, and if I had been paying better attention, you guys would have had more of a heads-up."

"Is Weaver okay?" I asked, peering over Megan's shoulder to where Weaver lay sprawled on one of the benches, surrounded by medics.

"He'll be fine," Kate said. "The guy's a legend, and legends aren't killed by a shark sideswipe."

"I don't feel like it's fair to call that thing a shark," Garth said. "I mean, it must munch on great whites for breakfast."

"Better than having *us* for breakfast," I said, noticing for the first time that my legs felt like all my bones had dissolved and left me with nothing but mush and muscle. I sat down hard on one of the benches, trying to process everything that had just happened. Over the hum of the engines I could hear a faint slurping noise as the water around our feet slowly drained away.

Across from me four crew members were rapidly

welding large strips of metal over the hatch door with an impressive degree of precision that made me wonder just how many times something like this had happened. I was so distracted watching this choreographed performance that I didn't notice that Captain Reese had walked in until she was standing a foot away from me.

"Berkley, Kate, Ryan," she said, "nice work." I probably should have responded, but I just nodded numbly instead. "Are any of you going into shock?" she asked, turning so she could study each of our faces.

"I don't think so," I said. "What does shock feel like?" My head felt too full, as though being underwater with that massive shark had scrambled what used to be a perfectly good brain.

Captain Reese bent low to peer in both of my eyes. I'm not sure what she saw there, but she gave a decisive no and stood up. "I don't think you're in shock, which under the circumstances, is rather impressive. Well done." She turned to Megan, eyebrow raised. "Please report to my office," she said. "I would like to talk to you about the duties and responsibilities of a scout." Megan seemed to visibly shrink, but she nodded and walked out of the diving room.

"Now," Captain Reese said, "if you four recruits *are* all fine, I need you to report to the command hub up front. We are shorthanded up there, thanks to these repairs." She jerked her head at the busted hatch, her face grim. "Tell Officer Wilson that I'll be back as soon as I finish talking to Megan." We nodded and stumbled awkwardly to our feet so we could slosh our way out of the soggy dive room.

We made our way down the halls in silence, each of us lost in our own thoughts. Finally we arrived at the front of the sub, where the wide, expansive windows showed us speeding along at a breakneck pace. With the exception of Tank, who lay on one of the windowsills snoring peacefully, every crew member had the same intense look of concentration as they ran the *Britannica* at full throttle.

"Is the meg still following us?" Max asked Officer Wilson.

Wilson never even looked up as he nodded. "We're putting some much-needed distance between us. It should lose interest soon; if not, we have a couple more blood bombs we can shoot off. How are the repairs in the dive room?"

"Good," Max said. "The hatch is almost completely welded shut. Captain Reese said she'll be back as soon as she's done talking to Megan."

Wilson grimaced. "That girl's going to get an earful," he said, shooting a glance over at Max. "Maybe even worse than the one you and Luke got."

Max winced but didn't say anything, his eyes staring straight ahead as the *Britannica* rushed past schools of fish so quickly they were nothing but a silver blur.

"How long do you think it will take for a full repair of the door?" Kate asked quickly, in an obvious effort to take Wilson's attention off Max.

"Depends how soon we can surface," said Wilson. "It's a bad rupture this time. It's a miracle it shut, let alone held a seal to depressurize us. We're going to have to dock to fix it right." He turned and yelled to an officer on the other side of the sub, "Hey, Pete, how far away are we from a liner big enough to accommodate the *Britannica*?"

"Probably at least a day or two," Pete shouted back. "I'll check as soon as this thing stops tailing us. There goes the cetus mission. Weaver's going to be heart-broken."

"Weaver got hurt," I blurted out, and almost every crew member in the hub turned to look at me.

"He'll be fine," Max said loudly, digging an elbow hard into my ribs. "The meg nicked him and he lost some blood, that's all. He's definitely been through worse." The crew members' faces relaxed, and they returned to the job at hand.

"Sorry," I muttered as Max shot me a look. "Why was that wrong?"

"Because talking about injuries is the captain's job," he said. "Not yours."

I walked over to give Tank a quick scratch behind the ear, but he just let out a waffling snore and rolled over without even bothering to wake up.

"Now, are you four here to work or to drip on the floor?" Wilson said as he read some new bit of information on his screen.

"Work," we all said, and boy did we work.

Together we washed wet suits, mopped up the dive room, helped the sub's cook prepare supper, and scrubbed down the dining room tables. I fell into bed that night still smelling like the ocean and so tired I didn't even remember my eyes shutting.

I t was another week before we were allowed back in
the water on a diving mission. After what had to be
the most exciting first day in the history of first days, I
was thankful for the normalcy of our new routine. Mr.
Weaver returned to the classroom the next day, well-
bandaged and a bit pale but none the worse for his
near-death experience. Two days after the meg attack,
we found a grower ship that was large enough to pull
the *Britannica* out of the water to repair the hatch, and
it was a relief to walk around in the air and the sunshine again, even if only for a few hours.

Grower ships were some of the most prized on the
ocean, as they were the only source of non-ocean-
supplied food. Thanks to their previous life as aircraft

carriers for the military, they had large, flat decks perfect for cultivating most of the things that had made up the diet of the human race before the tide rose. Even though we weren't allowed to touch the tomatoes, peppers, kale, and potatoes that covered every available surface of the ship, being around all that green was comforting somehow, and I found myself wishing the hatch would take longer to be repaired. As it was, we were back in the water within hours, and I was once again saying goodbye to the sun. This time was easier, though, especially since the ship had sent us a basket of fresh produce that our cook, Brenda, promised to make last for the entire week.

The *Britannica* certainly didn't feel like home yet, but it was getting there. I discovered that I actually liked my morning chores with Hector. The old man was a bit of a jack-of-all-trades, and we made our way over most of the sub, fixing this, cleaning that, organizing, and generally keeping the submarine up and running. He had a gruff, no-nonsense personality, but he also told some really fantastic stories about the monsters he'd encountered during his time aboard the *Britannica*.

Sometimes I felt like I learned more from Hector than I did during Weaver's classes, although those were eye-opening as well. However, I quickly discovered that the two men had very different views about how monsters should be handled. Hector was of the opinion that every monster should be exterminated—he called it "nipping the problem in the bud"—a viewpoint that Weaver condemned in a thirty-minute monologue when I made the mistake of bringing it up in class. He called Hector's views "old school" and "closed-minded" and went on to explain that while that had been the original intent of submarines like the *Britannica*, the Coalition had quickly realized that they'd make much more progress toward protecting ships if they focused on researching monsters instead of killing them on sight. "We only attack a monster once it has attacked a ship," Weaver had said, mopping at a forehead that had broken out in sweat, something that happened often when he got overexcited about something. I'd never brought it up again.

Besides my mornings with Hector and classes with Weaver, Kate was turning into a great friend. She'd relaxed a bit of her "instruction-manual personality," as Max called it, and she had such an easygoing nature that sometimes I forgot that I hadn't known her for my entire life. Even Max was warming up to us a bit, although sometimes he made it hard to remember my resolution to give him grace when he didn't deserve it. The only part of the new routine that felt wrong was Garth. I wasn't sure if it was because the megalodon attack had freaked him out, or if he was just missing home, but he'd lost the happy-go-lucky part of himself that had made life on board the *Atlas* so much fun. It didn't happen all at once, and honestly it took me a while to notice, but every day he seemed to smile just a little bit less and laugh less easily. It was almost as though he was fading away like the tan on my skin.

"Are you okay?" I asked one morning as I watched him pick at his food. Garth never picked at his food, especially when it tasted as good as the stuff in front of us did.

"Hmm?" he said, looking up.

"Are. You. Okay?" I repeated, enunciating each word.

Garth shrugged. "Just missing our old life, I guess."

"What about our old life?" I said.

"The sun, for one thing," Garth said. "Diving, scavenging, my family. I even found myself missing Gizmo a little bit yesterday."

"No way," I said, shaking my head. "Now I know you're lying."

Garth cracked a half-hearted smile. "Fine," he said, "not Gizmo, but everything else. Don't you miss it?"

"Of course," I said, even as I felt a pang of guilt at the lie. I missed my dad and my brother, but everything else had faded into the background without my even realizing. Life on board the *Britannica* was new and different, and after a lifetime of unchanging sameness, it was refreshing. Besides, even if Captain Brown ever allowed us to return, I couldn't imagine going back to the *Atlas* knowing what I knew now. Sitting on that ship, waiting for the monster I'd unearthed to catch up to us, sounded like the worst kind of nightmare. I'd made a promise to myself that if I ever did get a chance to go back to the ship I'd called home for my entire life, I was going to go with a way for them to protect themselves.

From what I'd learned from Mr. Weaver and Hector, most ships were brutally unprepared for any kind of attack. Which, since attacks happened randomly and rarely, wasn't all that surprising. Most captains believed their duties lay in protecting their ships from the inevitable storms, pirates, fishing droughts, and ship damage, and they were unwilling to risk resources and time for something that might never happen. Besides, with the range of monsters that roamed the ocean, how was a ship supposed to prepare for an attack? It was no wonder so many captains like Captain Brown chose to keep the existence of sea monsters a secret.

"After years of believing sea monsters didn't exist, it's like I can't get away from them," Garth griped, jarring me from my thoughts.

"It's not sea monsters you want to get away from," Max said, sitting down beside us. "It's Elmer."

"Fine," Garth said, sitting back and throwing his hands in the air. "You're right. I don't want to deal with that mean old curmudgeon of a crustacean anymore."

"Fun fact," Kate said, plopping down beside Max.

"Octopi aren't crustaceans. They're mollusks."

"They are giant wet spiders," Garth said, and Max snorted so hard his water shot out of his nose and across the table. "They are!" Garth insisted. "It's like he sees me coming and is just waiting to do something awful when I get into his tank."

"That's because he *does* see you coming," said Max. "That thing's smarter than Kate."

"I'd be offended, but he's probably right," Kate said with a shrug.

"Do you think you could switch jobs with someone?" I said. "I bet if you weren't getting dunked daily, you'd be a whole lot happier."

"He asked me," Max said. "But I've cleaned out those tanks more than my fair share. Pass."

"Don't look at me," Kate said.

"Trust me, I'm smarter than that," Garth said.

"Fine," I said, setting down my fork decisively. "I'll switch with you, then. Besides, I've never even seen the large-specimen room, and it's about time."

"You haven't?" Kate said, eyebrow raised in surprise. "How is that possible?"

I shrugged. I'd been trying to get there ever since our first day on board, but life on the *Britannica* was so busy that finding a spare minute to poke around had been impossible.

"I'll switch," I said again. "But you owe me one."

"He's going to owe you more than one," Max said, and everyone glanced over at him to see if he would elaborate. He didn't.

Garth and I walked together to the back of the sub, and I had to smile a little as Garth whistled happily. He turned left to head toward Hector while I kept going straight. I realized as I walked that I'd never asked Garth what the other specimens were besides old Elmer the mean-spirited octopus. As I rounded the corner and saw what was in front of me, that oversight seemed really, really dumb.

The back of the submarine had a very similar feel to the hub, with its wall-to-wall glass, the only difference being that the glass in this room was part of eight floor-to-ceiling aquariums. I stood frozen as I took in the tanks. Some of them held creatures I was familiar with: a giant squid, a sea turtle, and an enormous octopus that had to be the infamous Elmer. The other tanks were more of a mystery. I walked up to the closest one and peeked in at the strange creature. Its head was similar to a pig's or a boar's, and it tapered back into a seal-like body with four elongated fins. Down the middle of its spine was a large ridge of spikes that looked lethally sharp.

The tanks just got weirder from there. A pencil-thin, snakelike creature that had to be thirty feet in length was twisted and knotted around itself so it resembled a big orange ball of yarn with eyes. Another tank held what looked like a three-headed sea lizard, while the last tank held a bizarre anglerfish with translucent skin that revealed its skeleton and a twisted network of intestines that made my own stomach feel queasy.

"Pretty impressive, right?" said a voice behind me, and I turned to see Weaver walking in holding two huge buckets of dead fish. He was wincing a little, probably from the still-healing stitches in his side, and I rushed over to take one of the buckets from him.

"Very impressive," I said. "What are all these . . . these things?" I said, searching for the right word to describe the contents of the tank and failing.

"A little bit of everything," Weaver said. "Some of them are creatures we captured and were unable to reintroduce to the wild—like Elmer," he said with a nod at the tank with the giant octopus. "Most of them we research and release," he said, jerking his head toward the tank with the piggish-looking monster. "The majority of sea monsters are much too large to keep in a tank, but every now and then we find a very young or unusually small specimen."

"I'd say this is unbelievable," I said, doing another slow circle to take in the tanks, "but ever since the attack on the *Atlas*, I'm in the believing business."

Weaver chuckled. "I've never heard it put quite like that, but I like it. Where's Garth?"

"I switched jobs with him today," I said, realizing for the first time that I probably should have asked permission before doing that. I bit my lip nervously. I'd seen what had happened to Megan after her scouting mistake, and scrubbing the floors of the sub on my hands and knees was not something I'd enjoy in the least. Captain Reese was kind but ruthless in her command of the ship, and I had no idea what an infraction like this would warrant for me or Garth. Wouldn't that be my luck, I thought glumly—I try to do something nice for my friend and it backfires completely.

"Well," Weaver said after letting me stew and fret for a moment, "that's not really how things are done around here, but if Hector is all right with it, I guess I am as well. Here." I had no idea if Hector would be fine with it, but I said a silent prayer that he would be as Weaver motioned to one of the buckets. "Take that and follow me," he instructed. I did as I was told, and he gingerly climbed the steps to the narrow walkway around the top of the aquariums, unlocked the top of the first one, and tossed in its occupant's breakfast. It was my job to cart up the full buckets and retrieve the empty ones, and it wasn't long before my leg muscles were burning. When we got to the tank with the long, thin sea creature that looked like a giant twisted ball of yarn, he paused and put on a large pair of protective goggles and then fished a pair out of his pocket to hand to me. I slid them on as he donned thick metal gloves that went clear up to his armpits.

"Stand back," he instructed me. "The fliexarmonious is poisonous." I didn't have to be told twice, retreating so far that my back bumped into the tank on the opposite side. I watched, wide-eyed, as Weaver pulled out what looked like diced squid and carefully slipped it into the tank. The fliexarmonious suddenly lunged at the small opening Weaver had made in the lid of the tank. Thankfully, Weaver was faster, sliding the metal lock bar back in place a half second before the thing could reach him. He did this entire thing without breaking a sweat. Meanwhile, my heart felt like it had just stopped.

"These creatures are still very much a mystery to us," Weaver said. "Other than what they eat, we don't know nearly enough."

"And all this research is to try to keep ships safe from attack?" I said.

Weaver nodded. "It may be too much to hope for, but if there is one common thread that could help protect us, it would be worth it."

"Right," I said, thinking again of my family aboard the *Atlas*. I'd always known that living on a ship was dangerous, with the unpredictable weather and the constant need to supply food and water to the people on board, but this new threat felt so much worse. You could prepare for the weather, and you could stockpile food and water in times of plenty, but there was no way to prevent a sea-monster attack.

Or was there? The part of my brain that liked solving problems seemed to shake itself a little as it woke up. Tinkering and fiddling with things had been a huge part of what made me *me* aboard the *Atlas*, but I'd left that all behind me since coming aboard the *Britannica*. Part of that, I knew, was because I'd been too busy trying to get used to this new life in sea-monster-infested waters, but I knew a bigger part was that on the *Britannica* I just didn't have the same access to junk I'd had aboard the *Atlas*. The biggest reason, though, was that the *Britannica* was all smooth and state-of-the-art, while the *Atlas* had been rust-riddled and patched. There was no need here for me to solve problems with my trivial inventions, so I'd pushed that part of myself aside, but maybe it was time to dust it off again.

"We've found a few things that work to repel specific monsters, but nothing universal," Weaver went on. "For example, magnets are great against a megalodon, but they also deter fish, and the last thing we want to do is set up a ship for starvation."

"What else?" I said.

"Let's see," Weaver said with a sigh. "Lights, loud sounds . . . we've even tried some chemical sprays, but nothing has worked. Or, if it does work, it is too damaging to the environment or repels fish."

"Wow," I said. "After all that you still think there is a solution out there?"

"I do," Weaver said. "All we've figured out so far is about fifty-seven ways *not* to repel a sea monster, and that's pretty useful information too!"

"Really?" I said, thinking back to Gizmo's "failure isn't an option" speeches. The fear of failure had been as natural as breathing on the *Atlas*, and here Weaver was acting like it was no big deal. Which, considering the stakes, seemed kind of insane. My mind was chewing this over when I felt something wet and thick slide down the neck of my shirt.

"Elmer! No!" Weaver bellowed, but it was too late. I felt myself being lifted into the air, and I screamed, thrashing and turning to see the thickly muscled tentacle of an octopus inches from my eyes. That was the last thing I saw before I was slam-dunked into ice-cold water. I came up gasping, only to be dunked again. I came up a third time just as something large and black flew past me and into the tank. Elmer let me go, and I managed to grab the edge of the tank and haul myself out as Elmer helped himself to the fish Weaver had thrown in.

Weaver hurried to help me to my feet and I stood there, spluttering in shock.

"Sorry about that," Weaver said. "I thought Garth

would have told you not to stand that close to Elmer's tank."

"Why isn't it locked like the others?" I asked, trying hard to keep the accusation from my voice and failing.

"Oh, it was," Weaver said. "But Elmer has a deft hand at picking locks. He's been known to unlock the other tanks as well, just for kicks."

"Some kicks," I said wryly as Weaver handed me a towel.

"He may actually like you," Weaver said. "Usually he inks the people that he dunks." I nodded, remembering the smelly, oily substance Garth had sported on more than one occasion. "If that stuff gets in your eyes, it burns like the dickens. It's also a huge pain, since every time it happens we have to completely drain and refill Elmer's tank, or it would eventually poison him." He gave me a sympathetic smile as I stood dripping all over the floor. "Come on," he said. "It's time to show you the less glamorous part of this job: meal prep."

As I disemboweled dead fish and chopped up squid, I couldn't help but agree with Max—Garth definitely owed me more than one. While we worked, Weaver explained that Elmer was a rehabilitation failure. They'd found him tangled in an abandoned fishing net and brought him into the specimen area due to his huge size, thinking he might be a relative of a monster they called the goliath. He'd healed quickly, but when they tried to release him, he just wrapped himself around the submarine like a barnacle and refused to leave, jamming himself back inside the hatch anytime it opened, until they gave up and let him stay.

"Sometimes I think he's studying us just as much as we're studying him," Weaver said, and I stopped filleting the fish I was working on to look at him, but it was impossible to tell whether Weaver was serious or joking.

Once we were done, Weaver opened up a metal drawer in his small supply room and pulled out a tooth roughly the length of my arm.

"Um, thanks?" I said awkwardly as I inspected the tooth's impressively pointed end.

Weaver chuckled. "You're welcome," he said. "But that isn't a 'welcome to the large-specimen lab' present. I need you to take that up to the hub and give it to Captain Reese. If she isn't there, she'll be in her office."

"Okay," I said, holding the thing out as I headed for the door.

"Point the tip down," Weaver called absentmindedly as he peered down at his tablet. "Wouldn't want you to trip and impale yourself."

"Right," I said as I flipped the tooth, "definitely wouldn't want that." I carried the tooth out the door and headed down the hallway.

"Whatcha got there?" said a voice behind me a

minute later, and I turned to see Kate walking down the hall wearing a greasy pair of coveralls.

"Do you really think I know?" I said, eyebrow raised. "I'm just doing my best not to become a human kebab."

Kate snorted. "Working with Weaver is rarely dull." She looked me up and down, taking in my still-dripping clothes. "I see you've met Elmer."

"We met," I said, trying to keep the grump out of my voice.

"Regretting switching with Garth?" she asked, keeping pace with me as I gingerly turned left and maneuvered the giant tooth down yet another hall.

"Sort of," I admitted. "What are you up to today?"

Kate shrugged. "A bit of this, a bit of that," she said. "I don't like to stay with one job too long. I get bored easily. Twitchy." I nodded: it was a personality trait of hers I'd noticed on more than one occasion. Sitting next to her at the mess hall drove me a bit nuts because she would bounce her foot the entire time, like if it just went fast enough, she might be able to take flight.

"I'm surprised you signed on for life inside a submarine, then," I said, gesturing as best I could to the close walls of the hallways. The tooth wobbled a bit in my hands, and I quickly tightened my grip on it again.

"You sound like my mom," Kate said. "She thought they'd send me back in a week, that I'd bounce off the walls, but as long as we get to go out on diving missions every now and then, I'm fine. Besides, Captain Reese lets me keep my duties pretty varied. Sometimes I help Brenda in the kitchen; sometimes I help Wilson in the hub; other days I work in the engine room. I used to do the large-specimen room, but then you and Garth came aboard and the workload lightened a bit." She glanced over at me, tucking a strand of red hair behind her ear. "So what do you think about life aboard the *Britannica*? Are you wishing you'd picked the work ship instead?"

I shook my head. "No. I just wish I'd had a chance to say goodbye to my family. I left things in kind of a mess, and I'm not even sure if they know that I'm alive."

Kate grimaced. "I can't imagine," she said, then brightened. "But you are alive. Which means you may get to see them again someday—you never know! So make sure you don't fall on that tooth," she added with a wink as she waved goodbye and turned right as I turned left.

"Everyone keeps saying that, like I'd do it on purpose," I muttered, my arms trembling from the strain as I turned the final corner and entered the hub. A quick glance around showed that Captain Reese was nowhere to be found, so I turned and walked over to her closed office door. Propping the tooth gingerly against the wall, I knocked and waited. Nothing. I knocked again, a bit louder this time. Still nothing.

I glanced back over my shoulder at the handful of crew members currently engaged in steering the submarine. By this point I knew most of the crew aboard the *Britannica* by name, and I noted that Ed, Tom, and Jim were all on duty along with Wilson. The first three were still strangers to me, but I knew enough about Wilson's prickly personality to guess that he wouldn't take kindly to being interrupted. I fidgeted nervously, wishing that Megan or Ryan or one of the other teenage crew members were around. They were always willing to answer a question or lend a hand, something I'd relied on more than once when Hector had assigned me a task that was over my head.

Feeling a bit lost, I knocked one more time and then tried the doorknob. It turned, and I eased it open and poked my head inside. The office was empty, but I quickly popped my head back out, not sure what to do now. Should I just wander around, hoping to find her? Go back to Weaver and apologize for being terrible at this job? Neither of those seemed like a great option, so even though I felt weird about being in there when the captain wasn't, I grabbed the tooth and stepped inside her office so I could put it on her desk.

I was just turning to leave when I spotted the screen of her computer. Displayed across her monitor was a large map of the ocean with a few small lights blinking on the screen. I leaned in, quickly spotting the tiny iridescent miniature of the *Britannica* as it made its way around the now-submerged heel of Italy. It wasn't the only illuminated vessel on the screen, though, and I inhaled as I found the *Atlas* moving off to the left of the screen. Without even realizing I was doing it, I reached out to touch the tiny ship that I'd called home for my entire life, a stab of homesickness lancing through me so sharply I felt tears press against my eyes.

I stood there for a minute, staring, before it occurred to me that it was odd for the *Atlas* to be on the captain's computer. There were thousands of ships out there, and hundreds in the *Britannica*'s precinct alone—why keep track of the *Atlas*? I noted that there were a couple of other ships on the map. More interesting than that, though, were the tiny sea monsters, each no bigger than my thumbnail. Some of the names I recognized from Mr. Weaver's lessons, while others were completely new. As I looked at each one, making a mental note to look them up in my encyclopedia that night, I saw a name that I recognized all too well— the red hydra. Captain Reese had mentioned on our first day on the *Britannica* that they'd managed to get a tracker on the monster that had attacked us, but I hadn't realized that she could see its location with this level of accuracy, and I realized with a rush of fear why the *Atlas* was on her map.

I reached out with a trembling hand and placed my thumb on the hydra and my pinky on the *Atlas*. They were far too close for comfort, and as I watched, I saw the tiny monster get a hair closer to my ship, to my family. I took a step back, feeling numb. Somehow I'd gotten carried away in adjusting to my new life aboard the *Britannica* and let the fact that a sea monster was stalking the *Atlas* slip to the back of my mind. I hadn't forgotten about it, not at all; it just had seemed like some problem that would be solved eventually. Now those two little images on the screen made that problem immediate and terrifying. Captain Reese was tracking the monster in case it caught up with the *Atlas*, and from what I'd read in the encyclopedia, it was only a matter of time until that happened.

My time to figure out a way to protect my family wasn't in some distant future, when I'd gotten all the ins and outs of life aboard the *Britannica* figured out. The time was now—yesterday, even. I had no idea how I would do that yet, but I did know a good place to start.

11

The next morning, I slid into my now-customary spot at the mess-hall table.

"Nice to see you dry," Max said, smiling wickedly.

"It's nice to be dry," I said. The day before, I'd had the joy of walking into the mess hall still sporting soaking-wet clothes thanks to Elmer's "nice to meet you" dunking. It had been embarrassing, and I'd smelled faintly of rotten fish for the remainder of the day, but the look on Garth's face when he caught sight of me had almost made it worth it. He'd tried to hide his grin for a second before giving up and letting it take up his entire face, showcasing the dimple in his left cheek that I hadn't seen since we'd left the *Atlas*. I'd made a mental note to make sure that smile made an appearance again soon.

"Don't worry," Garth said glumly as he plopped down into the seat beside me. "I'm sure I'll be wet soon enough."

"Want to switch jobs again?" I asked, and Garth paused with a bite halfway to his mouth to stare at me like I'd lost my mind.

"What?" he said.

"Man," Kate said, shaking her head. "I knew you were nice, Berk, but I didn't think you were *that* nice."

"No one is that nice," Garth said, leaning in to peer at me suspiciously. "Not even you. What are you up to?"

"Nothing," I said.

"Utterly unconvincing," Garth said, leaning back and crossing his arms as he stared at me.

I stared back, doing my level best not to let my face give me away. Garth had been my friend long enough that he could tell when I was lying, and although I did want to switch jobs, I wasn't exactly telling the whole story, either. For one reason or another, I still hadn't told Garth what I'd learned that first day about the hydra that had attacked the *Atlas*. Which, considering I'd made a habit of telling Garth pretty much every-thing for as long as I could remember, felt wrong on a lot of levels. I just kept justifying it by reminding myself that he already knew how important it was that we made it here, and that terrifying him about a monster stalking our families' ship wasn't going to do anything but worry him. If I was honest with myself, though, it was really because telling Garth would make it that much more real, that much more terrifying, and my brain already felt overloaded.

Garth just kept staring at me, and Max and Kate shot each other a look and then went back to eating their breakfast, leaving us to it. I shook my head, trying to put my thoughts together. Garth wasn't going to believe a lie. Ultimately, I decided that the truth, or a version of it, at least, was my best option.

"Fine," I said, holding my hands up in surrender. "It's because I want to spend more time around the sea monsters."

"Because you like smelling like fish and having near-death experiences?" Garth said.

"It's just that, well . . . that's why we're here. Right?" I said. "To learn everything we can about sea monsters so we can figure out a way to protect the ships?"

"And you don't get enough of them in Weaver's class?" Kate said. "Gosh, by the time class is over, I'm so tired of hearing about the three-headed this and the forty-foot-tentacled that, I could just scream."

I shrugged. "I just figure being around the real thing would be helpful."

"Hey," Garth said, holding his hands up, "I'm not

complaining if you want to switch. That's fine by me. I'm with Kate—I get more than my fill of sea monsters in Weaver's class."

"Don't forget about the never-ending research assignments," Max chimed in. "Those are a barrel of laughs." Suddenly there was a loud, blaring beep overhead, and everyone in the mess hall froze in anticipation.

"Code five. I repeat, we are about to experience a code five," said Captain Reese's voice over the loudspeaker a moment later. "Report to your stations immediately." There was a burst of static, and the loudspeaker went quiet. The room stayed frozen for another heartbeat, and then everyone seemed to move at once. For a second the entire room was filled with the scraping of chairs, the shouting of panicked voices, and the pounding of feet as everyone took off running in a different direction at once.

"What's a code five?" I asked, scrambling to my feet to follow Kate as she whipped out of the mess hall and down the closest hallway.

"We're about to be swallowed!" Kate yelled back over her shoulder.

"Swallowed?" I said. There was no possible way I'd heard her correctly. Kate took a sharp left, and I raced past the hallway and had to double back to catch up with her as she hurtled into the dive room. Six crew members I now recognized as part of the *Britannica*'s diving crew were already there in various states of dress and undress as they worked to get what looked like thick hazmat suits on over their regular gear. Kate flew into action, tightening a strap here, helping with a flipper there, and I took my cue from her and jumped into the fray. I zipped up wet suits, sprayed defogger inside face masks, and handed out what appeared to be long, sheathed knives to the divers.

"We haven't had a code five in months," someone said. "The last time we got swallowed it took us an entire day to get out."

Kate was suddenly by my side, carrying over her shoulder six black dive belts, which she shoved into my arms. "Here," she said. "Give everyone one of these."

"We've been swallowed before?" I said, still not believing that this was actually happening. There was another loud beep overhead, and we all froze to listen as Captain Reese's voice came back over the loudspeaker.

"Prepare for impact!" she yelled. Everyone grabbed on to something, and Kate yanked me down next to her. A second later the sub jolted violently to the left, and I watched in horror as the small circular windows that flanked either side of the hatch went from the dark blue of the ocean to pitch-black. We really had been swallowed.

My brain was still fighting to process the concept as the dive crew did one last gear check and hit the button to open the hatch. Kate and I stood there panting and sweating as the door slid shut behind them, and we heard the whir of the water entering on the other side.

"Come on," Kate said. "We have a debriefing to get to."

"A what?" I said, walking over to the closest window and peering out. The lights of the *Britannica* shone on either side of me, but there wasn't much to see besides a murky darkness that made me uneasy.

"Debriefing," Kate repeated, grabbing me by the arm and dragging me out of the dive room. "Don't you want to know what swallowed us?" I followed her numbly, not really sure how you even began to answer a question like that.

"Swallowed," Garth said a few minutes later as we sat around the table in Weaver's classroom for our debriefing. His face was the same color as the white shirt he was wearing, and I could see the slight tremor in his hands despite the fact that he had them folded in front of him so tightly his knuckles were white. "Like something just ate us?" he said.

"It's one of the downsides to hunting sea monsters," Max said with a shrug. "Sometimes they hunt you."

"You're playing this awfully cool for someone who almost passed out the first time this happened to you," Kate said.

Max opened his mouth to reply and then shut it

again and smiled a bit sheepishly. "Happens to the best of us," he said. He glanced over at Garth. "So, see? There's your silver lining of being swallowed. Eventually, you get used to it."

Weaver looked up from his tablet then, practically bouncing with excitement, and we all fell quiet.

"Who can tell me what a leviathan is?" he said.

"A gigantic sea monster mentioned in the Bible," Kate said.

"Very good," Mr. Weaver said. "Now, depending on the translation you choose and the book of the Bible you're looking at, the leviathan is depicted as everything from a dragon to a serpent. The one thing all the descriptions have in common is the size of the creature. For that reason, we call all the colossal sea monsters we encounter leviathans. Simplifies things."

I raised my hand, and Weaver nodded at me. "But how do we get out of it?" I asked. This felt like a really crucial bit of information, and frankly it irritated me that no one had mentioned it yet.

"Unfortunately, we probably have to kill it," Kate said.

"I wouldn't exactly call that unfortunate," Garth said.

"It is," Weaver sighed. "Being swallowed is usually a bad sign that a monster is dangerous to ships and other submarines." Garth shot me a wide-eyed *can you believe this?* look, and I just shook my head.

"The good news is that now that we are inside it, it

will be much easier to kill. We've had to help out other submarines with leviathan attacks, and incapacitating one from the outside is ten times as difficult. Which is why we seem to encounter so many of them. They have very long life spans and no predators."

"So we are going to kill this thing and then get out?" I said.

"Yes," Mr. Weaver said. "If we simply blasted our way through the creature's stomach and rib cage to escape, the creature would be so enraged it would rip the *Britannica* to shreds. Instead we send out our dive team to do some reconnaissance. Once they have located the vital organs, we will know where to focus our attack. After the creature is dead, then we make our way out by force."

"Sounds easy enough," I said dryly.

"The tricky part is that we can't spend too long in the stomach," Weaver went on, "or the acid will damage the sub."

"So that's why the dive team had those suits on over their regular diving stuff?" I asked as my own stomach flopped uncomfortably. "Because they would get digested otherwise?"

"Gross," Garth said. "Please tell me that whatever you need us to do doesn't involve stomach acid?"

Mr. Weaver smiled. "Luckily for you, Garth, this type of mission isn't one recruits assist on." Garth sagged in relief, and I waited for the same relief to wash over me, but it didn't. To my surprise I felt a slight pang of disappointment. "Since it appears things are pretty well covered, I'd like all of you to report to the hub. You'll have a front-row view of the proceedings, and I'd like a report from each of you on Tuesday about the various techniques that you witness. Captain Reese thinks we will be able to be out of this creature within the hour, so you better hurry."

With that we were dismissed, and we headed single file to the front of the ship.

"Swallowed," Garth grumbled. "Unbelievable. This never would have happened on the *Atlas*."

"I wouldn't be so sure about that," Max said. "We think ships get swallowed every now and then. I mean, we don't have proof, since any ship that got swallowed wouldn't really have much of a chance to call for help, but some of the small ships do disappear mysteriously."

Garth looked over at me, and I knew we were both wondering if the *Atlas* would qualify as a small ship. Kate and Max fell in step together in front of us, and I noted absentmindedly that Max's limp was becoming a lot less pronounced.

"Think our families are okay?" Garth said after a second, and I glanced over at him.

"I hope so," I said. "I feel like Captain Reese would mention to us if something happened to the *Atlas*." Garth nodded, and I felt the guilt tug at me again for keeping all the information from him. What I needed was a plan, something definite about how to protect the *Atlas*, and then I could tell him. "Hey," I said, "I never even got to ask you how your day with Hector went. Was he mad we switched?"

Garth shook his head. "He said that as long as I worked hard, he couldn't care less. Still, I felt like a fish out of water with all the stuff he had me doing. I miss scavenging."

"Why?" I said.

"For one thing, I was good at it," he said with a sheepish grin. "For another, you and I got to work together. I feel like I barely get to talk to you except for meals."

"That's true," I said. "Well, meals and when we get swallowed."

We made it up to the hub, which felt weird with its pitch-black windows and brightly lit interior. The headlights were shining on what had to be the pink, undulating side of the creature's stomach, and I shut my eyes and took a deep breath to steady myself.

"Welcome," Captain Reese said, turning from the monitor she'd just been studying. "How's everyone's morning going?"

"It's been better," Garth said, plopping down on one of the benches where we'd sat on our first day aboard the *Britannica*. Through the front window we saw six tiny lights approaching through the darkness, and a few moments later the divers I'd helped gear up swam into view. One of them flashed the hub a thumbs-up, which Captain Reese returned, and they swam around to the newly fixed hatch. There was a loud beep, and the large computer monitor in front of Captain Reese suddenly showed a diagram of what I assumed was the inside of the creature.

"We're in luck," Captain Reese said, stepping forward to study the diagram more closely. "We are very close to the heart, and by cutting straight down, we can avoid most of the bone structure on our way out."

"This isn't happening," Garth said faintly, his face an unfortunate green color.

"Shush," Max said. "It's almost time for the good part." The intercom next to Captain Reese chirped, and I heard a crew member report that all the divers were back inside the *Britannica* and the charges were secured.

"Thank you," Captain Reese said, her face all business. Something moved to my left, and I saw Tank leap into Garth's lap and settle in. Did he know who needed him the most? Or was it just a lucky coincidence? I didn't have time to ponder that thought, though, because Captain Reese was making a sub-wide announcement.

"Brace yourselves," she said. "We will initiate our exit and detonate the explosives the dive team set pretty much simultaneously." She glanced back to make sure that we were all seated and nodded in approval. "Ready the saw," she said, and Officer Wilson pushed a few buttons on his monitor. There was a low whirring noise as four large silver disks appeared in front of the *Britannica*. From where I sat, I could see the metal disks begin to spin rapidly in the murky water.

Max leaned forward excitedly, and I covered my eyes. A second later I felt the *Britannica* make contact with something—probably the thing's stomach, since we'd have to get out of there before we could exit the beast altogether. I shoved the thought away, pretty grossed out by the whole thing. There was a terrible screech, probably from the creature itself, and I heard Garth make a gagging sound beside me. I kept my eyes squeezed shut and put my hands over my ears to block out the noise. I felt someone gently pry my hand off my ear, and I looked over at Max, who smiled at me.

"The worst is over," he said. "Trust me, you don't want to miss this."

"Detonate the charges," Captain Reese said, and Officer Wilson pressed a button on his computer. Suddenly the entire ship shook as something exploded behind us, and then we were out, leaving behind the murk of the creature's stomach.

"Time to get some distance from this thing," Captain Reese said, and I was practically thrown backward in my seat as the *Britannica* surged forward and away. A minute later the sub came to an abrupt halt, and Captain Reese spun the wheel so we faced the opposite direction. There was a whistle of appreciation from behind us, and I noticed that the entire crew of the *Britannica* was standing along the back wall of the hub, some of them still dressed in wet suits.

I turned to look out the window and saw what had caused the whistle. There, falling slowly toward the bottom of the ocean, was the thing that had swallowed us. I blinked hard, trying to understand what I was looking at. It was enormous, probably three times the size of the *Britannica*, and jet-black. I would have said it was some kind of whale if it hadn't had so many flippers and such a long tail.

"Where's its head?" Garth asked.

"There," Max said, pointing to one of the ends. "I think."

"How in the world can you tell?" I asked, squinting hard.

"A lot of practice," he said with a shrug.

"Can we stay to study it?" someone asked, and I turned to see Weaver standing with his nose practically pressed to the glass as he watched the thing fall.

"Not this time," Captain Reese said with an apologetic smile. "We received a distress call from the *Alamo* right before we were swallowed. Apparently, they are having some trouble with a couple of giant saw-mouthed skeplars. Swallowing set us back a couple of hours, but if we hurry, we may get there in time to help."

"All right," Mr. Weaver said with a sigh. "Seems like such a waste, though. I've never seen one quite like that."

"And let's hope we never see one again," Captain Reese said. "Everyone return to your normal duties, please. You will be alerted if you are needed again."

"You better go find Hector," Kate said to me. "He doesn't like it when his helpers are late."

"Um," I said with a glance over at Garth. He grimaced.

"You honestly still want to do the large-specimen room after that?" he said. "It's okay. I'll let you off the hook."

I shook my head. "Leave me on the hook. I still want to switch."

Garth shot me a baffled look and shrugged but hurried down the hall after Kate. Weaver was talking animatedly on my left with one of the divers about their mission.

"Two hearts?" he exclaimed. "Well, that's simply

marvelous, isn't it? Do you think it had more than one stomach, too?" He smiled as I approached. "Are you here to remind me that we have a very hungry crew to feed that doesn't care one whit that they were a few inches of metal away from being a meal?"

"Something like that," I said as Weaver politely disengaged himself from the divers and, together, we headed back toward the large-specimen tanks.

"So how was your first swallowing?" he asked jovially. "It's quite something, isn't it?"

"It sure was," I said.

12

For two weeks, my morning duties felt like they consisted of nothing but chopping up dead fish and getting dunked in Elmer's tank. Switching with Garth was starting to look like one of my stupidest ideas yet, but I just couldn't shake the idea that if I was going to make a breakthrough when it came to sea monsters, I was going to have to actually *be* around sea monsters.

I didn't spend the entire time gutting fish, though. I also helped the sea-monster-ravaged ship the *Alamo*, and even got to be part of the diving team that went down to study the two monsters the *Britannica* managed to kill. They were small as far as sea monsters went, only about twelve feet in length, with no eyeballs and one giant, circular, tooth-studded mouth that

197

looked a lot like the mouth of a lamprey, the eel infamous for latching onto a fish and sucking it dry. The two that attacked the *Alamo* had decided to give the ship's metal hull a go, and they'd done some significant damage before we arrived on the scene. Another hour and they'd have managed to bust through, and the entire ship would have gone down.

After the debacle with the megalodon and getting swallowed whole by the leviathan, I honestly hadn't had a whole lot of faith in the ability of this sub to do anything but run away from a monster. This encounter proved me wrong. The electrically charged nets were fired, and they distracted the creatures long enough for the hunting team to get four harpoons through each one. Even Garth was impressed.

Later, when we boarded the *Alamo* to help them assess and repair their damage, we were treated like heroes. Still, the *Alamo*, a small fishing boat with only about twenty families on board, was going to have a hard time overcoming the attack. As I worked shoulder to shoulder with our crew and theirs to help mend the ship, I couldn't help but think that Weaver was right. There *had* to be a way to prevent things like this from happening.

With that thought in mind I started spending my hour of free time each night sitting with my tablet in front of one sea-monster oddity or another, studying the notes Weaver had had me transcribe on the creature and racking my brain about how in the world you could use that information to defend a ship. One thing I did know was that captains like Captain Brown of the *Atlas* needed to change their practices when it came to informing their crew about the sea-monster threat. It wasn't fair to anyone, especially the scavenging crew, to send them out into the ocean without all the facts. Although, I reasoned, there might not *be* a scavenging crew if they knew the whole story.

"What do you do in here all the time?" Max asked one evening after stumbling upon me staring down a rather ugly bat-winged eel monster we'd captured just that afternoon.

"Think," I said simply.

"You make it look painful," he said.

I shrugged. "It is sometimes." I noticed then that his arms were full, and I scrambled to my feet. "What is all that?"

Max glanced down at the oversized bucket he held, which was crammed full of bits of rusted metal, wire, screws, a broken face mask, and some shards of glass. "Junk," he said. "Is Weaver around?"

I shook my head. "He said something about talking to the captain and left about a half hour ago."

Max sighed. "Shoot. I was hoping to hand this off to him."

"Why are you handing him junk?" I asked.

"He likes to pick through everything before we throw it out," he said. "He thinks we're wasteful. He's got a whole storage closet full of this stuff. Who knows what he plans to use it all for?"

"Really?" I said, perking up. "I haven't seen that yet."

"You aren't missing out," Max said. "It's just junk. I heard a rumor once that Weaver used to store it all in the ceiling before Captain Reese caught him and made him pull it out. Fire hazard."

"I'll give it to him," I said, holding out my hands. Max was happy enough to hand over the bucket, and turned to leave.

"Hey, Max," I said, glancing up from the bucket.

"Yeah?" he replied, turning around.

"Your limp's gone," I said.

Max glanced down at his foot and shrugged. "I guess," he said, turning to go again.

"Max?" I said again, and he huffed and turned around, eyebrow raised. "I'm glad it's gone," I said. "I don't know what happened with your friend, the one who left, but I do know that having a physical reminder of it every day must have been really hard." My own guilt for the danger in which I'd put my family and the rest of the *Atlas* crew often felt like a weight around

200

my neck, and I didn't have the constant reminder of it like Max had had. He studied me a second, opened his mouth as though he was going to say something, and then changed his mind and closed it again before walking out of the large-specimen room.

I waited until his footsteps had disappeared down the hall before upending the entire bucket onto the floor. Max was right, a lot of the stuff was junk, but I pulled out a few bits of twisted metal and screws and placed them carefully in a pile by my knee. Elmer watched me through the glass of his tank, and I held up a bent and rusted wire to show him.

"See this?" I said. "This is how I create a lock that you can't pick!" Elmer flicked one of his large tentacles up and out of his tank, where it slapped noisily against the outside of the glass. "Just wait, old man," I said, smiling as I pulled out a few more pieces that I might be able to use. My brain was already churning, and even though this wasn't the problem I'd camped out here to figure out, it was a problem I might actually be able to fix. Besides, I knew from experience that sometimes I got my best ideas when I was working on something else. Who knew, maybe this smaller problem would help me figure out the one that felt heavier by the day. If nothing else, I'd figure out a lock that kept me from taking a swim in Elmer's tank.

"I figured I'd find you in here," Garth grumbled a

few days later as he plopped down next to me in the large-specimen room. We'd ended up with a free hour before lunch thanks to Weaver getting called away by Captain Reese, and I'd decided to use my time wisely. Today I'd situated myself with my back against a tank holding a large sea turtle with a damaged shell we'd rescued two days ago. The tank I sat against varied, but I always made sure I was well out of Elmer's reach, since I hadn't figured out a working lock yet. I had my four failed lock prototypes laid out in front of me, each one slightly mangled from Elmer's rough handling.

"Still no luck with this?" Garth said, picking up the closest one and turning it in his hand. I'd used the rusted remains of an old fishing reel, five pieces of wire, four screws, and a seashell, but Elmer had made short work of it. After Max had delivered the bucket of junk, I'd asked Weaver about his personal stash, and he'd been more than happy to show me the storage closet jammed from floor to ceiling with all the cast-off bits and pieces that went into keeping a sub like the *Britannica* running. I'd been given free rein to use what I wanted, and I'd taken full advantage. I was surprised to see Garth, though, since the large-specimen lab was one of his least favorite places on the sub.

"What are you doing here?" I said.

"Gee, thanks," he said, dropping the lock so it clanged loudly, making a few of the monsters jump inside their tanks. He went to stand up, and I shot a hand out to stop him.

"I didn't mean it like that," I said. "You know I didn't. It's just that I know you aren't a huge fan of this particular room."

Garth sank back down and picked up another one of my failed locks, fiddling with it absentmindedly.

"Well, it's not like you come looking for me," he said. "I've barely seen you since we got swallowed."

"Now there's a sentence I bet you thought you'd never say," I said in a vain attempt to lighten my friend's mood. Garth just grunted and kept fiddling with the lock as he stared across the room at Elmer's tank. I let him stew, knowing he'd spit out whatever was bothering him eventually if I just left him to it. I picked up my newest lock attempt and tightened down a bolt with my fingers.

"Why do you think he wanted to stay?" Garth finally said, breaking the silence.

"Huh?" I said, looking up.

Garth jerked his chin at Elmer. "Think it's because he wanted to make my life miserable?"

I snorted. "Don't flatter yourself."

"I don't get it," Garth said. "If I had a choice, you can bet I'd be back on the *Atlas* yesterday."

"We had a choice," I reminded him. "We could have taken our chances with the work ship."

"I'd say that at least on the work ship we wouldn't get swallowed, but that might not even be true," Garth said glumly.

"I miss the *Atlas* too," I said. "But I think we're here for a reason. I think we can figure this sea-monster thing out."

"You really think we can figure out a problem that's been stumping the Coalition and their top-secret fleet of submarines for years?" Garth said. I winced—when he put it like that, it really did sound dumb.

"I don't know," I said, chucking the half-finished lock in my hand back into the bucket of potentially useful junk I'd accumulated from Weaver's stash and had taken to bringing with me on my visits to the large-specimen room. "Probably not. I mean, I can't even make a stupid lock to keep an overgrown octopus in his cage."

"If anyone could figure it out, it would be you," Garth said after a long moment of silence had lapsed between us. He shifted uneasily as Elmer circled his tank. "Is his tank locked now?" he asked.

I nodded. "One of my most recent attempts."

"Then why are you still working on locks?" He gestured to the one I'd just thrown in the bucket.

"Just wait—you'll see," I said with a glance over at Elmer.

"Okay," Garth said, and we both sat there and watched as Elmer's tentacles probed the lock I'd created.

After a minute, he said, "You don't feel, I don't know, trapped down here? Claustrophobic?" I looked away from Elmer to blink at him in surprise. If anything, that was exactly how I'd felt aboard the *Atlas*, although I'd never quite been able to put it into words. It was a feeling I hadn't had since coming aboard the *Britannica*. Before I could figure out how to respond, I heard a now-familiar rattling sound coming from Elmer's tank.

"Duck!" I said to Garth, shoving his head toward the floor.

"What?" he said, but a second later the lock I'd put on Elmer's tank went whizzing overhead and hit the tank behind us with an earsplitting clang.

I sat up, taking my hand off the back of Garth's head.

"Ha!" I said to Elmer. "You missed me again." Garth sat up and was just retrieving the newly mangled lock when Weaver bustled in, appearing flustered.

"Ah!" he said, spotting us, relief on his face. "I've been looking all over the place for you two. Come on. We have to get suited up."

"Suited up for what?" Garth said.

"To dive," Weaver said, flapping his hands at us impatiently. "I'll explain later—just hustle."

Together Garth and I clambered to our feet and rushed out of the large-specimen room. By the time we made it to the dive room, Kate and Max were already geared up and tapping their feet impatiently.

"Where have you two been?" Max said, running a finger around the neck of his wet suit. "I'm sweating buckets in this thing."

"Sorry," I said, jamming my feet into my own wet suit. "How were we supposed to know we were diving today?"

"You weren't," Weaver said from directly behind us. "No one knew."

"What's out there?" Garth asked warily. We all turned to stare at the hatch. It had been fixed since the megalodon attack, but it was still pretty banged up.

"Do you remember the hydra that attacked your ship?" Weaver said.

"Yeah," Garth said dryly. "Rings a bell."

"The diving crew found one of their nests unexpectedly while looking for traces of a kappa spotted in the area. A nest is a rare find, and I want to bring the eggs into the *Britannica* for study and observation." He rubbed his hands together in excitement. "Here." He handed each of us a large mesh bag.

"Um, not to be disrespectful or anything, but is swimming into a hydra's nest the safest idea?" Garth said, practically taking the words out of my mouth.

"Not to worry," Weaver said. "The dive team is trailing the parents to attach trackers. So we know for a fact that they are over a mile away. They'll be able to give us ample warning of the parents' return, allowing us to get safely back to the *Britannica*." Even as he reassured us, he was handing out some of the lethally sharp spears I'd seen the dive team take on missions. I tried to shake off the uneasy feeling the spear gave me as I carefully strapped it to my back.

"No harpoon gun?" Max said, looking disappointed.

"Do you remember what happened the last time you used a harpoon gun?" Weaver replied, eyebrow raised.

"Yeah, yeah," Max grumbled.

"What happened the last time he used a harpoon gun?" I whispered to Kate.

Kate grimaced. "Let's just say that if Mr. Weaver hadn't been paying attention . . . there probably wouldn't *be* a Mr. Weaver anymore," she said as water began spilling rapidly into the hatch.

We emerged into the blue of the ocean, and I felt my heart soar as I momentarily forgot why we were diving today. Weaver didn't forget, though, and began quickly paddling away from the ship and toward a large rock outcropping directly in front of us.

"These particular monsters like to live in dark caves," Weaver told us, forever the teacher. "They are very territorial and don't like other creatures invading their space."

"Berkley could have told you that one," Garth

chimed in. "For the record, they also don't like having things dropped on their heads."

"Does anyone like having things dropped on their head?" Kate said.

Weaver paused outside the entrance to a large dark cave and flicked on his headlamp, motioning for us to do the same. We followed his orders, and he quickly disappeared into the cave. I gave one final look behind me before following. I knew Weaver had said that the hydra parents were far away, and that the dive party was tracking them, but I still felt twitchy. It reminded me yet again of the time bomb ticking until the day the monster I'd accidentally unearthed was able to track down the *Atlas*.

I forced myself to shake off thoughts of my family for the moment as all my attention was currently needed to navigate the rocky interior of the cave. Weaver told us to stop about twenty feet in, his headlamp throwing the clutch of sea-monster eggs into the light. Each oblong-shaped egg was about a foot and a half long with light turquoise flecks, and Weaver immediately scooped one up and deposited it in Kate's outstretched bag.

"Remember, as soon as you have your egg, swim for the sub," Weaver said. "We don't have long, and these are much heavier than they appear and are going to slow you down." He wasn't exaggerating. When my own egg plunked into my bag, I almost lost my grip on the thing.

"Don't drop your egg," Max said, a bit of the old snark back in his voice. No sooner had the words left his mouth than the rocks he'd been bracing his flippers against shifted, and he threw his arms out to steady himself. The egg Weaver was handing him fell, and I lunged for it along with Mr. Weaver, Max, and Garth. The result was an uncoordinated jumble of arms and diving equipment that accomplished nothing but jarring Mr. Weaver's face mask clear off his face. Blinded by the salt water, he fumbled for a second as he struggled to replace the mask and clear it of the excess water. The egg, meanwhile, slipped through all of our grips and hit the rocks. A thick crack opened along the top of the shell, and a second later a high-pitched whistle reverberated through the water. I clapped my hands over my ears as the squeal finally came to a stop a few moments later.

"Uh-oh," Garth said, and there was something about the way he said it that made it clear he wasn't talking about the busted egg. I looked up to discover that his face mask had a fracture right down the center.

"You busted my mask!" Max said, his hand over his own cracked mask.

"No, you busted mine!" Garth shot back.

I was distracted from their bickering by Mr. Weaver, who'd finally succeeded in getting the last of the water from his own mask. "Swim for the submarine!" he gasped.

"But the eggs," Max protested.

"Are less important than you two surviving this dive," Weaver said. "If your masks break, and from the look of those cracks it's only a matter of time, you'll be in big trouble, and an egg will only slow you down. Now go!" I'd only heard Weaver bellow like that one other time, and it had been when the megalodon was bearing down on us. Both boys hesitated for a half second, but then they followed orders and turned to make their way out of the cave. Max had a hand clutched to his mask, and I wondered if he'd started taking on water. The thought was unnerving, and I watched them for a half second longer before turning back to the nest.

Weaver looked at me, his own face mask heavily fogged from its brief saltwater fill. "I need to make sure the boys make it back. Grab your egg and let's go," he instructed as he scooped two eggs into his own mesh bag. "This is just a theory, but I'd bet anything that the noise we heard when the egg broke is as good as a siren song for the parents, and I guarantee they are heading back this way as we speak. Hurry!" With that he swam after the retreating figures of Garth and Max.

There was one egg left, and I quickly rolled it into my bag and hefted it in my hands. It was heavy, but not unmanageable.

"Berkley!" Weaver's voice bellowed in my ear. "Get out of that cave! Now!" I whirled and kicked hard for the cave entrance.

The first thing I spotted upon exiting the cave were the hatch doors closing behind Garth and Max. This made me feel both relief and fear for my friends. If the boys couldn't wait for Mr. Weaver and me to get there before closing those doors, then their masks must have started leaking. I said a silent prayer that they'd made it inside in time. It would be a few minutes before they would be able to open up the hatch for us again, and I knew I had to be waiting outside it when they did. Mr. Weaver was already halfway back to the submarine, and I was about to follow him when Captain Reese's voice filled my ears.

"Berkley, Weaver, take cover. The dive team just sent a report that the adults are heading our way."

I froze, my eyes scanning for the monsters as Mr. Weaver changed course and dove for the ocean floor, where he disappeared behind an outcropping of rocks. I was about to make for the same outcropping when I spotted the parents.

If I'd never seen a hydra before, I might have mistaken the quickly moving ribbons of red in the distance for something else—maybe a school of fish or a large eel—but of course I had seen a hydra before. They were still pretty far off, but I knew immediately that I'd never make the outcropping with my heavy load. They were coming on too fast, so I turned and headed back the way I'd just come.

"Not the cave!" Mr. Weaver yelled, but it was too late to do anything else. I'd just have to make it work. I kicked hard, letting the weight of the eggs pull me downward. At the last second, though, I spotted what appeared to be a crack in the rock a few feet to the right of the entrance and changed course.

"Three hundred yards and closing fast," Captain Reese's voice said in my ear. I reached the crack and grimaced when I noticed it was much smaller than I'd first anticipated. I shoved the bag into the hole, maneuvering the eggs so they'd slide in one at a time, and gave them a good shove so they rolled toward the back.

"Two hundred yards," Captain Reese said. I fumbled to unfasten the large spear from its spot across my back and gripped it firmly in my right hand before shoving my feet into the crack and sliding in the same way I slid into the covers on my bunk every night. Thankfully, the crack was deeper than it was wide, and with a bit of wiggling and shifting I was able to get myself all the way inside with a good twelve inches to spare.

"One hundred yards," Captain Reese said. She didn't have to tell me, though. I could see them clearly now, and I felt my breath freeze in my lungs. I clenched my teeth together to keep from screaming. The monsters were a bit smaller than the one I'd unearthed in the old elementary school, but that didn't make them any less terrifying. For one thing, there were two of them; for another, they were streaking toward the cave entrance with their mouths open, fangs exposed. Weaver's theory about the broken egg looked like it was a pretty solid one. They seemed furious as they focused on the cave with a single-minded intensity that could only mean one thing—they knew their young were in danger.

The one on the right was smaller, probably the female, but wickedly fast as she shot through the water like a streak of red lighting. The male beside her had a thick mane of black hair that started at the top of his head and made its way down his fifteen-foot length. The female flew past my hiding spot and into the cave entrance, and I felt the rock around me tremble as she thrashed against the walls of the cave. Tiny bits of rubble fell around me like rain, and I winced as a particularly large piece hit the side of my head and glanced off. A moment later I saw a thin stream of red as it floated away.

"Mr. Weaver?" I said. "Can hydras smell blood like a shark?"

"I'm not sure," Mr. Weaver said. "Why?"

"Just curious," I said lamely as I watched the water in front of me turn a hazy red from my bleeding head.

The male monster had turned to investigate the *Britannica*, mouthing experimentally at the metal exterior of the submarine. Even from where I hid, I could see his teeth scraping long scratches in the *Britannica*'s iridescent finish. I was so busy watching him that I didn't notice that the female had emerged from the cave until her face was completely blocking the entrance to my hiding spot. I screamed as she attempted to shove her snout inside, and I tried to push myself farther away, but there was nowhere else to go. I could feel the eggs behind my feet shift, and I knew that if I broke them now, I'd be in even bigger trouble.

Captain Reese and Mr. Weaver were chattering simultaneously in my ear about poisonous fangs and poor eyesight and the importance of staying where I was because the dive team was on its way and they'd be able to help, but I could barely hear them above the scraping of teeth on rocks. The female's snout was mere inches from my head, and I knew she was going to get to me before the dive team ever got to her. I tried to think of a way out of this, but panic was fogging my brain, and I screamed again as another sizable chunk of rock fell away, giving the monster one more inch I couldn't spare. I squirmed backward again and felt something hard press against my shoulder. Turning my head, I saw the spear I'd unhooked from my back and stuck in beside me. It wasn't much, but it was something.

I tore my attention away from the open mouth and razor-sharp teeth and focused instead on shimmying the spear up from its spot along my side until I had it in my hands. I thought for a second about the harpoon guns Max had mentioned, and I wished he hadn't screwed that one up for everyone. It was no use mourning what I didn't have, though. The spear would have to be enough.

I only had one shot at this, so I had to make it good. I waited as the monster rammed her nose inside the hole again and winced as I felt the rush of water from her snout blast my face. One more go at the rock and she was going to be able to yank me out of my hiding place by the top of my head. She pulled her snout back out and opened her mouth to grind at the rock, giving me a clear view down the back of her throat. This was my chance, and I took it. I thrust my spear out with as much force as I could muster in the cramped space, sending its pointed end directly into the soft pink throat of the monster. She immediately jerked backward, her head thrashing angrily from side to side, the spear protruding from her mouth as the water around it turned red.

Behind the thrashing female I saw the male suddenly jerk sideways as three harpoons hit his side in rapid succession. The dive party had arrived. So much for just attaching trackers, I thought grimly as I watched the male go down with two more harpoons protruding from his side. Of course, I knew full well we couldn't leave these two monsters alive, not now, not after they knew we were responsible for killing and capturing their eggs. I felt terror rush through me again, although this time it was for my family on the *Atlas* being stalked by a monster just like these two, only without a dive team to save the day.

The female was hit by a diver's harpoon and went limp, probably since my spear had done a decent amount of damage already. Even as she sank lifelessly to the bottom of the ocean, I still couldn't quite believe that I was alive. Weaver emerged from his hiding spot a moment later and handed his eggs to a member of the dive team before turning to swim toward me.

I knew I could come out, I knew the coast was

clear, but somehow I couldn't get my limbs to cooperate. It wasn't until Mr. Weaver's friendly face peered inside at me that I was finally able to move. I extended a hand and he grabbed it and pulled. I slipped out and got my first look at the damage the female had done to the rock in her attempt to pry me out of my hiding spot like a turtle from its shell.

"Whoa," I said as I took in the huge gouges and chunks that had been removed.

"No time to celebrate," Captain Reese's voice said in our ear. "The cleanup squad is arriving." Weaver and I turned as three sharks emerged from the gloom of the ocean, no doubt attracted by the thick streams of blood emerging from the dying sea monsters.

"Darn," Mr. Weaver said, "and here I was hoping to bring the class back out for a quick inspection and dissection. Come on, then, Berkley—we'd better get back to the ship so they can close the hatch. Besides, your head's bleeding, and if we hang around too long, those sharks are going to notice."

I put a hand up to my head. I'd forgotten about the cut from the rock, and I felt thankful for the bleeding sea monsters that were taking the spotlight off me.

"My eggs," I said, suddenly remembering why we'd gotten into this mess in the first place, and I ducked into my hole headfirst to retrieve the mesh bag with its bulky contents. Weaver grabbed one side as I grabbed the other, and together we swam them back to the *Britannica*.

"What about the egg that got cracked?" I asked.

Weaver shook his head sadly. "It's most likely dead. Shame, I would have liked to collect the entire brood."

The dive crew flanked us on either side, harpoon guns ready in case the ever-increasing number of sharks decided they would rather have fresh diver instead of dead sea monster for lunch. I felt my stomach roll as the sharks ripped into the monsters. We made it back to the hatch, and everyone piled in. There was a quick head count to make sure no one had been forgotten, and then the button was pressed, and the doors began to close. The hatch sealed shut, and I was sure I wasn't the only one to breathe a sigh of relief. The water slowly drained away, and a minute later we were back inside the *Britannica*.

13

"**N**ear-death experience, and we still have to schlep these stupid eggs back to the large-specimen lab," Max grouched as we made our way down the hall, each of us gingerly clutching a sea-monster egg.

"I wouldn't get all fussy about your near-death experience," Kate said from behind me. "If you can even call a cracked face mask a near-death experience. Berkley is the one who almost got digested today."

"Don't remind me," I said.

"Where are we supposed to put these things again?" Garth asked with a grunt as he adjusted his grip on the egg he was carrying.

"Weaver said there was an empty tank next to

Elmer's," Kate said. "I heard him talking to Captain Reese about all the possibilities the hatchlings might have."

"Possibilities?" Garth asked skeptically. "What possibilities?"

I found out the next day when I walked into the large-specimen room to begin the now-familiar task of prepping breakfast for sea monsters. Weaver was standing in front of the tank full of eggs, his hands behind his back as he bounced excitedly on the balls of his feet.

"Endless possibilities! Endless, I tell you!" he said as a way of greeting when he saw me. He clapped his hands together. "One bite from an adult can paralyze a whale. If the young are even half as potent, we could use that poison as a weapon when defending a ship."

"Um," I said with a nervous glance at the tank with its clutch of eggs, "can I volunteer someone else to help with that particular project?" It hadn't even been a full twenty-four hours since I'd been attacked, and my heart still hadn't climbed down out of its hiding place inside my throat. It was the second time I'd come face-to-face with a hydra and lived to tell the tale, and I had a feeling the whole "third time's the charm" thing wouldn't exactly work out in my favor. "Besides," I said, "how exactly do you plan to harvest their poison?"

"That's the sticky part," Weaver said, brow furrowed.

"Morning, young'uns!" boomed a voice behind us, and I turned to see Garth and Hector standing in the doorway to the large-specimen room holding a huge bag filled with what looked like empty glass balls. Just like on the *Atlas*, glass was used pretty much everywhere on board the *Britannica*. One thing humans had a surplus of after the Tide Rising was sand, after all, and I knew from my time working with Hector that he was a pretty expert glass blower. The shimmering orbs had each been created by Hector blowing air down a thick metal pipe into a red-hot ball of molten glass, a sight that was both impressive and slightly frightening.

"Young'uns?" Weaver chuckled. "Who are you calling a young'un, old-timer?"

Hector laughed and came over to peer into one of the nearby tanks. The thin sea monster that always attempted to escape stared back at him with bulbous black eyes and writhed unhappily.

"Now, that one's ugly as sin," he said, taking off his hat to scratch his head. "Are you destroying it?"

"No, just researching, learning, and discovering," Weaver said flippantly, even though I knew a comment like that probably had him boiling inside. Weaver got attached to his sea monsters, despite the fact that a few of them routinely tried to kill him. "What brings you two to the large-specimen room this fine morning?" he asked, turning to smile at Garth. "I know it wasn't because Garth here missed the place."

"That's an understatement and a half," Garth grumbled with a wary look behind him at Elmer, who chose that moment to lunge at the front of his tank, making Garth jump. I stifled a laugh, and even Hector's lip twitched into a half smile.

"We came to bring you these," Hector said, depositing the bag of large glass balls on the floor. "It's that time again."

"What time?" I said.

"Blood-bomb-making time," Hector said.

Garth grinned wickedly. "I had to help make these on my second day on board. No trade-backs." Elmer lunged at the front of his tank again, and Garth flinched.

Hector rolled his eyes. "Come on, twitchy," he said. "We have work to do."

"Have fun!" Garth called over his shoulder to me. I stuck my tongue out at his retreating back, all the while reminding myself that it had been *my* brilliant idea to switch jobs. I glanced over at Elmer as I grabbed two of the orbs that we would fill with the bloody guts and remains of the fish we cleaned for the monsters, and I could have sworn he winked at me.

"Next time you have my permission to dunk him

and ink him," I said as I followed Weaver out.

The eggs hatched a week later. I was in the large-specimen room during a rare window of free time, notebook in hand, when I noticed the first crack and hurried to get Weaver. Kate, Max, Garth, a good chunk of the dive crew, and Captain Reese ended up all piling into the room to watch as, one after another, five tiny sea monsters emerged from their speckled shells. I observed the creatures with mixed feelings. While I had to agree with Weaver that this was fascinating, part of me was a bit disgusted by the whole thing. A full-grown one of those things was hunting down my family at that very moment, and now I was expected to take care of these babies?

I'd never have said it out loud, but I wished I'd just smashed the eggs instead of risking my life to get them back to the sub. A job was a job, though, and since Weaver insisted the newly hatched monsters be fed immediately, I found myself standing in front of half the crew, dutifully handing a bucket of live fish to Weaver as he carefully unlocked the lid of the tank and dumped in the lot. The tiny sea monsters, each about the thickness and length of my arm, swarmed the poor fish, biting them with their tiny needle teeth and then waiting for the fish to go stiff before swallowing them whole.

"Are you picturing how close we came to getting bitten by one of these? Twice?" Garth said.

I nodded as the miniature monsters twisted and writhed around one another, their tiny teeth flashing. A rumbling growl came from the floor, and I glanced down to see Tank eyeing the new monsters warily, one lip curled up in a snarl. He wasn't a fan of the sub's new additions either, and I crouched down to rub him behind the ears. "You and me both, buddy," I mumbled.

"Any ideas yet for how to extract the poison?" Captain Reese asked, leaning close to the tank to inspect the small red monsters.

"Working on that," Weaver said. "I'm thinking that extraction by capture, like they used to do with rattlesnakes before the Tide Rising, isn't a great option. The odds of getting bitten are a bit too high. Even an adolescent hydra could stop a grown man's heart. I'm still trying to design something that will work."

"I bet you could come up with something," Garth whispered in my ear, and I glanced over at him, eyebrow raised. "Give up on figuring out the lock for Elmer's cage, and figure this problem out first."

"What are you two talking about?" Kate said, jamming her head in between us.

"Probably how nosy you are," Max said.

"I think Berkley could figure something out," Garth

said so loudly that I cringed and shot him a dirty look. "What?" he said in mock confusion. "You and I both know you could. You're great at that kind of stuff."

"You're welcome to try," Weaver said with a smile. "Lord knows we could use all the help we can get."

"See," Garth said, proudly clapping me on the back. "You can thank me later."

"I wouldn't hold your breath," I muttered as everyone dispersed back to their regular chores. I stayed in front of the tank for a while longer, watching the young sea monsters swim. Maybe Garth was right; maybe I *could* figure out a way to collect the poison. And, who knew, maybe that was the weapon that could save my family. If nothing else, it was something to get my mind off the fact that we were still light years away from figuring out a solution to the bigger sea-monster issue. Elmer lunged against the front of his tank, but I gave him a level stare, eyebrow raised.

"You don't scare me, sir," I said. "And don't think I'm giving up on a lock for your tank, because I'm not. I'm going to stump you yet."

He flicked a tentacle in a way that seemed to say that he wasn't too impressed with me, either, and sulked to the back of his tank.

I spent the next week trying to figure out how to get poison from a sea monster without getting poisoned by a sea monster. It was a tricky bit of business, much trickier than an octopus-proof lock, which I still hadn't given up on. Whenever I got frustrated with one project, I'd turn to the other, and by now I had an entire bucket of locks that Elmer had successfully mangled. Weaver's stash of junk was good, but it had its limits, and I found myself longing for the bits of junk and clutter that were always so readily available to me as a scavenger. Of all the stuff we'd bring up from the bottom of the ocean, only about forty percent of it ever ended up being usable. The rest was usually unceremoniously dumped back into the water for the next salvage crew to dredge up.

"Why do you look like you just ate some bad fish?" Garth asked one day as he slid into the seat next to me with his breakfast.

"I miss scavenging," I said, putting my newest lock attempt down in disgust.

Garth paused to peer down at it before looking up at me. "Poison collector or Elmer lock?"

"The fact that you can't tell shows just how well this is all going," I said.

"Sorry," Garth said. "But you really miss scavenging? I thought it was just me."

I smiled. "I think maybe we miss it for different reasons. I'm missing the choice bits of junk we used to bring up."

"See," Garth said, throwing his hands up in mock exasperation, "that's why you were a crummy scavenger. The point was to find *useful* stuff, not junk."

"Ha-ha," I said. "You know what I mean. Weaver's stash of odds and ends is better than nothing, don't get me wrong, but it's pretty limited."

"You've probably used half of it making locks," Garth said, turning my newest attempt over in his hands before looking up at me hopefully. "Do you think they'd let us go out on a scavenging mission sometime? Just a little one when the dive team is off hunting down some obscure monster?"

I shook my head. "Probably not. The *Britannica* has more important missions than finding junk that's more user-friendly."

"I guess that's true," Garth said grudgingly.

"Remember that charybdis yesterday?" I said. "That ship, what was its name again, the *Maria*? It would have gone down for sure without us."

Garth nodded. "Weaver said that was an adolescent; the adults are twice that size."

I let out a low whistle. "Can you imagine?"

"Unfortunately, yes," Garth said with a shudder as the rest of the group headed our way with their own breakfasts.

"What's up with you two?" Max said, sitting down next to Garth.

"Missing our old life," I said. "Specifically our access to lots of junk."

"Weaver's stash isn't enough?" Kate said around a mouthful of breakfast.

I shrugged. "Not really."

"Well, you know," Kate said, leaning forward conspiratorially, "I've always heard that he has a secret stash somewhere on board."

"That's a legend," Max said. "I heard that one at the same time someone told me that Wilson sings French opera on the toilet and that Tank once battled a kronda monster and won."

I snorted, sending my recent sip of water spewing across the table. I spluttered and coughed as Kate pounded me on the back. "Opera?" I finally choked out. I heard the click of toenails behind me as Tank leaped onto the seat beside me and gave my face a worried lick. "I'm fine," I told the little dog as I handed over a bit of my breakfast, which he snarfed happily.

"Sorry," Max said with a rare smile. "Sometimes I forget you guys are new."

"Really?" Kate said, eyebrow raised.

"Really," Max said, turning his back on her in an obvious brush-off. "You could always ask him about the secret stash," he said. "You never know, maybe you'll debunk a myth."

"Maybe," I agreed, taking another bite of my breakfast.

I walked into the large-specimen room a half hour later to find Weaver inside one of the newly empty tanks with a scrub brush and a bucket of soapy water. The tank's previous occupant, a bakunawa, had been released the day before.

"Good morning," he said, his voice echoing slightly off the glass walls of the tank. "I thought I'd get an early start on this, as we may need the tank sooner rather than later. Why don't you begin dicing up the squid?"

I nodded but hesitated, shifting from foot to foot as he went on scrubbing. He noticed a moment later and paused, setting the scrub brush back in the bucket to consider me.

"What's on your mind?" he said.

"Have you made any headway in collecting the hydra's poison?" I said.

Mr. Weaver sighed and shook his head. "That idea might not end up panning out," he said. "They are just too lethal, and one slipup could end a life."

"Well," I said, "I've been working on a few ideas, and while the stuff you've let me use from the storage closet is great and everything, there are still some things I need that just aren't there."

"Oh?" Weaver said.

I nodded. "I know we can't exactly waste time on scavenger missions, but is there anywhere else on the ship where spare parts are stored? I promise I won't take anything without running it by you first."

He considered me for a second. "You heard about my secret stash, didn't you?"

"Maybe," I said, glancing down as I felt my face flush with embarrassment. "I also heard about singing opera on the toilet, though, so I wasn't sure if it was true."

"Oh, Wilson?" Weaver said with a grin. "That one's completely true. The man can sing like you wouldn't believe. Here," he said, and something jangly and silver came flying over the top of the aquarium. I caught it and looked down to find the thick ring of keys he carried with him at all times. They were what he used to open each of the specimen tanks as well as the supply room and his own classroom, and while I'd seen them plenty of times, I'd never actually held them before.

"The tiny one with the blue dot on it is for the door that takes you behind the tanks in my classroom," he said. I quickly found the key he was talking about and held it up. I'd been helping to clean and feed the occupants of those tanks for weeks now and knew the door well. It was built seamlessly into the wall of tanks: three of the tanks actually swung inward on a hinge. Essentially Weaver's classroom was a small room—made almost completely of aquariums and tanks—situated inside a bigger room that allowed him to service all those tanks from behind. It was kind of ingenious. Behind the tanks was a narrow three-foot hallway that wrapped around the room and functioned as Weaver's office, workroom, and storage.

"The bank of drawers next to the bait sink is where I've kept leftover bits of this and that over the years—anything that doesn't fit in that tiny storage closet Captain Reese lets me use. Why don't you paw through it and see what you can find?" he said.

I glanced down at the keys, feeling excited but also a tad guilty. "Are you sure you don't need me here?"

"The squid that needs chopping can wait," he said with a smile. "I won't be done for another half hour or so anyway. Have fun." I hesitated for another half second and then nodded and rushed from the room. My mind buzzed as I hurried down the hall and took a left toward the classroom. I was almost there when the alarm went off, freezing me in place. I shut my eyes tight as I waited for the announcement, praying we weren't about to be swallowed again.

The sound system crackled and then Captain Reese's voice came over the line. "All available crew please report to your superior for instructions. We are under attack." And that was it. The alarm stopped blaring, but the flashing red light made it clear the emergency wasn't over. We were being attacked, but by what? Usually Captain Reese gave specifics when it came to a sea-monster attack, but she hadn't said anything this time. Why? Kate was suddenly careening past at a full sprint, Max close at her heels.

"What's going on?" I said.

"Didn't you hear? We're under attack," Max yelled over his shoulder. "Come on! All recruits are supposed to report to the hub." I dashed after them as they went sliding into the front of the hub. I skidded to a halt behind them and gasped. The entire place was in an uproar, with everyone seeming to yell at once while Captain Reese stood in the middle of the chaos giving orders, her face tight and strained. What was going on? I wondered. Then I saw it—through the panoramic front window of the *Britannica*, a huge black submarine came into view.

"Pirates," Max breathed beside me. "I was worried about that."

"Pirates?" I said, turning to stare in disbelief at the large skull and crossbones painted on the side of the strange submarine.

"What's going on?" Garth said, coming to stand beside me. "Captain Reese looks more stressed than when we were swallowed. What can be worse than being swallowed?"

"That," Kate said, pointing out the front window as the black submarine fired something cylindrical and black. It hurtled through the water toward the *Britannica* and the crew erupted, shouting orders. There were also a few terrified screams.

"Pull up, hard!" shouted Captain Reese above the mayhem, and the crew rushed to comply. Everyone stumbled and grabbed on to something as the nose of the sub suddenly veered upward, sending the floor into a steep climb. I was lucky enough to be close to one of the wall benches and grabbed on. I noticed a small cream-colored blur as Tank slid past, his nails scraping uselessly at the metal floor. Max reached out with his foot and stopped his slide long enough for Kate to grab the little dog and tuck him safely under her arm.

A moment later I felt the entire submarine shudder as whatever it was hit us.

There was a flurry of activity as the crew checked various monitors. The *Britannica* leveled out momentarily, and I could see the black sub turning to track us.

"Pirates," Garth croaked beside me. "I never thought about underwater pirates!" Captain Reese must have called out another order, because suddenly the *Britannica* plunged downward, sending anything not bolted to the floor sliding the opposite way that it had just come.

"I think I'm going to be sick," Garth said. My ears popped in protest at the quick change in pressure, and I winced.

"Why don't we just outrun them!" I heard Wilson yell above the fray.

"We can't," Captain Reese replied, her voice tense. "The dive team is out on a research mission. We've called them back, but until they are safely inside the hatch, we can't go anywhere." The pirate submarine fired at us again. The *Britannica* turned hard, but the missile still made contact, sending a tremor through the metal under our feet.

"You four, with me," came a harsh bark behind us, and we turned to see Hector motioning us to follow him. Since there didn't seem to be much we could do in the hub, and we knew better than to argue with Hector, we followed, Kate still holding a very disgruntled-looking Tank under her arm.

"Where are we going?" I asked as the *Britannica* rocked hard to the left, and we all threw our hands out to steady ourselves on the narrow passage walls.

"Damage control," Hector said over his shoulder. "That first missile nicked us, and we're taking on water."

"*Nicked* us?" Garth said. "You don't *nick* a submarine. You *sink* a submarine." Before he could say

234

anything else, Hector had thrown open a door, and we all hurried into a storage room I'd never seen before. Instantly my feet were wet, and I looked down at the six inches of water that had already accumulated. Three of the sub's engineers I recognized from the incident with the megalodon and the busted hatch were there, desperately trying to weld large swaths of metal over the small hairline leak in the side of the *Britannica*.

"I take that back," Garth said. "Maybe you can nick a submarine."

"Less chitchat, more work," Hector snapped. He turned to me and Max. "You two grab the hose out of the closet in the dive room, attach it to the drain in the floor, and bring the other end back here. We need to start getting this water pumped out of here, or it won't matter if we get away from those blasted pirates." He turned to Garth and Kate. "And you two go grab the hand pump. I believe it's in the storage closet next to the captain's room. Now go!" We went, practically colliding as we all tried to fit out the door at once.

"Leave the dog!" Hector bellowed, and Kate looked down at Tank in surprise, almost like she'd forgotten that she was holding him, before plopping him down in the water and dashing out the door after Garth. I followed Max through the quivering halls of the sub, all the while trying not to think about what was happening to make the floors tilt like that. It only took a minute to attach the hose to the dive-room drain and drag it back to the small flooded room. Garth and Kate arrived a moment later with the pump. It was big and clunky and took two people on either side to work the handle back and forth, and it wasn't long before my hands were raw. I didn't mind, though. I was glad to be doing something, anything, as the *Britannica* continued to jerk this way and that.

The crack in the submarine was patched in about ten minutes, and we started to make some actual headway on removing the water. It felt good, since up to that point the water had just kept creeping higher up our ankles to our calves, despite the fact that we were pumping so hard and fast that my blisters were getting blisters. Satisfied the leak was patched, the sub's engineers grabbed their tools and practically flew out of the room, most likely headed toward another breach. The thought made my insides roll, but I just kept pumping, trying to take reassurance from the cool metal under my hands and the bulldog that was alternately picking up one foot and then another, as though if he got just the right combination, he'd be able to free himself from the freezing cold seawater. I'd stopped feeling my own feet a long time ago, or I probably would have been doing the same.

The water was down to an inch or two when we heard an earsplitting bang, and the sub jerked hard to the left. Everyone lost their footing and went down, even Hector, whose veteran sea legs almost never wobbled. As we scrambled to our feet, Hector held a hand to his lips, motioning for us all to be quiet. We did what he asked, listening hard for whatever had made his face go tight like that.

"Kate and Berkley, go check the dive room," he instructed. "That sounded like something just happened with the hatch." Max quickly stepped in to take my place at the pump next to Garth while Hector took over the other side single-handedly, his thin arms pumping with a strength I hadn't realized he still possessed. I didn't have time to marvel, though, as we hurried for the door. "And girls," Hector said, and we paused to look back. "I have a bad feeling about this. Be careful."

Kate nodded and slipped out with me at her heels. The hallway had its own inch or so of water, and I felt my stomach flop as I noticed that it was coming from the front of the submarine. I said a silent prayer that the engineers were getting it patched up as we sloshed back toward the dive room. We were about to round the corner when Kate stopped so abruptly I ran right into her. She stumbled and shot me a look as she held her finger to her lips. I nodded and followed suit as she pressed herself against the wall and crept closer to the dive-room door. I heard it then: voices, and not any that I recognized. I had been around long enough to know that no one on board talked with the harsh rasp I was hearing now.

"Put down that harpoon gun or your buddy here will lose his other ear," someone snarled, and I swallowed hard as Kate turned to me with wide eyes.

Pirates, she mouthed. I nodded. We'd been boarded, and from the sound of the scuffle and the shouting, the dive crew had been ambushed. That thought alone was unnerving, as I'd seen them make short work of a two-headed aphant without breaking a sweat.

"Someone has to tell the captain," I hissed as quietly as possible. Kate nodded, and together we slipped back down the hallway. As soon as we were far enough away, we broke into a dead sprint, the icy water splashing up around our feet as we flew back. Rounding a corner at top speed, I ran directly into someone. I barely stifled a scream as Hector shot out a hand to keep me from falling.

"I was just coming to make sure you two were all right," he said. "What's happening?" Kate skidded to a stop beside me, and between the two of us we managed to splutter out what we'd heard. Hector's face was grave as he listened, his eyes sparking angrily.

"We have to tell Captain Reese," I finished.

"You let me take care of that," he said, turning to Kate. "Do you remember the protocol for a hostile take-over?" Kate nodded. "Good," Hector said. "Follow it. Go tell the boys, and stay out of sight. Do you hear?" Before we could answer, he'd gathered the hose he'd been carrying and rushed down the hall. Kate and I watched him go, too shocked to do much else.

"Did I just hear you guys tell Hector that we'd been boarded?" Garth said as he sloshed down the hall.

"I heard hostile takeover," Max said.

"Shhhhhhh," Kate and I both hissed as the boy's voices echoed down the hall.

Max immediately dropped his voice. "But that's impossible. We've never been boarded before."

"It's not only possible; it's happening," Kate whispered back with a nervous glance over her shoulder. "Hector went to warn the captain." She looked like she was about to say something else, but then she stopped and really looked at the two boys. "Wait a second, why aren't you two still pumping?"

"Hector took the hose," Garth said. "He said we'd done all we could do in there, and he was going to track down the engineers."

"Oh," Kate said, and then shook her head sharply and refocused on Max. "Hector said it was time for the protocol."

"What protocol?" I asked, although secretly the

thought of having a protocol was incredibly reassuring. Even if it was a protocol for pirates.

A loud thump came from the hallway behind us, and Kate put a finger to her lips and shook her head.

"No time," she whispered. "We have to go to ground. Hide."

"Where in the world do you hide aboard a submarine?" Garth said, his low voice still somehow coming off as a yell. I had to nod in agreement. The *Britannica* was large by submarine standards—huge, even—but every nook and cranny of the place was being utilized. There was a low woof behind us, and we turned as Tank came trotting down the hall, the water sloshing up around his chest. I reached down and scooped up the sopping-wet dog. I didn't know much about pirates, but I doubted they had a soft spot for chubby dogs. As I picked him up, I heard a faint jangle in my pocket, and I remembered Mr. Weaver's keys. I turned back to the group, Tank tucked firmly under my arm.

"I know where we can go," I said. "Follow me." Together we slipped down the hallway. It was time to go into hiding.

"So now what?" Garth said, shifting uncomfortably in the cramped space behind the classroom aquariums.

"Now we wait," Max whispered. I'd led everyone quickly and quietly down the halls of the *Britannica* and into Weaver's abandoned classroom, where I'd unlocked the two small metal knobs along the wall and swung three of the tanks forward. Garth had stared at this process in openmouthed amazement, and I didn't blame him. I'd been in this classroom countless times, and I'd never noticed the small hairline seam in the wall that indicated there was a hidden door—until the day Weaver had unlocked the thing to show me the proper way to clean the tanks.

"So tell me more about the protocol," I said as soon as the door was bolted behind us.

"I'm surprised Weaver never reviewed it with you," Kate said. "Basically, we are supposed to go to ground, like I said. Hide and try not to let the pirates spot us. Captain Reese won't give them a list of who's on board, and most submarines don't have any kids, so they won't expect us."

"But why did they board us?" Garth asked. "What are they hoping to get?"

"Anything and everything," Max said grimly. "The *Britannica* has cutting-edge technology that makes every other submarine out there look old and outdated. They'll do one of two things. Strip the *Britannica* of everything they can use, or"—he glanced nervously at Kate—"abandon their submarine and take ours, keeping just enough crew alive to run it."

"I don't like either of those options," Garth said.

"Well, let's hope it doesn't come to that," Kate said. We stood in the dark, taking that in for a minute, as we stared out from behind the tanks into the classroom beyond. Finally, Garth broke the silence with an elbow to my ribs.

"Why didn't you ever tell me the backs of the tanks were two-way mirrors?" he hissed in my ear. "Do you know how many times I picked my nose in here when

I thought I was alone? Mr. Weaver was probably watching me the entire time!"

"Shhhhh," Max hissed, holding up a finger. "Someone's coming. They may not be able to see us, but these tanks aren't soundproof." Garth snapped his mouth shut and we stood frozen as the sound of footsteps got closer. A moment later the door to the classroom slammed open, and we all stiffened as two men and a woman stalked in. All three of them were dressed in tattered, worn clothes liberally spotted with stains. The men were both bearded and hunched, with a lean, hungry look to them that made the hairs stand up on the back of my neck. The woman's hair was black and matted into straggly chunks that hung almost down to her waist. All of them were armed to the teeth with an odd assortment of knives, swords, and spears.

"Nobody in here," growled the first man, spitting something red onto the lab table.

"What kind of freak show were these people running?" the woman said, spinning slowly to take in the tanks. "What is that thing?" she said, thrusting a finger at the exact tank we were all crouched behind, and I flinched back even though I knew she couldn't see me. "Looks like a big glob of snot," she said, her beady brown eyes peering closer. I held my breath and glanced down at Tank, who was sitting at my feet, his teeth bared in a silent snarl, and said a prayer that he wouldn't decide to bark and give us away.

"Think we can eat it?" asked the other man.

"You must really be hungry to eat that thing," said the first man.

"I'm not just hungry—I'm starving. This place better have some edible grub."

"Did you see the size of the crew?" said the women. "This sub is funded by somebody with deep pockets. I bet they have rations coming out of their ears."

"What do we do with these things, then?" asked one of the men as he ran a long, jagged knife down the front of one of the tanks. I clapped my hand over my ears to keep out the painful squeal of metal on glass as the women chuckled.

"Whatever we want," she said. "This is your new home, boys. We better make it comfortable."

"As long as this one doesn't have rats on it," said the first man. "I hate rats. The ones on board the *Piranha* are so gutsy they don't even have the decency to wait till you're asleep to nibble on ya." With that they slammed back out of the room, and we listened as their footsteps retreated down the hall.

"This is bad," Garth said.

"Ya think?" Max snapped.

"Stop it," Kate said. "Bickering isn't helping. We need a plan."

"Do you think we've lost control of the sub?" I said.

Kate shook her head. "It doesn't look good. Even if Hector managed to get to the hub to warn the captain and the rest of the crew, it's not like anyone walks around armed."

"Maybe they should," Garth said.

"Don't be dumb," Max said. "The only threats we ever face are outside the submarine. What good would it do to carry weapons inside? Can you imagine the damage a harpoon gun could do in here?"

"Especially in your hands," Kate said, and Max paused mid-rant to glare at her.

"It's useless to debate something we can't change now," I said. "Hector told us to stay out of sight and to follow the protocol, so that's exactly what we're going to do. We say hidden and assess the situation, help if we can, escape if we can't."

"Escape where?" Garth said. "We're at the bottom of the ocean, in what we all know full well to be sea-monster-infested waters, with no clue how far away the nearest boat might be."

"I'd never bail and leave the rest of the crew in the hands of pirates," Max said.

Garth made a face at Max. "I was being hypothetical."

Max nodded. "If the pirates have gained control of the *Britannica*, the first thing they're going to do is go over this place with a fine-tooth comb, trying to find all of the crew. Chances are they're armed to the gills. If we give it some time, they may relax a bit, and we'll be able to get the jump on them." We all looked to Kate to see what she'd say, but she just shrugged.

"So it sounds like the odds are that the only people who aren't captured right now are standing in this room," I summarized, more for my own spinning head than for their benefit. "That means it's up to us to figure a way out of this mess. Now, I don't know much about a submarine getting taken over by pirates, but I do know that the first thing you do when you're trying to solve a problem is figure out what your resources are."

"This is a bit different from laying out a bunch of junk before putting together some harebrained invention," Garth said.

"Is it?" I challenged. "It feels awfully similar. Now, what does everyone have on them?" One by one we turned out our pockets, revealing a hodgepodge of stuff. Max had three kelp bars, which we promptly divided up, since it had been a long time since breakfast. I had Weaver's key, Kate had nothing but some lint, and Garth had a tablet.

"Garth wins," Max said, snatching the tablet out of his hand. "We might be able to communicate with some of the crew with this."

"How do you figure?" I said.

"Did those pirates look intelligent enough to steer something like the *Britannica*?" Max said, eyebrow raised.

"They didn't look like they could steer themselves out of a bucket," Garth said.

"Don't underestimate them," Kate warned. "They did manage to take over the *Britannica*, and as far as I know, that's never happened before."

"Good point," Max said, "But I'd still bet just about anything that they can't work our technology, which means we might be able to get a message out to Captain Reese or Wilson. What we need to do is find a way to turn the tables and get the *Britannica* back in our control, and getting in touch with them would be a good start. I'll check and see if Captain Reese managed to get a distress call out. Maybe there is another sub nearby that could help us."

As he began tapping away at the tablet. I slumped down to the floor next to Tank and ran a hand over his head.

Max looked up a moment later and shook his head. "I've managed to access the captain's account. No distress signal went out." I was about to ask how in the world he'd managed to get into the captain's account that fast when the tablet suddenly beeped and we all jumped.

"Seriously?" Kate said. "You didn't think to put it on silent?" Max just glared at her and hit a button on the side of the tablet before looking back down at the screen. His forehead bunched in concentration as he read whatever new information had just popped up. Kate leaned over his shoulder to read as well and let out a low whistle.

"What?" Garth said. "Don't do that—just spit it out."

"Well," Kate finally said, "you know how it kind of seems like this particular situation couldn't get much worse?"

"It couldn't get any worse," Garth said.

"It could," I said. "We could get swallowed."

"Did we get swallowed?" Garth said.

"No," Max said. "So, I guess that's kind of good news. However, the *Britannica* just got a pretty serious distress call from a nearby ship that's being chased by a sea monster."

I nodded and wondered if the crew on board knew they were being attacked, or if their captain was like Captain Brown on the *Atlas* and had kept them in the dark until it was too late. Ships needed a way to defend themselves, I thought for what felt like the thousandth time since learning the truth about the sea-monster situation. A distress call that went out after an attack had already begun wasn't nearly enough.

"Tell them that we're really sorry about their luck,"

Garth said, interrupting my thoughts, "but we have enough problems at the moment. We can't even help ourselves, let alone anyone else."

"The ship is the *Atlas*," Max said.

For a second I didn't think I'd heard him right, but from the way all the blood drained out of Garth's face, I knew it was true. I launched myself off the floor to look over Max's shoulder and saw the very same map I'd spotted that time in Captain Reese's office. There was the tiny blinking *Atlas*, and right behind it was a tiny hydra.

"Everything I just said, I take it back," Garth said. "We have to help. We have to do something. How far away are they?"

"Fifteen miles south," Max said, consulting the tablet.

"How fast could we make it there?" I asked, unable to take my eyes off the tiny blinking ship.

Max shrugged. "Under normal conditions? Fast. But we don't have control of the sub. Plus we have no idea how much damage we sustained in the attack."

"Well, we aren't neck-deep in water," Kate said. "So the engineers must have been able to bandage it up."

I felt a surge of anger and frustration at Kate and Max as they calmly discussed the fate of what had been my entire world for essentially my entire life. My family was on that ship, and they'd never seemed more fragile or horribly out of reach than they did in that moment. "We have to do something," I said, my voice tight.

"Understatement of a lifetime," Garth said simply, his hands pressed tightly together in front of his face like he was praying.

"I agree," Max said. "But we can't do anything to help your ship until we help the *Britannica*. I know you're worried, but your ship has been able to keep ahead of the hydra so far, so, who knows, they may be able to hold out a while longer. They got away from it the last time."

"The last time, we were there," I snapped. Max's eyes narrowed, and he sat back down with a huff of frustration. Garth sank down to sit next to Max, looking defeated, but I hesitated, glancing back through the tanks at Weaver's empty classroom.

"What?" Kate whispered. "Do you hear someone coming?"

I shook my head as I took in the sea creatures anxiously circling in their tanks. For a second I thought that they could somehow sense the wrongness of the situation, but then I realized they were just hungry. I glanced over at the small clock on the wall behind me and saw that it was way past the time the animals usually had breakfast. With a huff I turned away from the group on the floor.

"Where are you going?" Kate said.

"To do my job," I answered stiffly. I needed to think, and the habit of routine was calling me like a siren. The small walkway behind the tanks extended along the perimeter of the room, and I edged my way around, stepping over the random buckets and pieces of equipment that Weaver kept stored back here. On the far side I found the three narrow tanks that Weaver stocked with the baitfish and other sea life that he used to feed the creatures that made their home in his classroom. The minnows flashed with a silver shimmer in the water, and I grabbed a net and scooped some of them into a bucket. Someone reached out to take the bucket from my hand, and I jumped before noticing that it was only Garth.

"Let me help," he said quietly. "It's better than sitting and doing nothing."

"I can't stand it," I whispered. "The *Atlas* is in trouble and we're supposed to just sit around and wait to see how things play out? No thanks."

"I know," he said. "But we're kind of stuck. Kate and Max said it was protocol or whatever."

"I don't care about protocol," I hissed. "I care about protecting our families. What was the point of spending all these weeks learning about sea monsters if we can't do anything when one attacks our ship?"

"We couldn't have known the *Atlas* would get attacked again," Garth said.

"I knew," I said. It was time to come clean. Garth blinked at me in surprise and then set down the bucket and crossed his arms across his chest.

"Explain," he said, so I did. Out of my mouth came a flood of words, starting with the description of the hydra I'd found in the sea-monster encyclopedia our first morning aboard.

He listened and then turned away from me to stare unseeingly at the tank in front of him. "You could have told me, you know," he said. "I'm not some fragile sea-shell that can't handle things."

"I know," I said, feeling guilty. "And I should have. I just wasn't sure how to process it myself, and I didn't want to worry you. You seemed to be having a hard enough time adjusting to life on the *Britannica*."

"That's because I hate it down here," Garth spit. "I miss the sun, I hate getting dunked by that stupid octopus, and diving without salvaging feels pointless. Besides that, I've almost been eaten I don't know how many times, and weirdos like Weaver care more about their precious monsters than they care about us half the time. Do you know there are days where I've seriously considered asking Captain Reese to just drop me off at the nearest work ship?"

"You can't mean that," I said, reeling from Garth's confession. I'd known he wasn't particularly happy aboard the *Britannica*, but I thought things had gotten better after we'd switched jobs. Although, honestly, I'd also kind of stopped paying much attention. "I'm sorry," I said.

"For what?" he said. "It's not your fault I hate it here."

"It's my fault you're here in the first place," I said. "Just like it's my fault that the hydra is after the *Atlas*. If I hadn't dropped one of my dumb inventions on that monster's head, none of this would have happened. We'd still be living on the *Atlas*, working as scavengers."

"Maybe," Garth said. "Or maybe we'd be dead."

"I'm sorry," I said again as I scooped the tiny silver minnows into the bucket Garth was holding. He opened his mouth to protest, and I held up a finger before he could talk. "I'm sorry for not noticing how miserable you were," I said.

"It's fine," Garth said. "I was working really hard to hide it from you. I didn't want to make us both miserable." With that we made the rounds to each of the tanks. The creatures inside thrashed happily as they devoured their meals. I found myself smiling despite the situation, and I realized that, like Weaver, I'd actually gotten a little attached.

What would happen if the pirates took command of the *Britannica*? Would they let these creatures starve?

I realized with surprise that the thought made me feel a bit ill. We'd faced more than our fair share of deadly sea monsters, and I didn't feel bad at all when the diving crew brought one of those down in order to save a ship, but we also came across monsters that weren't really all that monstrous. It was one of the reasons I actually enjoyed working with Weaver every day. It was satisfying to study a living mystery and then release it back into the ocean to live its life. However, the idea of pirates troubling themselves with releasing monsters back into the ocean was laughable. It had been pretty clear that they had no knowledge of sea monsters, and I realized that, compared to them, I was now somewhat of an expert. For the first time since I'd boarded the *Britannica*, I didn't feel like a complete rookie.

Just in time for everything to go south, I thought sourly as we finished up the last tank and headed back to the sink to hang up our buckets.

"Now what?" Garth asked.

"I wish I knew," I said. Garth sighed, leaning back against the cabinet next to the sink. As he did, he bumped into the large metal bucket I'd been using to store my failed lock attempts, and I watched in horror as it wobbled and started to fall. I lunged for it, but even as I reached a hand out, I knew there was no way I could reach it in time. It tipped and hit the metal floor with an earsplitting bang before bouncing to crash noisily into the cabinet, and a cascade of locks clattered across the floor. Kate and Max came flying around the corner to see what had happened. Max stepped directly onto one of the locks, and his foot shot out from under him. His arms flailed for a second before he went down, almost taking Kate with him. Garth and I stood frozen in horror, both of us with our hands uselessly outstretched from our failed attempts to keep the bucket from tipping.

"Smooth," Max hissed as he gingerly pulled a lock out from under himself. Before he could even get back to his feet, the door to the classroom burst open again, and we all went silent as more pirates rushed in. These four were slightly better kempt than the first three, but they had the same angry look to them that reminded me eerily of a hungry shark.

"You're sure the noise came from in here?" a heavy-set male pirate said as he turned this way and that, taking in the seemingly empty room.

"I'm sure," said a red-haired woman as she walked around the room, peering in each of the tanks. I said a silent prayer that all of Weaver's specimens had finished their breakfast. The woman continued her inspection as the other three grumbled something and stomped back into the hall to look for the source of the noise. I held my breath as the woman passed the tanks we were hiding behind. I expected her to leave then, but she stayed, standing in the middle of the room, studying the tanks. While the first group of pirates had seemed rough and crude, she had a cunning look to her narrowed eyes that made my skin crawl. It was as though I could see her mind work to solve the puzzle of the tanks and the noise. After what felt like an eternity, she finally left, and we all sagged in relief.

Sorry, Garth mouthed, but Max just shook his head and pointed to the floor, making it clear that Garth's walking-around privileges had officially been revoked. Garth did what he'd been told, sinking sheepishly to the floor. I sat down next to him, feeling more than a little responsible, and leaned back, only to sit up again as the knob of the cabinet dug into my back. I realized that I was leaning against the very cabinet Weaver had told me to come check out.

Our conversation that morning about creating something to collect the hydra's poison seemed ages ago. I'd been hoping to find a sponge that I could carve into the shape of a fish and somehow seal so that when the little monsters bit it, their venom would be collected without risking a human life. It probably would have worked, I reasoned, but we had bigger problems now. We were outnumbered, and we didn't have a single thing we could use to defend ourselves.

I opened my eyes and looked again at the row of tanks in front of us, filled with their strange assortment of the bizarre and the unusual. I hoped those stupid pirates did try to eat the hidden-fanged loogie. They were right, it did look like a harmless blob of snot, but it had teeth the size of steak knives. Lucky for them that Weaver kept the monsters under lock and key, or the loogie might just have taken off one of their dirty dumb hands, I thought. The loogie blinked its bulbous eyes, and I smiled as an idea pushed its way through all the worry clouding my brain. That idea felt just like one of the sunrises I'd witnessed standing at the rail of the *Atlas* as the darkness was peeled back to reveal the hope of a new day.

"Thanks," I whispered to the loogie as hope shook itself like a wet bird and puffed inside my chest. If I played it right, we might just be able to save the *Atlas* as well as the *Britannica*.

15

Everyone slept on the floor that night using their arms as pillows. We took turns staying awake to stand guard. I was slightly surprised to see just how many locks I'd made in my attempt to stump that mean old mollusk Elmer. In total I'd made over thirty different prototypes, but only eleven of them had actually worked. Although, it was really more like ten since Elmer had crushed one into a compacted metal ball that refused to be uncrushed no matter how hard I tried. It wasn't enough. We needed at least twice this many, and unfortunately, I only knew of one place to get them. Finally I reached over and shook Garth awake. He sat bolt upright so fast that we nearly cracked heads, and

I could see his wide, panicked eyes in the dark as he looked around for a potential threat.

"Shhhhh," I said. "Everything's fine."

"Are we still hiding from pirates?" he whispered back. I nodded and he scowled, rubbing at his eyes. "Darn, I was hoping that was a nightmare. What's up? Is it my turn to take watch already?" I shook my head, glancing over with a tug of guilt at the sleeping forms of Kate and Max. If they knew what I was planning, they'd probably try to stop me, but then again, it wasn't their families' lives in danger as we sat around waiting for a good time to try the impossible.

"Do you trust me?" I asked. Garth nodded without hesitation, and I smiled at him in the dark. "Follow me," I instructed, "and watch out for buckets."

"You're not funny," he whispered back as we carefully maneuvered around our sleeping friends and over to the door. I unlocked it and swung the tanks inward so we could slip out, making sure to lock the door behind us with Weaver's key ring.

"Where are we going?" Garth whispered.

"The large-specimen room," I whispered back. "I have an idea, but we need a few supplies from there if it's going to work."

"Whatever you say," Garth said, and together we tiptoed to the classroom door and pressed our ears against it. I couldn't hear anything but the thrumming of my own heart, so I eased the door open and slipped out into the hall. The floor was no longer covered in an inch of water, but it was damp enough for me to see that the water wasn't too much of a distant memory. I could hear the rough rasp of unfamiliar voices coming from the front of the sub, and closer still the grating rumble of someone snoring, but there wasn't a pirate in sight. Knowing that that wouldn't last long, I jerked my head at Garth to follow me, and together we crept down the *Britannica*'s now-familiar hallways, taking care to stop and listen before turning every corner. Every muscle in my body felt like it had been stretched to the breaking point as we made painfully slow progress back to the large-specimen room. Despite one close call, where we had to duck inside a storage closet moments before two pirates rounded a corner, we managed to make it there in one piece. I eased the door shut and locked it. Hopefully it would deter any nosy pirates, or at least slow them down.

"Whoa," Garth said. I turned from the door to see what he was making a fuss about and gasped. The tank that had held the adolescent sea pig was shattered, the water inside spread across the floor in a mottled puddle. We'd only had this particular monster for a few days, and I'd found something almost charming in its smashed-in snout and fat flippers. It was harmless, according to Weaver, feeding mostly on the vegetation that grew on the ocean floor. Of course, if you stuck your arm in its tank, it would probably try to rip it out of its socket, but you couldn't really blame it for that. Now it lay prone in the middle of the mess, and I covered my mouth in horror as I took in the deep slashes and gouges along its bristly sides. I glanced away as my stomach rolled.

"Why do you think they killed it?" Garth said.

"No clue," I said, crouching down to inspect the sea pig. Its long tusks were stained with blood, which I hoped belonged to a pirate.

"What supplies do we need?" Garth said.

I shut my eyes and willed myself to focus. "The locks off all the tanks, and any extras Weaver has in the supply closet . . ." My voice trailed off as I caught sight of the supply closet for the first time, the key ring I'd been preparing to use falling uselessly to my side. The supply-closet door had been pried open and was hanging loose and crooked on its hinges. I peered inside gingerly to find that most of the well-organized contents of the tiny room had been trashed.

"Weaver's going to cry when he sees this," Garth said, coming up behind me.

"Let's just find what we need and get out of here,"

I said as I carefully stepped over the broken glass of a blood bomb. In a matter of minutes, we were loaded up with all the locks I could find, and I headed toward the stairs that led to the tops of the tanks, intent on the large metal locks that Weaver used to secure the tanks. That's when I spotted Elmer, thrashing angrily.

"What's with him?" Garth said, pausing to eye his old nemesis warily.

"He's hungry," I said. "He probably thought we were here to feed him, since I doubt Weaver had a chance to feed anyone before this whole mess started. He's missed his breakfast and his dinner."

"Don't even think about it," Garth warned, but I turned around and hurried back to the supply closet. I heard Garth groan and mutter something behind me, but I was already rushing around the room, pulling out the refrigerated fish we kept on hand in case we weren't able to bring in fresh.

"You can't be serious," Garth said when I came out a minute later and thrust a full bucket at him.

"I am," I said. "Weaver won't thank us if all these guys die of starvation. Now help me, and we can have this done in two minutes."

"He won't thank us for getting caught, either," Garth whispered, but he grabbed his bucket and dutifully followed me up the small steps that led to the walkway around the top of the huge tanks. Thankfully, the other aquariums were still intact, and I quickly took the lock from each one and slipped it into the empty bucket beside me, before easing the tank lid open just far enough for Garth to slip in the occupant's food. We made our way around until there were only two tanks left: Elmer's and the baby hydras'. I decided to save Elmer for last since he and Garth had a dicey history, but despite our utter lack of time, I still found myself hesitating after I confiscated the lock from the hydras' tank.

"You want to just let those starve?" Garth said. "Because if so, I can totally get on board with that."

"You've been hanging out with Hector too much," I said, glancing up.

Garth scoffed. "You're probably right, but don't act like it hasn't crossed your mind."

"It has," I admitted. "But Weaver thinks their poison might be useful. I mean, what if they *are* the key to creating some kind of weapon the ships can use to defend themselves?"

"Don't fall in," Garth cautioned.

"You're not funny," I said as I carefully flipped open the top of the enormous tank. I peered at the excited, writhing bodies of the baby sea serpents. They knew by now what the opening of the tank meant, and they were hungry. Garth dutifully handed me the bucket of dead fish, and I emptied it into the tank, watching as the little monsters ripped into their meal.

A second later there was a surprised yelp, and I looked back to see a thick tentacle wrapped around Garth's ankle. Elmer had unlocked his tank again. Like I expected, he yanked Garth off his feet and into his tank, dunked him mercilessly, and shot out the customary cloud of ink, covering him from head to foot. Garth was pawing at his stinging eyes as Elmer lifted him by the leg back out of his tank, but instead of dropping him unceremoniously to the floor, he moved his muscular tentacle over toward me. I saw what was about to happen like it was going in slow motion, and it took everything in me not to scream as Elmer released Garth directly over the tank full of poisonous sea monsters I'd just whipped into a feeding frenzy. I lunged forward, trying to grab Garth, but it was no use. He careened past me and into the tank headfirst. I plunged my hand into the water after him, only to jerk it out a second before one of the monsters could latch on to my forearm. Garth spluttered to the surface a moment later, and I grabbed him and hauled him out of the tank.

"How many times were you bitten?" I asked, but Garth just coughed, choked, and pawed at his ink-filled eyes. I frantically searched my friend for the telltale puncture wounds that would mean he was as good as dead. Even one bite could stop a grown man's heart—that was what Weaver had told us. Well, Garth wasn't a grown man, and if he'd been bitten by one hydra, he'd probably been bitten by all of them, based on their reaction to the fish I'd just thrown in.

"Stay here," I said to Garth, leaping to my feet. "I'm going to get help." Even as I said it, I realized there was no help to get. Pirates had taken over the *Britannica*, and even if they hadn't, I knew there wasn't any help I could get fast enough. For a week I'd watched the hydras bite into fish, which went rigid a second later. Any minute now my best friend was going to die, and it was going to be all my fault.

I was halfway down the steps when Garth's voice stopped me in my tracks. I whirled to see him flapping a hand at me to stop as he coughed up another mouthful of water. "Wasn't bitten," he managed to choke out between coughs, and I stopped in my mad rush to look back at him.

"What?" I said.

"I wasn't bitten," Garth said again. "Not even once. I would have felt it."

"Are you sure?" I said, hurrying back to his side.

"Well," he said with a half-hearted grin, "I'm not dead yet, so yeah, pretty sure."

"That's a miracle," I said, amazed as I looked back down into the tank, remembering my own near miss as I'd tried to grab him.

"It was," he said, getting to his feet. He gave Elmer a glare, but the octopus was skulking near the back of his tank and ignored him. "Why does his ink have to sting?" Garth asked. "And reek? It wasn't enough that he tried to kill me—he had to blind me and make me smell like a dead animal, too?"

"Sorry," I said feebly as my best friend attempted and failed to wipe the mess off his face.

Elmer looked over at me, and I held up a finger and shook it at him. "You and I are going to have a talk," I said, but he just blinked at me in a very unimpressed sort of way. I glanced back down at the neighboring tank, where the baby monsters were still furiously finishing off the last of the fish. I turned to Garth.

"But why didn't they bite you?" I said. "They should have." Garth just shrugged as my brain churned. There was a puddle of murky water surrounding us, and I ran my hand through it, looking at the oily ink left on my fingers. Garth was right: it did smell a bit like a rotting animal of some kind. "I wonder . . ." I turned back to Garth. "Give me your shirt," I commanded.

"Gladly," he said, yanking the ruined garment up over his head. My heart racing, I got down on my hands and knees to mop up every last bit of the ink-stained water. That done, I approached the edge of the hydras' tank and carefully dipped the end of the shirt in the water. The monsters immediately flinched back, cowering against the far wall of the tank, as far as they could get from the inky shirt. I pulled it back out, my mind abuzz with possibilities.

"What are you doing, exactly?" Garth said.

"I have a hunch," I said, clambering to my feet. I needed to know if the hydras were a fluke or if Elmer's ink repelled *all* sea monsters. Well, I reasoned, there was one way to find out. I walked across to the tank that held the ribbon-thin monster so fond of trying to kill Weaver, and I shook my head. I'd already gotten lucky once today; I wasn't going to push it by trying it on that guy. Instead I went over to a tank that held a small mortagog. We'd caught it about two weeks ago, and I'd enjoyed getting to see the mysterious creature up close. It had a large, blocky, almost hippo-like head, with four sharp tusks that curled back around its stocky body. Its body was smooth and streamlined, like a seal's, but its two giant front flippers came complete with thick talons that had scraped the glass of the tank so badly it would need to be replaced. Its back half was more aquatic in nature, streaming back into a thick powerful tail.

This mortagog was small, only about six feet in length, and not even a year old, according to Weaver. It had been tricky to feed, since it liked to crank its head up in an attempt to rip off the hand that was delivering dinner, but I didn't need to stick my hand in its tank—just Garth's shirt. It only took a moment for me to carefully slip the inky-covered shirt inside. The mortagog peered up at the strange new item in its enclosure, sniffed, and then let out an eruption of frightened bubbles from its huge nostrils as it thrust itself backward and away.

So maybe it wasn't just a fluke, I thought jubilantly as I hurried over to try the same experiment on the dogfish specimen we'd brought in last week. It took three more monsters shying away from the shirt like it was on fire to convince me once and for all. I felt a grin spreading over my face. I had something here. I wasn't sure what, exactly, or how we could use the ink, but I knew this information was important. The problem was that unless we got the *Britannica* out from under the control of the pirates, I couldn't tell anyone about this realization to find out just how important it might be.

I hurried back to where Garth still sat rubbing at his stinging eyes, and I thrust the shirt in his face. He flinched and glared at me.

"If I wanted it, I wouldn't have given it to you," he snapped.

"I figured it out," I said. "Elmer's ink, it's like some kind of sea-monster repellent or something."

"And that saves us from the pirates how?" he said.

"It doesn't," I admitted. "But we definitely need to tell Weaver about it."

Suddenly I felt something wet wrap around my ankle, and I turned to see that one of Elmer's tentacles had snaked out of the top of his tank.

"Don't even think about it," I said, giving it a firm smack. He flinched, yanking the tentacle back inside the tank. Realizing I'd almost just gotten myself dunked, I quickly hurried over to confiscate the lock he'd so deftly picked.

"Come on," I said, dragging Garth to his feet. "We need to get back to Kate and Max before they think the pirates got us."

"Right," Garth said, but he still paused on the way past Elmer's tank to glare at the sulking octopus. "Repellent ink or no repellent ink," he said, "you, sir, are a jerk." Elmer just flipped a tentacle at him and slithered up the side of his tank. "Doesn't it make you nervous to leave all these tanks unlocked?" Garth said, glancing around in concern.

"No," I said. "These guys are the least of our worries. Besides, if we end up failing, at least we give them a fighting chance against the pirates. Now grab your stuff and let's go." Garth shook his head but did what he was told, stooping to grab the buckets of locks. As Garth peeked his head out into the hallway, I couldn't stop myself from blowing Elmer a quick kiss.

We slipped back through the hidden door in Weaver's classroom a few minutes later, and I almost screamed in surprise to find Max waiting for us, his arms crossed across his chest. His expression changed when he caught sight of the ink-covered and shirtless Garth.

"You risked all our lives so Garth could get dunked by Elmer?" he said incredulously as I carefully locked the door behind myself.

"No," Garth said, setting down his heavy bucket, "that was just a perk."

"What's going on?" Kate said, rubbing sleepily at her eyes.

"I have an idea," I said, holding up my heavy bucket of locks.

"Is it a good idea?" Max said. "Because we can't really afford any mediocre ideas at the moment."

"It's a long shot," I admitted.

"We are currently under the control of a bunch of pirates," Kate said, "and the sub's only hope is a group of four kids. I'm going to say anything is a long shot."

"Okay," I said, nodding. "Here's the first thing we do."

16

The clock in my head ticking down the time since the *Atlas* sent out its distress signal was obnoxiously loud, and I rushed to explain my idea. The entire time I talked, I was laying out locks, the ones I'd made as well as the ones we'd managed to obtain from the large-specimen room. To Max and Kate's credit, they listened to my entire rambling spiel without interrupting. When I'd finally run out of words, Max picked up the closest lock, which happened to be one of my first Elmer prototypes, and rotated it in his hands.

"It might work," he finally said, looking up. "I say we do it."

Kate let out a quiet whoop, and we sprung into

action. After talking through our route—and a few contingency plans if things went south—it was time to move. As we queued up behind the door to the classroom, I glanced over at everyone and took a deep breath that did nothing to settle my tingling nerves. Man, I hoped this idea wasn't going to get all of us captured. Everyone must have been thinking something similar, because Max turned to face us, bucket in hand.

"What is it?" Kate said. "Are the pirates coming back?" Max shook his head, shifting a bit as he glanced over at me and Garth.

"I think I owe you two an apology," he finally said.

"For what?" I said, surprised.

"For rooting for you to fail," Max said. "For telling you at every turn that you wouldn't make it here. I was wrong. Even if this crazy plan of yours doesn't work, you guys have more than earned your spot here."

"Wow," I said, not sure what else to say.

"Took you long enough," Kate grumbled. "Now, if you're done with your deathbed confession or whatever that was, can we go?"

"Right," Max said, blushing a bit. "Sorry, let's go." With that he slipped out the door, followed by Kate and Garth. Since I was keeper of the keys, I was the last one out, and I carefully relocked the door so that the pirates wouldn't stumble upon Tank by accident.

We made it down the first hallway without seeing a soul, and though I could hear voices and yelling
coming from the direction of the hub, we'd already
decided that we needed to head there last. We took
a left and paused outside the door to the dive room.
Voices were coming from inside, and Max quickly shut
the door so I could slide one of the locks into place.
We'd barely gone a few steps when a surprised yell
came from inside the room, and something thumped
uselessly against the locked door. There was no turning
back now.

Our biggest obstacle was being so severely outnumbered. That and the fact that we were unarmed.
We couldn't do much about the unarmed bit, but we
could level the playing field and eliminate some of the
pirates from the equation, at least until we could free
some crew members and even out the odds. On the
way to and from the specimen room with Garth, I'd
taken careful note of which rooms had pirates inside.
We moved down the hall, spreading out to attach locks
to the crew's bunk rooms, the bathrooms, the mess
hall, and even a few large storage rooms just in case.

We made it to the large-specimen room without incident and paused to regroup as planned. As I glanced
around at my grinning friends, I began to think that
we might actually have a chance. Suddenly there was

a surprised shout, and we all whirled to see two men walk in.

"What's this? Kids?" said the one on the right. He had a similar pinched look to the pirates we'd seen earlier, except his face was more worn and wrinkled. He was also missing a rather large chunk of his nose, which gave him a lopsided appearance.

"No one mentioned there were kids on board," said the other, who had a matted red ponytail and squinty blue eyes. "The captain's not going to like getting lied to. Somebody's head's gonna roll."

"We better bring 'em up front with the others," said the first pirate. My friends and I instinctively took a few steps back toward the tanks.

"Hold it right there!" boomed the second pirate as he stalked toward us.

"Hold this!" Max yelled as he chucked one of my larger prototype locks at the man's head. Max's aim was good, and the man barely managed to duck as the lock missed his head by centimeters and hit the tank behind him. He stood up, his face a mask of fury, as Max grabbed another lock and pulled his arm back.

"Nobody move!" bellowed the first pirate, and I looked over to see a sword being held to Garth's neck. I froze as the man pointed his free hand at Max. "Drop it," he said, and Max let the lock he'd been about to launch fall to the floor with a resounding clang.

Garth took a giant step backward, and the pirate with the sword to his neck snarled and kept pace until he had Garth pinned against one of the tanks.

"Don't move again," the pirate growled as he pressed the sword blade into the soft skin on Garth's neck. Garth flicked his eyes upward. We all followed his gaze as three huge tentacles launched themselves over the edge of Elmer's aquarium. The man stumbled backward in an attempt to get away, and dropped his sword as Elmer grabbed him and dumped him into his murky tank. Black ink shot out, and the pirate thrashed to the surface, screaming as he clawed at his eyes. Garth picked up the fallen sword and pointed it at the other pirate. This probably wouldn't have gone well, seeing as Garth had never held a sword in his life, except that Kate chose that moment to give the distracted pirate a quick kick from behind, which sent him sprawling just long enough for Max to disarm him.

The aquarium Weaver had been cleaning the morning before was still empty, and with nowhere else to put the pirates, we crammed them inside. They didn't go easily—even with one of them blinded, they put up a fight that earned Garth a black eye and Kate a bloody nose. I used Weaver's keys to bolt the top of the aquarium lid with one of the locks we'd collected, smiling at the two pathetic figures inside.

"You know," Garth said as he scooped up the locks that had tumbled from his bucket, "if you had told me ten minutes ago that I'd owe my life to Elmer, I wouldn't have believed you. Thanks, man," he said, turning to give Elmer's tank a salute.

"We are almost out of locks," Max said, hopping down from where he'd been triple-checking the lock on the pirates' tank.

"That's okay," I said. "The locking-pirates-in portion of this whole thing is over. We need to start turning the tables, or the ones we locked in are going to bust their way out."

"It sounds like the rest of them are in the hub," Kate said, and she took stock of the weapons we'd managed to get our hands on: two swords, three knives—one so rusty it seemed almost unusable—and a thin rope the first pirate had had looped around his waist like a belt.

Max turned to the two pirates in the tank and tapped on the glass. "Hey, ugly and uglier," he called. "How many of you are aboard the *Britannica*?" The pirates just yelled back at him, using words that I'd never heard before but that didn't sound at all complimentary.

"I'm surprised no one else came back here to see what those two were yelling about," Kate said. "That whole encounter wasn't exactly subtle."

"You spoke way too soon," Garth said, peering down the hall. "Get ready."

The words had barely left his mouth before five more pirates burst through the door. It took them a second to take in the situation—a group of kids they'd never seen before, and two of their comrades locked inside a giant aquarium. As though we'd planned it, we backed up toward Elmer's tank, and the cranky old octopus did not disappoint. The pirates rushed toward us, and within a moment three of them were airborne and headed toward Elmer's tank. Between the four of us, and a very lucky slip and fall by one of the pirates right before he would have put a pretty nasty gash in Kate's leg, we managed to disarm the two pirates Elmer hadn't managed to blind in his inky tank.

There was a lot to be said for the element of surprise and a trigger-happy giant octopus. The pirates were ink-blind and utterly confused by the time we had them disarmed. Unfortunately, we'd run out of tanks to put them in. Instead we tied them up with the rope we'd confiscated as well as some of the wire we used to string fish. Garth had the bright idea of hooking them to the front of Elmer's tank.

"If they move, dunk them," he instructed the gigantic octopus.

"You know he can't understand you, right?" Max muttered as Garth rejoined our group.

"You know that, and I know that," Garth said quietly. "But those pirates don't know that."

Max snorted and shook his head. "Time to move," he said. Everyone headed out, but I hesitated in the doorway, looking back at the tied-up pirates, worried they'd get loose. Elmer chose that moment to lunge at the front of his tank, and all five of them screamed. I smiled and shook my head as I hurried after my friends. It was time to take back the *Britannica*.

We could hear the hub before we saw it. The rough chorus of voices with the occasional sound of something shattering made it clear that the pirates were making themselves at home. I glanced nervously at my friends. So far my idea to use the locks had worked out far better than I ever could have hoped, but despite our efforts, we were about to be outnumbered. The second I thought about hesitating, though, I remembered the emergency call from the *Atlas*, and I felt my resolve harden into an icy rock inside my chest. These pirates were standing between me and helping my family, and they were going to live to regret it.

As we got closer, we slowed our pace, creeping

along the hall until the only thing separating us from the hub was the spiral staircase that led up to the entrance hatch I'd come down on my first day.

"Let me ask you again," said a male voice so low-pitched it reminded me of thunder. "What is the pass code to the controls of this submarine? Keep it a secret much longer and you're going to lose a crew member. I might even let you pick which one." I felt my stomach give a sickening roll. Max held a finger to his lips, and we peered around the corner.

I saw the situation in a split second. Captain Reese was standing in front of the control panel, a pirate's sword pressed to her neck, the pirate in question looming over her. While the rest of the crew looked gaunt, he appeared well-fed and powerful, and I knew instantly that he was the captain of the pirate submarine. Four of the *Britannica*'s crew members, including Wilson, were untied, sitting hunched in front of their control panels while armed pirates loomed over them. From Wilson's sour face and crossed arms, I could tell they'd been at this a while. I scanned the room for the rest of the crew and spotted Hector, Weaver, the three engineers who had patched up the *Britannica*, Megan, Ryan, and the rest of the teenage crew members tied up and gagged against the far wall. I jerked my head back, hauling the others with me. I held my finger to my lips and motioned for them to follow me. Max looked like he wanted to argue, but after standing for a second with his fists balled, he gave a sharp nod and followed me back down the hall. A few of the doors we passed rattled as the pirates trapped inside tried to get out. Thankfully, their shouts were muffled behind the thick metal doors.

I took a right and stood aside so everyone could pile into Weaver's classroom. I shut the door behind Garth and quickly locked it, turning to my friends.

"We are right back where we started," Garth said. "What gives?"

"Did you see how outnumbered we were?" I said.

"So?" Max said. "We're out of locks, and if we wait too long, the pirates we *do* have locked up are going to find a way to get out."

"We need to free Hector and Weaver and all the rest of the crew who are tied up," I said. Max opened his mouth to say something, and I held up a finger to stop him. He shut his mouth. "To do that, we need a distraction," I went on. "We need someone to sneak around the perimeter of the hub and get them untied while the pirates aren't paying attention."

"Too bad we can't snag Elmer and haul *him* into the hub," Garth said. "He is one heck of a distraction."

I smiled at Garth. "Great minds think alike," I said.

"You can't be serious," Kate said. "Elmer is huge! He'd chuck us through a window before he'd let us squeeze him down the hallway and into the hub. I was here when they tried to release him the last time—it took five adult crew members and three tranquilizers, and it was still a fiasco."

"I wasn't thinking about Elmer," I said. "I was thinking about these guys." I motioned around us to the tanks that were humming and gurgling with their strange occupants.

"Huh," Max said, spinning slowly in place. "That just might work. Which ones were you thinking?" The next five minutes were spent arguing the merits of launching the loogie at someone and hoping it managed to latch on versus releasing the poisonous double-headed beaked sea snake and hoping it didn't accidentally bite one of our own crew members. We eventually decided to hedge our bets and grabbed four of Weaver's more interesting pets.

Unfortunately, executing this part of my plan proved trickier than I'd anticipated, and at one point I found myself wondering if wrestling Elmer down the hall would have been easier.

The hidden-fanged loogie proved particularly troublesome. Garth had the misfortune of missing it with his first net swipe and paid the price. Thankfully, Kate remembered that the loogie hated bright lights, and she was able to get it to release Garth using a small flashlight she had judiciously slipped into her pocket. In the end we each had a bucket with a different specimen inside. Garth had chosen a stinging nettlefish, Kate had a baby dogfish, Max had the poisonous two-headed beaked sea snake, and I ended up with the loogie.

Buckets in hand, we jogged back down the hall toward the hub. When we got back to the staircase we'd hidden behind before, we stopped, and I carefully handed Garth the bucket containing the loogie. Kate handed her bucket to Max, and she and I slipped quickly past the entrance to the hub so we were standing on the opposite side of the doorway, pressing our backs tight to the wall so we wouldn't be seen. Max and Garth waited until we were in position, and then, with a curt nod, Max donned the metal armpit-length glove Weaver always wore when handling specimens, screwed up his face, and plucked the poisonous beaked sea snake from its bucket. A beaked sea snake was deadly with just one head, and Max flinched backward as both heads snapped at his face. He crouched down and carefully pointed the snake toward the hub and let go.

We stood frozen, waiting as the snake slithered inside. I said a silent prayer that the pirates would notice it and that the *Britannica*'s crew would stay out of its way. A second later someone screamed, and Kate and I made our move. I dashed around the corner at a full sprint, Kate hot on my heels, as Garth and Max burst into the room shouting and launching the contents of the last three buckets at pirates. I had no idea if the loogie had managed to grab on to someone, or if it just looked like Max had hurled some snot into the room, because my focus was on the small cluster of crew members we were attempting to free.

I skidded to a stop and crouched down beside Hector. Kate did the same with Weaver, and we began sawing at the ropes binding their arms behind their backs. Meanwhile, complete chaos had broken loose in the hub, but I didn't dare look up to see what was happening. If Max and Garth were captured, and they undoubtedly would be, our only hope was to have enough of the crew untied to turn the tide. The small metal lab scalpels we'd tucked into our pockets from Weaver's dissection cabinet were sharp but tiny, and it took longer to get through the ropes than I'd hoped, but eventually Hector's hands sprang free, and I handed him the scalpel, grabbed a second one from my belt, and started working on Megan's ropes.

I was halfway through when I felt someone grab me and rip me backward. Something sharp and metallic was pressed to my back, and I stiffened as I was hauled roughly to my feet by my hair. I yelled and twisted, kicking and biting with all my might, but it was no use—the grip just tightened. The hub was pure chaos, with some of the pirates battling monsters while others battled my friends. Captain Reese was slumped on the floor, but I saw with some relief that the crew members who hadn't been tied up had thrown themselves into the fight like their lives depended on it. Which, of course, they did.

"Berkley! Duck!" I heard someone yell, and I turned to see Weaver expertly holding the loogie by the tail. I obeyed, and I felt the slimy fish brush the top of my head before smacking into my attacker's face. The hands holding me let go, and I twisted away and back toward the tied-up crew members. To my surprise, the only thing left where they'd been sitting was a pile of ropes, and I turned just in time to see Hector pick up a tablet and bring it down hard over a pirate who was about to go after Wilson.

Within a few minutes it was over, and the crew of the *Britannica* was back in charge. Two of the medics were hunched over Captain Reese, and the pirates who weren't unconscious were being wrestled into the very same restraints they'd used on the *Britannica*'s crew. I glanced around, locating each of my friends, reassuring myself that they were all in one piece. Garth had a bloody nose, and the stinging nettlefish had apparently done a number on Max, but other than that everyone seemed okay. Weaver was hurrying around with buckets, expertly scooping up his precious specimens, a few of which were still attached to pirates. My surge of relief at the victory won was short-lived, though, as I spotted the clock on the wall. How long had it been since the *Atlas* sent that distress call? Had they managed to stay in front of the sea monsters tracking them? Were we already too late?

"Well, that was fast thinking," Hector said, coming up to clap me on the shoulder. "I was more than a little worried about you lot. By the time I made it up to the hub to warn the captain, those brutes had already gotten the jump on them. Got the jump on me, too, as a matter of fact," he said ruefully as he rubbed a large black-and-blue goose egg on the back of his head.

"We got a distress call," I said, my voice much louder and more high-pitched than I'd ever heard it before. "From the *Atlas*, my home ship."

"Mine too!" Garth pitched in from across the room.

"They are being chased and maybe even attacked by a hydra. Probably the same one that attacked them before. We have to help."

"I'm sorry, youngster," Hector said. "But there is no

286

way we can help anyone right now. Those pirates have wreaked havoc on this place. The captain's down, and who knows what the hatch looks like after they forced entry." He shook his head in disgust. "How these mongrels managed to infiltrate us that easily is going to haunt me until the day I die."

"Where is the pirate captain?" Kate asked, spinning in place as she silently accounted for the downed pirates.

"What?" Hector said, turning.

"Their captain," Kate repeated. "The one who hurt Captain Reese. Where is he? Did anyone get him?"

"The first mate is missing too," Hector said, turning to inspect the pirates.

"There they are!" Garth said, pointing out the front window. We all turned as five divers, each loaded down with what I recognized as the dive crew's weapons and various other bits of technology from the *Britannica*, swam by.

"We have to go after them!" Kate said.

Hector shook his head. "They'll be back in their rust bucket and firing on us before you're halfway there. That is, if they don't have a small crew on board already, just waiting for us to stick our necks out."

"Speaking of firing on us," said another crew member, "if we don't move, they'll do just that." Those who were able hustled to the *Britannica*'s controls and began flipping switches and turning knobs as they worked to wake up the submarine. Within seconds we were moving, angling up and away from the black submarine with its ominous skull and crossbones.

"Do you think they'd really fire on us, even with most of their crew still on board?" I asked as Kate came up to stand beside me.

"Pirates," she said simply, and I guess that was answer enough. A tense silence followed, with no sounds but the clank and grind of the *Britannica* as we worked to put some distance between ourselves and the pirate submarine.

"Good to see the *Britannica* didn't sustain any serious damage," Hector mused to himself as he bent low over the computer Captain Reese usually used. He looked up and glared at the pirate submarine a minute before shaking his head in disgust. "Here's hoping they won't be able to pilot their hunk of junk with such a small crew. Keep us at full speed," he instructed. I came up behind him and tapped him on the shoulder. He turned to look at me, and I stood up straight. I had no idea what my face looked like, but I was hoping it was conveying more determination than desperation, even though I was feeling both things pretty equally at that moment.

"The *Atlas*," I said, slightly surprised by the

command I heard in my own voice. "We *have* to go after the *Atlas*." He stared at me for a second, blue eyes intent, but he finally nodded.

"Wilson," he said. "Did those knuckleheads bang up our system too badly to look up that distress call the kids are talking about?"

"I'll check," Wilson said, and I held my breath as he rapidly typed something into his computer.

"Got it," he said. "We're actually headed in the right direction. We just need to bear north by a few degrees."

"Do it," Hector said. He turned to the medics still crouched on the floor. "How's the captain?" he asked. One of them looked up and shook his head, his face grim. I felt my heart sink as I realized we might lose her.

"Not to interrupt or anything," Garth said tentatively, and we all turned to look at him. "We have seven pirates in the large-specimen room we probably need to check on," he said. "Assuming Elmer didn't drown them for the fun of it."

"Yeah," Max said, "and we also have pirates locked in the bathrooms, the crew's cabins, the dive room, the mess hall, and a couple of storage rooms." He turned to me. "Berkley, where are Weaver's keys?"

"Here," I said, fishing them out of my pocket and tossing them to him.

"Right." Hector nodded, then turned to the crew assembled in the hub. He pointed to the dive crew. "Grab some of these pirates' weapons and three of you head back to the large-specimen room. The other two take Megan and see about the crew's cabins." The others were dispatched to the storage rooms and bathrooms, and everyone took off at a run.

"Wilson, do you need me up here? Or are you good?" Hector said. Wilson gave a thumbs-up, never looking up from his monitor. Hector quickly took stock of the remaining crew, and I noticed that many of them were sporting injuries of their own, whether from the first pirate invasion or from the recent take-back of the *Britannica* it was hard to say. Hector's brow furrowed, and then he shook his head. With a quick jerk of his chin at Garth and me, he turned and headed out of the hub.

"That means we're supposed to follow him," Garth said as he jogged past me after Hector. I didn't point out that I knew that already, that I had been the one to work with Hector first. I just followed. Hector zigzagged us through the sub and into the newly unlocked dive room, where we all skidded to a surprised stop. The place was a total and complete mess.

"Whoa," Max said, coming in behind us. "What did those jerks do?"

"More like what didn't they do," Weaver said, emerging from behind an overturned bench, the two-headed beaked sea snake in hand. The snake thrashed, but Weaver didn't seem to notice as he picked his way over the trashed diving equipment toward the door, the snake held a safe distance from his face. I tried to take in the utter destruction in front of me. The pirates had seemed to plan on making the *Britannica* their home, but they'd ruined almost everything there.

"This was their captain's doing," Hector said as he picked up a wet suit that had been slashed in half. "One last stab at the *Britannica* before he stole what he could and left."

"It could have been the pirates we locked in here too," I pointed out. "They had some time on their hands after we locked them in."

"What a bunch of jerks," Garth muttered as he inspected a shattered face mask.

Suddenly the intercom system let out a hiss of static, and we all froze in nervous anticipation. Wilson's voice crackled through a moment later. "We will be approaching the *Atlas* in less than five," he said. "I'm sending what's left of the dive team back to prepare."

Hector turned to Garth. "Run up to the hub and tell him not to bother. We don't have anything to hunt a sea monster with that isn't in pieces or damaged." Garth's lips pressed together in a tight line before he opened his mouth to argue. Hector raised an eyebrow at him, and Garth snapped his mouth shut and took off.

"So, what now?" I asked. "Send out the nets? A blood bomb? What?"

"We'll figure that out when we see what we're dealing with," Hector said. "If Weaver's put that snake away, we need him back here. With the captain down, we're going to need his expertise on the beastie."

"I can get him," Kate said, coming into the dive room just to spin sharply on her heel and head back out the door. I followed Hector back to the hub. The first thing I noticed when we walked in was that the pirates were gone. When we'd left, there had been a group of them bound and gagged against the far wall, as well as a few who had just been tied up right where they lay. I looked around to see where they'd been taken but didn't spot a trace of them.

"How's it look?" Wilson asked, glancing over at us, and I immediately stopped worrying about where the pirates had gone. All my thoughts turned to the *Atlas*.

"Worse than we thought," Hector said, bony arms crossed over his chest. "We won't be battling this monster from the water, that's for sure. Any gear they didn't steal, they busted to smithereens." I felt a fresh flash of fury at the pirates for crippling us so badly. If there had still been a few lying around, they might have received a swift kick just for spite. It would have felt good.

"If we can't battle them from the water, we battle

them from the sub, right?" I said. "There has to be something we can use."

"Let's hope," Wilson said with a grimace. "We got another distress call from the *Atlas* about a minute ago, and it sounds like they have more than one monster attacking them."

"Two?" I said, choking a little on the word. Garth sat down hard on the floor of the hub as the blood drained from his face.

"Let's hope it's not an alpha," said Weaver, coming up to stand beside us with Kate and a heavily panting Tank.

Garth let out a groan and covered his face with his hands. Tank let out a low woof, but even the little dog's presence couldn't do a thing to calm my nerves this time.

"Well, we're about to find out," Hector said as the shadowy outline of the *Atlas* came into view.

"Don't let us be too late," I whispered, and I reached out a hand to grip Garth's shoulder for support as the ship we'd called home for our entire lives came closer. I inhaled sharply as I saw the thick red bodies twisted around the *Atlas*.

"Three," Garth breathed. "There's three of them." Suddenly I wasn't numb anymore. The fear that had been holding me in place seemed to explode all at once, and I gasped as I felt a sensation that had to be similar to having a bomb detonate inside your chest. The monsters were doing everything in their power to dismantle the ship. I could already see a rainfall of supplies, crates, plants, and metal showering down to settle on the bottom of the ocean.

"Do something," I said, turning to Hector. "Shoot them, net them, something!"

Hector's face was grim. "We can't," he said.

"What?" Garth and I yelled simultaneously.

"He's right," Max said, his voice flat as he came to stand beside us. "The nets will just hit the ship, nothing for them to wrap around. If we fire a harpoon, the odds are we will hit the ship and do even more damage." I shook my head, my hand over my mouth. One of the monsters detached long enough for me to see its massive head as it swam swiftly under the ship and launched itself out of the water on the other side.

"That's what I was afraid of," Weaver said. "See the size of the one on the left? That's an alpha. The smaller two must be his mates."

"My family is on there," I said. "My dad and my older brother. Garth's mom and dad and his little sisters." Even as I said this, more familiar faces flooded my mind—the cook who always let Garth swipe an extra helping at breakfast, the guys who worked with Wallace and my dad in the engine room, my old teachers and the tiny kids who followed them around like a school of fish on field trips. Even Gizmo. The *Atlas* had been my whole world for almost my entire life.

"Fire a blood bomb," Hector said to Wilson. "Maybe we can lure them far enough away from the ship to use the electrical net and a harpoon." I wasn't sure if it was desperation or hope, but something made me cling to his words like they were the only thing keeping me from drowning. If we didn't do something, if I sat here, helpless, and watched the *Atlas* go down, life would never be the same again. Not ever. Wilson nodded and launched one of the glass domes I'd helped fill. It exploded twenty feet from the ship, and I held my breath as the water turned red, waiting for the monsters to take notice. They didn't.

Weaver shook his head. "I was worried that wouldn't work," he said. "Blood isn't a siren song for them like it is for a megalodon."

I noticed that Garth was still shirtless. While he'd scrubbed the majority of Elmer's ink off himself, there was still a thick blue strip of it along his hairline and down his neck and arms, and I remembered my realization about Elmer's ink back in the large-specimen room. I gasped as I felt an idea click into place like a missing puzzle piece. The ink was the answer. If a blood bomb could attract a monster, why couldn't an ink bomb repel one? My tongue felt thick in my mouth as I clutched at Garth's shoulder and swiped a finger through the blue stripe of ink on his arm.

"What?" Garth said, looking from me to the *Atlas* and back again. "What now?"

I grabbed Weaver's shirtsleeve, my knuckles white as I yanked at it to get his attention. He turned to me, eyebrows raised. "I know what to do," I said, holding my ink-covered finger up so he could see it.

"What?" Weaver said, brow furrowed as he squinted at my flailing hand.

"I know what to do," I said, louder this time. "During the pirate attack, I think I figured out a way to keep sea monsters away."

"That's right!" Garth said, his eyes wide. "How did I forget about getting dunked in the hydra tank?"

"You got dunked in the hydra tank and survived?" Max said.

"Spit it out," Hector said. "How do you keep a sea monster away from a ship?"

"Octopus ink," I said with a grin. "Come on." With that I raced out of the hub, down the hall, and back to the large-specimen room. I skidded inside a minute later and immediately glanced over to the tank we'd locked the pirates in earlier. It was empty now, and I made a mental note to ask Hector where exactly they kept prisoners on board the *Britannica*. Weaver, Garth, Kate, and Max came flying into the room behind me, and I pointed at Elmer's tank, which was full of blue-black octopus ink.

"Oh my," Weaver said. "We need to drain and refill his tank before he poisons himself. I held out a hand to stop him before he could head back to the control room and shook my head, breathing hard.

"Watch," I instructed, and raced up the stairs to the top of the tanks. Elmer's tank was still unlocked, and the ink had begun to pool in greasy slicks on top of the water. I plunged my arm into the tank and swirled it around until it was well coated with the oily ink. I pulled it out and showed it to the group below, who were watching me as though I'd lost my mind. Ignoring Weaver's cry of protest, I turned to the hydra tank and thrust my arm inside, praying that my experiments before hadn't just been a fluke. I waited, eyes closed, but nothing bit me. I glanced down to see all the monsters crowded on the far side of their tank in a writhing, unhappy mass.

"Amazing," Weaver said, stepping forward to peer in at the tiny sea monsters. "It's the ink?" he said. "How did you discover this?" Then he seemed to shake himself and looked up at where I was still crouched, armpit-deep in a tank of sea monsters. "Get your arm out of there now," he commanded. "You've made your point." I removed my arm and gave it a shake.

"I never thought of ink," Weaver said, walking up to look into Elmer's tank. "It makes sense, though. Otherwise these noble creatures would have died out long ago."

"That's awesome and everything," Kate said, "but how does that help your ship now? Do we throw Elmer at them and hope he inks them? Because I hate to break it to you, but like a lot of bullies, he may seem like a tough guy when he's on his own turf, but he's a great big wimp as soon as you shove him out of his comfort zone. Why do you think he's stuck to the *Britannica* like glue?"

"I'm one step ahead of you," I said, hopping down and running into the small workroom where I'd spent countless hours with Weaver. I snatched one of the empty glass orbs out of the crate Hector and Garth had delivered the week before, orbs that were supposed to be filled with blood to make blood bombs. I turned and held it up. "Why not an ink bomb?" I said. "If we shoot enough of these around the *Atlas*, it should repel the monsters away. At least long enough for the *Britannica* to get a clear shot, right?"

Weaver stared at the globe in my hand, turned to inspect Elmer's tank, and then looked back again. "It's worth a try," he said. "Of course, we'll have to figure out a way to concentrate the ink somehow, but boiling should do that."

"Let's move, then," Hector said. "The *Atlas* is running out of time."

Garth let out a whoop and ran to collect two of the glass globes before racing over to Elmer's tank. Elmer saw him coming, though, and before he could reach the stairs that led to the top of the aquarium, Elmer had hoisted him into the air and slam-dunked him into his tank, spraying a fresh spurt of ink out into the water. A second later he'd hoisted him back out and deposited him in a soggy pile on the floor in front of his tank.

"Don't even care," Garth sputtered, holding up his ink-filled globes triumphantly.

An excruciatingly long half hour later we were standing beside the blood-bomb launcher as Weaver loaded the ink-filled globes inside.

"I hope this works," Garth said as he handed Weaver another one.

"It has to," I said, not feeling the need to point out that we didn't have any other options. In total we'd filled ten globes, and I'd said awful things in my head about the pirates who had smashed the rest of them into sharp shards that crunched under our feet. While we'd worked, Kate had drained Elmer's tank and given him fresh water, something he seemed incredibly grateful for, although I warned him that if this didn't work, I might just take Kate's idea and launch him at the *Atlas* to see what happened. He'd been unimpressed with my threat, but since not much impressed Elmer, that wasn't at all surprising.

Now it was time to see if my idea was going to actually work. I stood, rigid, every muscle in me tensed to the point of snapping, as the inky spheres were loaded one by one into the launcher.

"That's the last one," Weaver said as he carefully slid the final globe inside. "Go tell Hector and Wilson to fire at will."

I turned and raced for the hub, flying down the halls so quickly they turned into a weird blur. Every second counted, and if this didn't work, then we were out of options.

"Fire!" I yelled, skidding to a stop inside the hub.

"You heard her—fire!" Hector said to Wilson, who nodded and pressed a button on his computer.

Garth slammed into my back a second later, and I could hear everyone else as they hurried in, waiting in breathless anticipation as the first ink bomb ever created was fired directly at the *Atlas*. A second later it made impact, and we saw the small burst of black discolor the water. Nothing happened. The three red monsters just went right on ripping at the ship, and I felt my heart sink inside my chest. It hadn't worked.

"Fire again," Hector said. "Aim the next few a bit closer to the big one there on the left. Maybe proximity matters more with ink than it does with blood."

Wilson nodded, although he didn't look even a little bit hopeful, and a rapid-fire succession of ink bombs rocketed toward the ship. One after another they shattered against the *Atlas*'s metal hull, sending their puffs of black into the water, obscuring the monsters momentarily as more of them broke and released their inky contents. The seconds ticked by agonizingly slowly as I watched my idea dissipate into the water, useless.

I was just shutting my eyes to block out the nightmare in front of me when the smallest monster suddenly detached itself from the ship. "It's working," I breathed as one after another the monsters backed off and put some distance between themselves and the ink-obscured *Atlas*.

"Nets!" Hector called, and the nets were shot out, trapping two of the three monsters, including the one Weaver had called the alpha. The third must have seen the writing on the wall, because it turned tail and fled just as the harpoons were launched.

I didn't realize that everyone around me was cheering until Garth practically knocked me over with an enthusiastic hug, whooping loudly into my ear as he released me to pump his fists in the air. I just stood there in a daze as first one and then another of the monsters sank to the bottom of the ocean, still tangled in the *Britannica*'s nets.

"It took all ten ink bombs," Weaver said beside me, hand on his chin. "I bet if we took longer to actually distill the ink and make it more potent, we could get it done in less. The trick will be finding enough gargantuan octopuses to harvest it from, and then educating and training the ships on how to use the ink to escape the monsters. Or," he mused, his face brightening, "I wonder if we could turn it into some sort of paint the ships could apply to their hulls, thereby preventing the attacks altogether. Oh, the possibilities of this are endless."

I was barely listening, though. Instead I was staring at the hull of the *Atlas* as the ink cleared. It was still floating. It was still intact. It had survived yet another battle, and now the only thing I wanted to do was go on board to see if my family was okay. Hector seemed to read my mind, because he came over to clap me and Garth on the shoulders as he instructed Wilson to surface and dock beside the *Atlas*. I was going home.

We'd saved the *Atlas*, but our delay had cost them dearly. As I climbed over what was left of the rail, I felt my heart sink.

"Whoa," Garth said, coming to stand beside me. The devastation made the attack that had happened during our scavenging mission seem like nothing. Huge chunks of the ship had been ripped apart, masts were leaning dangerously to the side, their sails tattered, and supply crates and plants were strewn around haphazardly, as though someone had hoisted everything thirty feet into the air and then dropped it. Which, I realized, was probably exactly what had happened.

Garth and I walked across the deserted deck in a

daze, picking up a broken piece of this or that as though we could somehow patch it back together by pure memory. Where was everyone? There were smears of blood here and there, but I didn't see any bodies except for the occasional mangled chicken. Panic started to push out the elation I'd felt just moments before. Where was my family?

"Berkley?" came a voice behind me, and I whirled to see my dad standing there, a look of baffled bewilderment on his face. I must have run to him, but for the life of me I can't remember dodging wreckage or maneuvering around the shattered pieces of the deck—it was as though I was instantaneously in his arms.

"Are you really here?" he said. "Alive? How is that possible?"

I was sobbing too hard to reply, so I just nodded as he hugged me hard. The deck was slowly filling as families came up to survey the damage. Captain Brown must have given the order for everyone to stay below until help arrived, I realized, and felt a fresh rush of gratitude that the *Britannica* had gotten to them in time. *Just* in time, I amended as I pulled away from my dad and took in the devastation again. How in the world would they be able to come back from this? To replace the lost supplies? The plants? The chickens?

Out of the corner of my eye I saw Garth being

hugged fiercely by his mother, and I pushed away my worries. The *Atlas* would rebuild and overcome. It was a ship full of survivors. It was what they were good at.

"You should be proud of this girl," Hector said, coming to place a hand on my shoulder. "If it wasn't for her quick thinking, we'd never have gotten here in time. She's pretty smart, this one," he said with a smile.

"You don't have to tell me that," my dad said, smiling back.

The next week was one of the hardest and the best of my entire life. The *Britannica* stayed docked with the *Atlas* as the crew helped rebuild and repair what the sea monsters had broken. In return the *Atlas* helped equip the *Britannica* with some of the supplies the pirates had wrecked and stolen. It felt good to work alongside my family and my new friends, shoulder to shoulder, and my face hurt at the end of each day from smiling so much. As for the pirates, well, we were lucky enough to flag down a passing work ship and hand them off, much to everyone's relief. They weren't a pleasant group to have on board, and I felt no pity as they filed onto the ship where they would work off their lengthy sentences.

"Octopus ink," my dad said, shaking his head as we stood in front of Elmer's aquarium. "Who would have thought that octopus ink could do all that?"

"Not me. I personally hated this guy," Garth said, jerking his head at Elmer. Elmer lunged at the front of his tank, and Garth took an involuntary step back and scowled. "Stop that," he said. "We're on the same team now, remember?" Elmer just flicked a tentacle dismissively and moseyed to the back of his tank. "He may be useful," Garth said, "but he's still a jerk. I won't miss you, either!" he yelled at the octopus, pulling a face.

I smiled sadly. While I had chosen to stay on with the *Britannica*, Garth had decided to rejoin the *Atlas*. I would miss him with every fiber of my being. He'd looked sheepish when he finally got up the nerve to tell me about his decision, and I'd felt my own heart sink, even though I'd known this was coming.

"They need everything," Garth had explained with a shrug. "The scavenging team is going to be more important than ever now, and with Gizmo gone, it will actually be enjoyable again." Gizmo and a few other officers had stolen one of the *Atlas*'s small boats and deserted the ship when it had become obvious that the hydras would catch them. I'd nodded as Garth talked and bitten my tongue to keep from begging him to change his mind. He had to do what was best for him, just like I did, and I wanted him to be happy. Even if that meant he was happy hundreds of miles away from me. I knew that it was only a matter of time before Garth took over Gizmo's entire department. He was that good. Besides, he'd be the only crew member who was also a bit of a sea-monster expert. The thought made me smile.

My dad cleared his throat, and I stopped staring at Garth's retreating figure to look at him, eyebrow raised. "This life," he said, gesturing around us at the huge tanks full of their weird occupants. "This submarine? You really want to stay?"

I took a deep breath and nodded. For the first time ever, I felt like I was really the captain of my own life, free to make my own choices, and it felt unbelievably good. Now I just had to convince my dad of that choice.

I'd had a chance by now to explain to him what had really happened during that first attack on the *Atlas*, and my story had made his face so red and tight I was worried he might explode. Captain Brown had no doubt received more than an earful on the matter, which had probably played a large part in him forgiving the debt he'd put on our heads. I could do what I wanted with my survival credits from here on out, and I knew what I wanted to do with them.

"I wasn't sure at first," I said, "especially right after I signed on, but I've grown to love this place and its mission. I'll miss you and Wallace like crazy, but I think this is where I'm supposed to be, what I'm supposed to be doing."

"You know how I said all that time you spent

mooning over the ocean was a waste of time?" Dad said with a smile.

"Yeah?" I said.

"I take that back," he said. "And I think you're right. This is where you belong, with a bunch of sea monsters." He chuckled and shook his head ruefully, as if he still couldn't believe it, before smiling at me. "So, what's next for the great sea-monster-hunting submarine?"

"Well," I said, "we're going to hunt down the hydra that got away after attacking the *Atlas*. I don't want it trailing you guys anymore. After that we're going to work on finding more gargantuan octopuses like Elmer. I mean, he's great, but he can't provide enough ink to protect everyone." I smiled as I remembered Garth's face when he'd heard that the plan was to fill the large-specimen room with Elmers. If he hadn't already decided to go back to the *Atlas*, that would have sealed the deal for sure.

"The applications for the ink seem endless," I said. "Weaver even thinks we may be able to apply it to the *Britannica* and avoid getting swallowed again."

"Swallowed?" my dad said, his face going pale. "Again?"

"Just kidding," I said with a nervous laugh.

"Good," he said, looking relieved. As we headed out of the large-specimen room, I could have sworn I saw

Elmer wink at me. I winked back—there were just some things that my dad was better off not knowing when it came to my new life.

We cast off from the *Atlas* three days later. I sat in the hub as a heavily bandaged but still very much alive Captain Reese directed the submersion. Tank was on my lap, and my new friends were on either side of me. Together we watched as the hull of the *Atlas* disappeared from view. Instead of the dread and second-guessing I'd felt the first time, I found myself feeling strangely hopeful. I'd miss my family and Garth, but that was okay. I knew that I'd see them again. I'd created a new family for myself aboard the *Britannica*. A family that felt just as much a part of me as Dad and Wallace did. Besides, this life that I'd chosen felt like a well-worn glove, perfectly shaped and comfortable. As the engines geared up and we sped away through the deep blue of the ocean, I couldn't help but feel like I was right where I belonged.

AUTHOR'S NOTE

So apparently I have a thing for sea monsters. Who knew? Not me. If you'd told me ten years ago that of the six books I've managed to get published that not one, not two, but *three* of them would include sea monsters . . . I would have laughed in your face. Well, maybe not in your face—my mother raised me better than that—but you get the idea. The inspiration for this particular sea monster–infested book actually surfaced in Italy of all places.

My husband and I got to slip away from our hectic life in Indiana with our adorably exhausting children for a week to celebrate our ten-year wedding anniversary in Italy, and I found myself confronted with a whole bunch of sea monsters. They were woven into tapestries at the Vatican and sculpted onto gorgeous fountains, and like any good overactive imagination, mine got carried away. As I listened to my tour guide at the Roman Colosseum explain that legend had it that the arena had once been filled with water for a mock ship battle complete with monsters, I began to imagine a girl forced to hunt down the sea monsters for that battle. I imagined her corralling the monsters, feeding them, and housing them in the complicated labyrinth of tunnels beneath the famous arena. I imagined her narrowly avoiding getting eaten, and ultimately triumphing as some sort of sea monster–wrangling master. Obviously, I didn't end up writing that book. The idea morphed, as ideas usually do, after visiting Venice, the sinking city.

Rumor has it that Venice, that beautiful city built on canals instead of streets, might someday be underwater thanks to ocean levels rising, and I began to wonder what would happen to the human race if *all* land went underwater. How would we survive? Could we survive? And, if we were forced out onto the ocean, what would we discover? I heard this astounding fact once that the human race has only explored 10 percent of the ocean, so my question was simple—*what might be hiding in the other 90 percent?* Was it possible that the sea monsters sailors described to those ancient mapmakers and fountain carvers were out there . . . if you knew where to look?

On my twelve-hour flight to Italy I finished off copy edits for *Glitch*, and on my twelve-hour flight home, I started writing *The Monster Missions*. In a lot of ways, *The Monster Missions* felt most similar to my first book,

Edge of Extinction: The Ark Plan, only instead of the remains of the human race retreating into underground compounds and tree houses, they'd fled onto boats and submarines. Replace dinosaurs with sea monsters, get rid of the compass and swap it out for a cranky giant octopus named Elmer, and you have *The Monster Missions*. In fact, when my writing group first read it, someone said, "Oh, it's *Edge of Extinction* but underwater." What can I say? I like my books filled with action and, apparently, monsters of some variety or the other.

I also wanted to mention that the fantastic Mr. Weaver who teaches the kids in this book is based on the real live Mr. Weaver who taught at Clay Middle School at the same time that I did. He was, and is, the best teacher I've ever met. He taught seventh-grade science, and his room was filled with tanks full of hissing cockroaches, albino frogs, snakes, and a snapping turtle the size of a truck tire—and that was just the live stuff. He had mounted animal heads, wasp nests, bird nests, interesting rocks, crystals, and a vast array of "treasures" his students had brought in for him over the years. (On one memorable day, he even dropped off half a human head in a suitcase to help me teach my students a lesson on Phineas Gage. By the way, if you want to look up a crazy real-life story . . . go read about that guy!) He was amazing, and he made science come alive for his students. When I sat down to write this book, I knew that the kids on the *Britannica* needed their own, literary, Mr. Weaver complete with a classroom full of tanks. The world needs more teachers like him, and I love that his teaching legacy will live on, at least a little, in the pages of this book.

I'm not even going to hazard a guess that this will be my last book involving sea monsters, because I would have assumed that *Edge of Extinction: Code Name Flood* was going to be my one-and-only foray into the world of monsters, and then I wrote *Hoax for Hire* and now the book you hold in your hands. If there is one thing I've learned from my writing career, it's that I shouldn't ever disregard an idea just because it's weird . . . because, as it turns out, all of my ideas are weird. But between you and me, I think the weird ideas are usually the best ones.

Until next time,
Laura Martin

ACKNOWLEDGMENTS

For all the people who came alongside me to make this book and every book before it possible. For my husband, Josh, who listened to me dream up a story about monsters during our ten-year anniversary and never once told me I was crazy. I'm incredibly blessed to have married a man who happily lives in the middle of a hot mess because every spare moment I have when I'm not chasing babies goes into chasing this writing dream of mine and not cleaning the house. For my parents and in-laws, who consistently step in to wrangle my babies so I can get my head above water and get things turned in on time.

For my writing group that is always willing to take the first crack at a rough draft and an even rougher idea, so that I can craft it into something better than it was before.

For my editor, Tara Weikum, who is so good at helping shape my books into the best possible version of themselves. I'm so grateful to be part of her team. For my agent, Jodi Reamer, who helps me navigate the publishing world without falling on my face. Thank you for your wisdom and guidance.

And most important, for the God who gave me a unique set of gifts and then waited patiently while I figured out how to use them. I remember well the days I prayed for the things I have now. Ephesians 3:20. *Now to him who is able to do immeasurably more than all we ask or imagine, according to his power that is at work within us, to him be glory.*

DON'T MISS THIS SNEAK PEEK
AT *VANISHING ACT*, THE SEQUEL TO *FLOAT*!

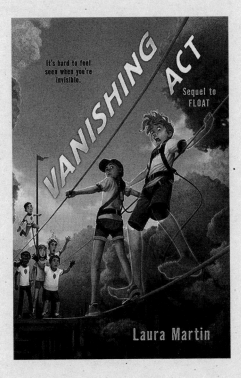

CHAPTER ONE

When I was little, I used to love playing hide-and-seek. I had three older brothers who were 100 percent normal, so they'd hide in normal places. Eddy would squeeze behind couches, Phil liked hiding under tables, and Charlie had a thing for curtains—you get the idea. I, however, would simply disappear. One second a scrawny kid with floppy blond hair would be standing there. The next second the only thing visible would be whatever clothes I happened to be wearing, which is probably why I got in the habit of ditching my clothes at a very young age. What was the point of being invisible if your T-shirt and shorts gave away your location?

If I was having a good day, I could make all of me disappear for the game. However, I didn't have good days very often, so usually just a chunk of me was invisible. If it was just a small chunk that wouldn't go invisible, like a hand or a toe, then I'd just jam the visible bit into a flowerpot or the dog food bowl. If it was something bigger, like my entire leg or head or something, I'd use everything from the trash can to my mom's favorite soup pot. Which, for the record, worked great until she tried turning the stove on underneath the soup pot. At which point I jumped out howling, only visible from the shins down, and got grounded for a week. Apparently, no one wants their kid hanging out naked in the same pot they make chili. After that, my mom tried to add rules to hide-and-seek, but you aren't allowed to add rules to hide-and-seek, even if "no naked kids in the soup pot" is probably a good one.

The games were epic, and I got pounded on for winning a lot. I didn't mind, though. When you're the youngest of four boys, getting pounded on by your brothers is just par for the course. Even when Charlie went to college, the first thing we'd all do when he came home to visit was play hide-and-seek, although I was the only one that hid these days. It was fun, but I didn't want to play today. It was a bad day. It was a day where I didn't exist.

Okay, that was being a bit dramatic, which, according to my mom, is one of my many talents, but still. She should try disappearing for an entire month and then we'd see who was dramatic. One month of looking in the mirror and not seeing myself look back. One month of getting tripped over by everyone in my family. One month of not being able to go out without getting stared at or terrifying the general public. If only my mom would let me tag along naked to the grocery store and the movies, it would be fine. No one would even know I was there, so no one would stare or scream or faint. Plus, as an added bonus, she wouldn't have to buy me a ticket.

"Please? I'm begging you," I said, folding my hands in front of me and dropping to my knees in front of my mother. She, of course, couldn't see the hands. Today I was just a walking-talking pair of Nike shorts and a blue T-shirt. Nike shorts and a blue T-shirt can't win anyone over.

"No," she said as she rubbed the back of her hand across her forehead. It was unusually hot for May in South Dakota, and my dad refused to turn on the air-conditioning.

"But why?" I whined. "I've been invisible for weeks. I'm not going to just become visible again this afternoon for the one hour we're at the mall. I promise."

"You can't promise that," Phil chimed in from his spot at the kitchen table. Of my three older brothers, he was the closest to me in age at seventeen, and he took a special pleasure in making things hard on me. I think he was still bugged about losing his status as the youngest when I'd come along unexpectedly thirteen years go.

"I don't need your help," I said, and stood up. If kneeling on linoleum wasn't helping my cause, I might as well stand. "Come on," I begged. "I leave for camp tomorrow, and I still need a bunch of stuff."

"Should have just ordered it all online," Phil said around a mouthful of pizza. I reached over and swiped a slice off his plate. Thanks to my invisible hand, it took him a solid five seconds to realize it.

"Give that back!" he said, and made a swipe for it.

"I already licked it," I said, "but fine, here ya go." I tossed it back on his plate. He made a face and shoved it away from the rest of his un-licked pizza.

"Mom!" he said.

"I didn't actually lick it," I said when Mom stopped unloading the dishwasher to stare daggers at me. Well, not so much at me, but at the spot where she knew my head was probably located. She was really looking right through me and giving the rooster clock on the wall behind me her signature Mom glare, but that didn't make it any less effective. She nodded and Phil pulled the offending piece of pizza back onto his plate and grumbled something that probably wasn't overly complimentary.

"Mom!" Phil said around his next mouthful. "I think I'd like to go to the mall. You know, just to browse. I'll be back by dinnertime." With that he stood up, jingling the keys to his new jeep in that obnoxious way that made me want to smack him, and taking his pizza with him.

"How is that fair?" I said, anger bubbling inside me as I watched Phil saunter across the driveway toward his car.

"No one said that you couldn't go," my mom said calmly, "but you have to go with clothes on. I don't feel like I should have to explain this to you again."

"You don't," I said. I folded my invisible arms across my chest and stood at the window, debating with myself. I glanced over at the tree where I used to set up the Mountain Dew cans for the squirrels. They'd really loved the stuff, but Dad had made me stop. Sometimes having a veterinarian for a father was fun, like the time he'd brought home a box of kittens for us to bottle-feed, and sometimes it was annoying, like when he lectured you about not giving soda pop to the wildlife. In my defense, I had no idea the crazy critters would get cavities.

"Can I go to the mall with Phil?" I finally asked.

"Sure," she said. "But if I hear about you going naked to fly under the radar, I may just call off camp."

"Whoa," I said, turning from the window. "You don't mean that. I have to go back to camp. The guys are counting on me to be there."

"And I'm counting on relaxing this afternoon without any phone calls from the mall security," she said, matching my tone perfectly. I was about to tell her about how my friend Emerson had accidentally floated all the way up to his mall's ceiling and that they'd needed four security guards and the fire department to get him back down again, but the roar of Phil's jeep interrupted my thoughts, and I realized that my ride was about to leave without me.

"Bye, Mom!" I said, grabbing my flip-flops off the mat by the door and spinning to go.

"Hold it," she said. I froze and turned back to look at her.

"Forgetting something?" she prompted, and I hurried over to give her a quick peck on the cheek. She managed to wrap her arms around my invisible shoulders and give me a quick squeeze before I was out the door and racing after the jeep that was already making its way down our driveway.

"Wait up!" I yelled, but Phil just kept going.

The *kiss the mom* rule was really going to mess things up for me this time, I thought grimly as I doubled my speed.

"Hey," Phil said, without even looking back as I finally vaulted through the open back of the jeep. "That took you longer than I thought."

"You could have slowed down," I wheezed as I fumbled with the seat belt.

"Could have," Phil agreed. "Didn't want to. You took your sweet time leaving the house."

"*Kiss the mom* rule," I said.

"You mean the Hank Rule," Phil corrected me. As the youngest, I should have been able to fly under the radar a bit more than I did. However, as the only family member that had a RISK factor, the government's clever acronym for Recurring Instances of the Strange Kind, I wasn't allowed to avoid any radars—mothers', governments', or otherwise.

Mom had instituted the rule after I accidentally got broadsided by my oldest brother's four-wheeler, and they'd had to spend two days in the hospital trying to instruct doctors how to stitch up my invisible bleeding head. Life was short, life was fragile, life wasn't guaranteed, so you'd better kiss your mother before you leave the house. Period. All my brothers had quickly

7

renamed Mom's new mandate the Hank Rule, since it was obviously put in place for me. They were 100 percent visible all the time and much less likely to die a horrific death. At least in theory, I thought grimly as Phil took a turn faster than was probably safe. Phil drove this jeep like he'd stolen it, and I wondered how long it would take the paramedics to realize there was another, invisible person in the car if he bent it around a tree.

Our family's farm was a good twenty minutes from the nearest mall, and I settled back in my seat as Phil turned up his radio. My hair whipped around my face and into my eyes, and I quickly snagged a baseball hat off the floor of the jeep and jammed it on my head to keep my hair out of the way. Yet another side effect of prolonged invisibility was the inability to get a haircut. Phil had offered to take his clippers to it and just shave the whole mess, but after the lost eyebrow incident two years ago, I wasn't going to allow that to happen again.

I reached in my pocket to pull out the list of supplies I still needed to get before camp the next day and felt the familiar thrill of excitement as I pictured the next few months.

Camp Outlier was my favorite place in the entire world, and after nine months of waiting and preparing, it was almost time to go back. I unfolded the paper and smoothed it out on my leg. It consisted mostly of sun-screen, bug spray, and some new shirts and hoodies. I'd never cared much about my wardrobe, but since it was literally the only thing people could see, I thought I might want to move it up the priority list.

I then pulled the other list out of my pocket, the list of requirements I'd given the guys at the end of camp last summer. I'd instructed them to destroy their list upon memorizing it, but I'd kept my original copy since my memory was absolutely horrendous. My dad always joked that it was lucky my RISK factor didn't involve detachable appendages, or I'd have lost my arms or head years ago. He was probably right. This paper was much more wrinkled and crinkled than the other one, since I'd crammed it in my pocket about a hundred times.

Red Maple men:
Before next summer you MUST, and I repeat, MUST have completed the following items.
Write me an email. Here is my email address. LifeListsRule127@gmail.com. I will then send around everyone else's email addresses so we can stay in touch. Oh, and if you have a cell phone, send me

the phone number too. I don't have one anymore after getting grounded for a prank-calling binge last year.

Be able to hold your breath underwater for at least two minutes. I have a capture-the-flag plan for next summer. Two words. Sneak attack. (Murphy, I know you crossed this one off your list already. Which is actually what gave me my brilliant plan. Thanks!)

Learn to juggle.

Murphy made me add this one. He wouldn't say why, but apparently, it's important that we can all run a six-minute mile. So start running, men. Gary—this includes you.

Learn how to dance. Not like lame dancing either. Go to YouTube. The Monarch girls won't know what hit them.

Age at least fifteen years by the time I see you again. I have my list of where you all left off, so no cheating.

Start lifting weights. No more string-bean arms for us. Chicks dig muscles, so I hear.

Learn how to quack and waddle like a duck. Kidding. Just wanted to see if you were still paying attention.

Start brainstorming an initiation night for when we're in Red Wood, and we get to harass the new Red Maple boys. It's going to be hard to beat eighties prom dresses. Although you have to admit, I looked good in mine.

Check out the picture I stuck in your envelope. I pulled some strings and had Chad make enough copies for all of us, you know, just in case you forgot how fabulous we looked.

Sincerely,

Hank

PS: After you've read and memorized this letter, either flush it or eat it. Whatever floats your boat.

I didn't need the picture in front of me to remember the glory of those eighties prom dresses. Mine in particular had been spectacularly horrendous, and I was kind of sad that I'd forgotten to bring it home from camp. It was going to be hard to top that initiation night, but I was looking forward to the day I got to welcome the Red Maple cabin into the brotherhood of camp by dragging them into the middle of the woods and forcing them to bond on their trek back to camp. The thought actually brought me up short, since the entire school year I'd been thinking about how great it would be to be back at camp and be a Red Maple man again, but I wouldn't be in Red Maple this year, would I? We'd all be moving up to the White Oak cabin. The thought made me a little sad.

Aging in real life had a bittersweet feeling that aging on a Life List didn't. A Life List, which was like a bucket list only way less depressing, was a way I'd come up with to really squeeze the most out of my life. A Life List was a list of everything from the challenges I wanted to tackle to the places I wanted to visit to the talents I wanted to acquire, and for the last couple of years I'd dutifully checked things off my list. Each item that I successfully checked off counted as a year in my Life Listing life. I was an old duffer in Life Listing years, well over a hundred, and I had no intention of stopping.

I pulled my Life List from my pocket. The list spanned five pieces of paper that I'd stapled and then re-stapled together more times that I could count. I ran my finger down the things I'd crossed off this past school year, and felt a bit smug about a few of the more daring items on the list. The thing with the snakes at school had been particularly tricky. I wondered if the other guys had held up their end of things and aged the fifteen years I'd stipulated in their letters. Murphy would for sure, although now that he'd lost the *I've got nothing to lose since I time travel and die before summer ends* mentality, he was probably a bit more cautious these days. Zeke and Anthony were also pretty reliable Life Listers, and I wouldn't be surprised if they aged double the required amount. Gary? Well, Gary was a grump and a half, partially because he routinely got himself stuck to inanimate objects and partially because he had the personality of a constipated toad. Sometimes when you told him to do something, it just made him *not* want to do it. I was pretty sure Emerson would follow through. He'd left camp a different kid than the one I'd met in the parking lot on the first day of camp. I smiled as I pictured my friend who'd gotten the double whammy of uncontrollable floating and a puke-inducing fear of heights.

Don't miss these books by
LAURA MARTIN!

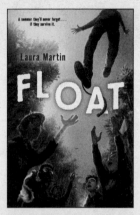